# THE
# *Onyx*
# TALISMAN

# Also by Brenda Pandos

*The Emerald Talisman*

*The Sapphire Talisman*

❦

*Everblue* - Mer Tales #1

*Evergreen* - Mer Tales #2
(Coming 2012)

# THE
# *Onyx*
## TALISMAN
### TALISMAN SERIES - BOOK THREE

# BRENDA PANDOS

OBSIDIAN MOUNTAIN PUBLISHING

Pandos, Brenda, 1972 –
The Onyx Talisman: A novel/by Brenda Pandos

Cover design and layout by the author herself.
www.designbybrenda.com

Published by Obsidian Mountain Publishing
www.obsidianmtpublishing.com
P.O. Box 601901
Sacramento, CA  95860

Summary: Julia waits for Nicholas' return while Phil, Scarlett, Katie, and Tyler take up residence in his house. Phil holds Julia's fragile psyche together while Scarlett plots for Julia's vampire-ending prediction to come into fruition. In L.A., Alora bides her time to retrieve her necklace. A war is brewing and there's more than one vampire who desires to overthrow the Prince of Vampires.

Printed in the United States of America
ISBN: 978-0-982-903384

1 2 3 4 5 6 7 8 9 10

*For Kristie,*

*Because you believed in me
and pushed me to do my best.*

*For all my fans,*

*Because you loved my characters as much as I do
and wouldn't let me off the hook.*

One life is all we have and we live it as we believe in living it. But to sacrifice what you are and to live without belief, that is a fate more terrible than dying.

*- Joan of Arc*

# Chapter One

"I need some ore," Phil said with a scrupulous grin behind his fanned out cards as his sexy dark eyes flirted directly with mine. "Anyone got any?" I marveled at his perpetually perfect shock of sandy blond hair.

Three ore cards mocked me within my undisclosed hand, along with a few others. If I traded my ore—which I really didn't need—he might win again. His smug aura told me he pretty much had this game in the bag; it was a matter of time.

"I'll trade for a brick?" he asked, his sharp canines revealed in his smile. No one budged, though I sensed a few were tempted. "Two bricks?"

Katie caved first. "Okay. Here."

Within moments of the trade, Phil switched out his city for a settlement, pleasure beaming from him like a strobe light.

"Nice," Tyler said with a twisted grin.

"Pschtt!" I nudged Katie in the arm, pretending to be upset. "Why did you do that?"

"I need a brick and Phil's sitting on a brick factory over there." She pointed at the game board and blew aside her black bangs tinged with florescent pink highlights.

*True.*

Tyler's turn was next. As I watched him palm the dice, my competitive side itched for Lady Luck to grace me this turn. Normally the rolls I needed came up all the time, but not in this particular board game of *Settlers of Catan*.

Scarlett sat off to the side, dark hair falling over her shoulders in glossy waves, and read her worn *Tales* by Edgar Allen Poe. The fact that she enjoyed the stories as much as she did gave me the creeps. Her mind-reading abilities had ousted her from playing any games with us—not that she'd play anyway.

Tyler blew into his partially closed fist. "Come on, karma! Papa needs a new set of shoes." He shot us a coy smile then winked at Katie.

I withheld my comment as Katie giggled and wove her fingers through his brown locks at the nape of his neck. If she got the karma she deserved, she'd lose every game. Quick as a flash, Katie grabbed his hand and kissed his fingers before he could fling the white cubes. The interruption discombobulated his throw, causing them to skitter across the table, and onto the floor. I peeked over Tyler's knee and watched a die move of its own accord from a four to a five.

Scarlett coughed. Her icy-blue eyes peered at us momentarily over the binding of her book.

"You so cheat," I accused Phil, who appeared bewildered.

"I didn't do it." Phil held up his hands—truth rolling off him in huge waves. "This is crap anyway."

"That was *so* a four." I pursed my lips and raised a brow as guilt billowed out of Katie like a hole in a balloon.

She snickered and waggled her eyebrows. "What?"

"Fine, it's a four. No arguing." Tyler pulled a face and finished his turn.

Katie's turn was next. I crossed my fingers for something I could use.

"Eight," she called out. While she traded out her cards and moved her pieces on the board, I playfully mad-dogged Phil. Our competitive sides quietly bantered with one another through our eyes. My turn was next. I only had one chance to finish him off. While feeling for the dice, I kept an eye on Phil when Katie's shock and sudden elation sliced through my psyche.

Her squeal, followed by her inhumanly fast flit around the table, upset the board onto the floor. Annoyed, I pushed away from the table and moved over to the couch opposite Scarlett, away from Katie's blatant display. Though she rarely won, I wouldn't indulge her poor sportsmanship with any type of congratulations.

Phil came over and sat next to me—a little too close, actually. His wonderful natural scent filled my lungs and tempted me to bury my nose in his neck.

"Awww, don't pout," he whispered in his golden honey voice.

A huge part of me wanted to lean over and kiss him right then and there, but I knew his powers of persuasion were running at a high level. I fought the temptation and pulled out my *iPhone* instead, searching for a text from my missing boyfriend Nicholas—an obsession I couldn't kick.

"I'm not," I said defiantly. "If I would have gotten one more turn, I would have won. Katie was *lucky*."

"I see." He touched the tip of my nose then pointed to my touch-screen. "Anything exciting happening at Drama High?"

With a smirk, I put the phone away in my pocket. "No. Not today. But that reminds me. My Dad's out of town this weekend and—"

"No," Phil said quickly, flipping from sexy to cold in an instant. "Out of the question. We've already discussed the dangers as a group, not to mention I will not escort you to L.A. without your father's knowledge. Not after what happened."

His words sent tiny pinpricks of pain radiating across my

chest. Every day I'd conspired a way to get Phil to take me to L.A to see Nicholas and every time he'd tell me no. All to his benefit, of course. Without Nicholas around, Phil got all my attention. I couldn't complain. Alora had resurrected him from the pits of Hell and he'd practically become a saint.

But what I did hate her for was the fact she'd awakened Nicholas' vampire side by feeding him blood. She'd hoped, by turning him to the dark side, he'd retrieve her talisman from me so she could become invincible. The plan almost worked until Phil defected from her rule and saved me in the nick of time.

The horrific family reunion came to an end once Preston, Nicholas' father and avenger of evil, came to the rescue and took his wayward wife and son back to L.A. with a promise to rehabilitate them. The only thing I'd received to even suggest he was on the mend was a letter stating he missed me and a reassurance he'd come home soon. That was a month ago.

Lyrics to a song he wrote about me were sent as well. They lay hidden safely in my pocket, practically falling apart from all the times I've read them.

*Down by the ocean tide*
*the still of the moonlight*
*Its come at the right time*
*The moment we caught eyes*

*The sun hits your eyelids*
*an hour too early*
*and your heart starts racing*
*too quick for the morning*
*Ill equipped*
*for pretty sights*
*we're just ships*
*passing in the night*

*Just say the words*
*and I'll be right over*

*I'll meet you*
*at your bedroom roof top*

*The porcelain doves*
*chime above the highway hum*
*serenade the setting sun*

*I'm caught in your balcony breeze*

*Turn around*
*the winter jasmine crowns are born*
*they're waiting for a head to adorn*
*a pretty little head like yours*

*a pretty little little head like yours.*

*Ill-equipped*
*for pretty sights*
*we're just ships*

*passing in the night*

I'd continually looked for clues to what he was thinking when he wrote them. But all I could decipher was that separated ships never docked at the same time. Was that how he saw our relationship? Something that could never really be?

I curled my arms across my chest and huffed. His words promised he'd meet me on my bedroom rooftop. But when? Where was he?

"I can't keep doing this day after day. I have to find out something," I finally said with clenched teeth.

"I know." Phil looked at me tenderly while he massaged my shoulder, infusing me with his stress-releasing charm. "Patience, my dear sweet Parker. Patience."

I slid up against his chest. Whether I liked it or not, Phil did make me feel better. My spirit mended in his presence and I was beginning to need him—like a drug. I shut down my empathy and closed my eyes so I didn't have to watch Katie and Tyler snuggled up together on the opposite couch as they started a movie. She of all people didn't deserve the happiness wafting around us and lately my jealousy was getting the better of me. I didn't want to be a love buzz-kill, but their blatant displays often rubbed raw the longing in my heart.

But, for some reason, I always returned to hang with the Fab Five. Sam, my supposed BFF, had all her free time sucked up with her boyfriend Todd. So, I had no choice but to melt into the coven's regular routine where my melancholy mood was understood, for the most part. Phil and Katie were our sober vampires, Tyler and I were the inducted humans, and Scarlett was the token shape-shifting half-vampire den mother—a very motley group. After school, Tyler and I would hang out at Nicholas' abandoned house where Phil and Katie hid during the daylight hours.

"Do you have homework?" Phil asked while petting my hair.

"Mostly studying for finals," I murmured. "I also need to finish my history report."

Phil scoffed. "So glad I never have to finish high school."

I nudged him in the side. "Brat."

After a few minutes and with much reluctance, I slid down onto the floor and opened my backpack. My report wasn't going to write itself. Phil continued to try to distract me by playing with my hair, but he eventually succumbed to the movie.

I started to read about Betsy Ross, the subject of my report, but my mind drifted. The group didn't know, but I'd devised a new plan to see Nicholas. Sam and I were going to Disneyland for a few days as soon as school was out for summer. She'd scored tickets from her aunt and during the trip, somehow, someway, I'd get to Preston's house and see Nicholas in person. I had to.

I refocused my attention back to Betsy Ross when I felt it. A storm of rage sped towards Nicholas' house and whomever the feelings belonged to, they weren't about to let a door stand in their way from getting inside. I stood up, eyes glued to the sunlight-blocking barrier as I held my breath, hoping that someone was Nicholas.

"Parker, what's wrong?" Phil asked before Scarlett's warning screamed in our minds.

*"Hide!"*

The sudden movement of vampires escaping the scene launched my notes into the air like confetti, leaving Tyler and me alone to deal with whoever was about to come through the door.

# Chapter Two

Heart filled with hope, I sprinted to the door and threw it open. My feet skidded to a halt and I squinted up into a shadowed face, the silhouette shorter than I expected. My eyes took a moment to adjust in the full light of the sun.

"Julia?"

My brother's voice crumbled my anticipation into a ball. "Luke? What are you doing here?"

"What am I doing here?" He sneered and looked past me into the darkened living room, then grimaced once he spotted Tyler.

"Hey." Tyler stood and plunged his hands into his pockets. The guilt painted on his face didn't help matters.

"I'll be right back, Tyler." I shooed Luke off the porch before shutting the door.

We faced off for a moment as I slowed my rapid breathing. Luke's angry brown eyes bored holes into me.

"Dad knows I'm here. What's the big deal?"

"I called and you didn't answer."

I pulled my phone out to prove he didn't call. The missed call warning stared back at me.

"Oh. I didn't get it."

"Who's *that* guy?"

Suspicion ebbed off him in small bursts, infusing my anger with pity.

"Tyler?" I laughed. "He's just a friend. We're waiting for the others to come at any moment for a study group."

"Study group? Here? Whose house is this anyway?"

I propped my hands on my hips. "It's a friend's cabin. Really, it's no big deal."

Luke's anger hovered on the surface. He kept glancing at the house, shooting big brother lasers into the siding with his eyes.

I touched his arm. "Luke, you don't have to worry. Nothing's going on. I'm not like that."

His cheeks flushed at my correct assumption. He shuffled his feet against the dirt walkway. I wasn't sure if I should be hurt or flattered he cared about my honor, but I couldn't entirely be upset. Dad must have put him up to checking on me. I wanted to tell them both to chill and stop being all parental. In just a few short weeks, I'd be a senior in high school and practically an adult. I could handle myself.

"Last time your phone didn't work, you did need help . . . or have you forgotten already?"

I bit my lip. He was right. In September, I'd run out of gas after work and almost fell off a cliff walking home in the woods. My phone had become a casualty in the mishap. But of course, I'd left out a small detail when explaining the story of how I'd sprained my ankle; that a vampire stalked me and Nicholas came to my rescue.

"Since you've fixed my gas gauge, everything's been great. And I haven't been in the forest since that happened . . ." *and I wear a vampire warding talisman,* ". . . so."

Luke tilted his head. "Still."

I rolled my eyes. "Okay, well. As you can see I'm fine and if it makes you feel any better, I'll turn on my ringer so I don't miss your call. Can I go now?"

He squinted, pausing for effect. "I guess."

"You guess?" I playfully stuck out my tongue.

Luke still remained firm though my answers should have lessened his worry. I pulled out the big guns and pushed some peace his way to loosen him up. He finally produced a smile.

"You should open the blinds in there and let in the sun. What are you trying to do? Become vampires or something?" He shoved his hand into his pocket and pulled out his keys.

"Ha. Right." An unnaturally high pitched chuckle trilled from my lips as I punched him in the arm. "Will do. I'll be home later."

He rubbed his arm with a crease in his brow and spun on his heels. I waited until he drove his Blazer down the gravel driveway out of sight. Dad was seriously going to get a lecture for siccing Luke on me when he should have been the one calling if he was worried.

"I'm opening the door," I called out as a warning in case Phil or Katie were within reach of the sunlight I'd let in.

"What was that about?" Katie asked after peeking around the corner once I'd locked the door behind me. "Big brother's watching you. Dun, dun, dunnnnn."

"Nothing." I collected my papers from the carpet and rearranged my workspace on the dining room table behind the couch.

"Hmmm . . . Seems Luke needs something to do."

I ignored her and tapped my pencil on the paper, trying to pull together my thoughts.

Scarlett, who had shape-shifted into cat form at the sign of danger, curled up in the corner and gave herself a bath. Tyler started the movie again and the general curiosity died down, except for Katie.

She hung over the back of the couch, her face in her hands. "How did he know you were here?"

I glared at her inquiring eyes and bit my tongue. Years of unexpressed frustration from her rudeness bubbled to the surface. "It's no big deal, okay? He needed something."

"And he couldn't call you?"

I cocked my head to the side. "My phone was on silent, as if that's any of your business."

"Must have been important for him to drive all the way here." Her brow arched.

"It was."

"And?" Her big dark eyes bore holes into me while I remained tight-lipped. When I didn't cave, she pulled a face and slithered down the leather into Tyler's lap. "Well excuse me for asking."

Her catty tone sent a hurricane roaring through my stomach. She didn't care about me or Luke, or if something bad might have happened. She only asked because she feared being discovered. But the audacity for her to question me, especially after I'd secured her a hideout and protected *the secret* with my life was unconscionable. With shaking hands, I began to throw my things into my backpack.

"Wait." Phil appeared at my side and took my wrist. "Are you leaving?"

"I can't be in the same room as her right now," I whispered, noticing she didn't even care I was upset.

"She didn't mean anything. Please. Don't go."

His rich buttery voice tasted dreamy to my ears. But I couldn't stay. Her churning curiosity told me she had more crap to vent and my patience was growing thin.

"The movie is distracting me from studying. I'll see you tomorrow."

Phil took ahold of my bag and led me into the kitchen instead of the front door. I only put up a partial fight, enamored by his tenacity to keep me there. He stopped and gave me his spine-tingling grin for extra measure.

"Parker," he said, smoothing aside my bangs. "We'll figure out something with Nick. Don't let it consume you."

"It's not that." *Well, it is, actually, among everything else.* I looked away, wishing I could say what I wanted to out loud.

His dark satiny eyes grabbed my attention and I almost accepted the invitation to enjoy his delectable kiss when Nicholas came to mind. *If only I were single.* I backed away quickly, realizing my emotional roller coaster made fighting him off a struggle today. I had to leave before I did something I'd regret later.

"I'm doing my best. See you tomorrow." I placed a quick peck on his cheek and stole my bag from his shoulder.

My hair moved away from my neck and his lips grazed my ear lobe for a second. "Bye, Parker. Miss me."

I cracked a smile.

When I opened the door, he was gone—far away from the sunlight.

The drive home left me worse off than I'd hoped. All the things I should have said to Katie came to mind, including the confrontation I'd wanted to deliver for years. What if Tyler knew the truth about all her pre-vampire failed manipulation attempts to gain his attention? It was only after her sexy vamp-makeover did he finally notice her.

But I couldn't let Katie take the brunt of my anger. Alora was to blame for all of this. She'd acquired the venom serum and turned Katie in an attempt to lure me into her coven. When that failed, she captured and converted my half-vampire boyfriend—her long lost son—over to the dark side by force feeding him blood.

I clutched the talisman Nicholas gave to protect me. It was all she'd ever wanted. Well, that and her son. This whole time he'd thought she'd died after his birth. Preston had lied about the fact he'd changed her into a vampire and when she wouldn't agree to remain bloodless, Preston kidnapped Nicholas as a baby and ran.

How, after all that drama, could they become one big happy vampire family? Something else had to be preventing him from coming home. But what was it? I feared the worst. Did he not care for me anymore?

Pulling in front of my house, I stomped unnecessarily hard on the brake and slammed the transmission into park. The uncertainty was driving me crazy. Luckily I didn't have to wait long.

I picked up my phone and texted Sam.

**- Totally can't wait till Disneyland! Summer is HERE! Need to get out of this town!**

I waited, hoping she'd call me back, instead of texting. The phone remained silent in my hand. After no reply, I pocketed it, grabbed my backpack, and hauled myself inside. She must have been with Todd, like always.

I'd learned my lesson the last time I'd called. Todd did everything in his power to distract her from talking to me. She'd promised to call back and forgot. If Nicholas were here, I wouldn't have minded and would be distracted myself. Without him, I'd become a third wheel.

But our adventure to Disneyland was going to be the two of us. We'd drive down and stay at her aunt and uncle's who lived in Anaheim. And sometime, during the four-day trip, I'd steal away to Beverly Hills and visit Nicholas. One more week. I couldn't wait.

As I entered the house, my phone buzzed with a return text.

**- Me neither!!! Whoot!**

I closed my eyes and smiled as my heart fluttered in anticipation.

Inside, Luke watched TV, apparently over his bout of parental protection. The aroma of chili wafted from a pot on the stove—one he'd expect I'd wash later. But chili didn't tempt my taste buds. After the painful afternoon with Katie, *Ben and Jerry's brownie batter* ice cream was far more appetizing. I grabbed the half-eaten pint from the freezer and headed upstairs.

In my room, I sprawled on the floor and pulled out a leather journal from between my mattress and box spring. I trailed my fingers over the embossed cross-shaped dagger on the cover—the same emblem Nicholas had tattooed on his bicep. I closed my eyes and inhaled the rich leather, transported to the comfort of his arms wrapped tightly around my body while I nuzzled his coat. I imagined my fingers tangling in his soft dark locks. The pages flipped open to the middle, my fingers dancing over the words he'd written last fall.

*September 13*

*Today was a disaster. In my attempt to trail Lavin, I put Julia in harm's way. She'd run out of gas and her phone must have died, so she walked home through the forest. Her courage astounds me sometimes. Anyway, somehow she knew to run when Lavin found her. But she fell off the cliff. If she had died today, I would have snapped. I was just in time to catch her.*

*But to see her and hold her. God, it took everything in my power to keep from kissing her. She's just so beautiful. It's so wrong. But it feels so right when I'm with her. Of course she asked a million questions. I don't know if telling her I killed a mountain lion was such a good idea.*

*But luckily she's okay. I agreed to see her again, but now I know I can't.*

*This is going to kill me.*

*September 14*

*She's waiting for me right now and I can't go to her. It's driving me crazy. I know it's the right thing to do, but I can't stand it. I can't help thinking she probably hates me and never wants to see me again. I can't stand hurting her, but it's for the best. If any vamp were to know I care for her like I do, they'll torture her to torture me for all the slayings I've done. I could never live with myself if anything ever happened. AnneMarie's death nearly killed me. Julia will move on. She'll find another guy. And when she does, I'll make sure he's worthy of her, and if he isn't, I'll rip his arms off.*

*It's better this way. It has to be. It needs to be. It will be. I just need to stay focused so I don't do something stupid.*

*DAMN IT! I need to hunt something. Now!*

*September 16*

*Kill all vamps, Nicholas. That's your rule. And because you've broken it and decided to keep Lavin alive so he'd lead you to the coven, Julia knows you exist. Stop feeling sorry for yourself. You had to be short with her, not only because you were worried the bloodsuckers would get away, but because you can't have her harboring feelings for you. She'll recover and so will you. When you allow yourself to get attached, you get sloppy. You hesitated to spare her feelings and then you lost their scent—AGAIN.*

*That's why you have rules. Stop messing around, otherwise you're going to have bigger problems on your hands.*

I held the journal to my chest, remembering back to those first days together. If only I'd known the truth. He'd felt just as horribly as I had. Our connection was so much deeper than just one mission of mercy, no wonder I couldn't let him go. But it was all right there. Every encounter, every heroic deed the last eleven years of my life since he'd vowed to be my guardian when Mom died. He was trying to do the right thing every time.

I tucked the journal away and pulled out my school notes instead. Though his words made me feel better, the longing never stopped. I snuggled up on my bed and rested my head on my arm. So much to do, so little time before finals next week.

Hours later, the rap on the window broke the narcolepsy my homework had induced. I opened my eyes with a start.

"Parker," Phil quietly called. "Invite me in."

I blinked, groggy and unsure of the time. In the window, the moon tinged Phil's wayward blonde hair with golden strings of light. "You're invited in."

He slid the glass the rest of the way open and stepped inside quicker than my eyes could register. "Why do you do that?"

"Do what?"

"Un-invite me?"

I yawned and moved all the stuff scattered across my bed into a pile on the floor. "I don't."

"Really?" Phil moved towards me and sat down. "That's weird. Maybe the invite has an expiration date."

"Maybe." I chuckled and crawled under my covers, aware that only a thin sheet separated his body from mine.

If Nicholas saw us at this moment, he'd rip Phil's head off. They already had quite the jealous relationship going on, and Nicholas had killed him once. But his visiting and occasionally staying the night was harmless. And after reading Nicholas' journal again, I knew who my heart belonged to. I'd never let myself kiss Phil no matter how good I knew it would feel.

"You okay?" he asked, rubbing my shoulder and smoothing back my hair.

"Meh," I groaned, curling into the pillow and closing my

eyes. "If I talk about it, I'll just get all riled up again."

"And you're far too adorable when your angry," he said, a smile in his voice.

With all my energy focused on Nicholas, I'd forgotten how pissed I'd been at Katie.

"You're crazy." I leaned into his hands as his touch sucked all the tension out of my tired muscles. "It's just not fair. Katie has never gotten what she deserves and acts as if the world revolves around her. She hasn't even said thank you to me for letting her stay in Nicholas's house. Then she rubs her romance in my face when she knows I'm missing him."

Phil took his hand away and sighed. His longing radiated out, mingling with mine, and my words stabbed me in the gut. While I pined for Nicholas, Phil longed for me, a wish that would never come into fruition. The guilt tore into my illusion of our friendship. Once Nicholas did return, Phil most likely wouldn't stick around. The thought of losing him killed me. How could I survive this? I scooted away from him, adding a little space between us.

"The Fab Five isn't so fab," I said, burying my face into my pillow.

"I can talk to her."

"No, don't. It's over."

Silence lingered, the tension building. He knew what I wanted and I knew what he wanted—a recipe for disaster. We needed to stop pretending everything would always be like this. That we'd be close. That he could come over anytime he wanted at any hour in the night and talk. That I'd eventually accept Nicholas wasn't returning and become his.

Without a word, Phil popped off the bed and reappeared at the window. "Well, I just wanted to make sure you were okay. I'm sure you're tired, so . . . I can go."

I bit my tongue to stop myself from asking him to stay. "Yeah. Big day tomorrow. Thank you for checking on me."

He nodded and disappeared, disappointment fluttering out the window with him.

# Chapter Three

"So, about next Friday. Is everything cool with your aunt?" I asked, trying to gain Sam's attention and failing miserably.

Her gaze lingered exceptionally long on Todd as he walked away from us toward the cafeteria line with Tyler.

"Hmmm? Oh yeah. It's cool," she said, taking a seat at our table.

Beyond the few measly minutes before class started, I never got time alone with her anymore and I wanted to discuss the details before the guys returned. Not to mention, I didn't want Tyler to overhear. My plan was privileged information, and the Fab Five was only on a "need to know" basis.

"It's awesome she got us those park hopper passes. Helps when you know Tinkerbell personally, right?"

Sam laughed. "Yeah, and she got an extra one for Todd too."

The blood drained from my cheeks. "Todd?"

"Oh." Sam looked at me, guilt wafting out. I pulled my feelings radar in tighter. Whatever she had to say, I didn't need to feel her excuses as well. "I was hoping that would be okay."

I looked away, swallowing the bitter pill. How could she do this? We'd been planning our girls' getaway for months now—just us.

"That's okay, isn't it? I was thinking we could ask Tyler to come, too."

"Tyler?" I wrinkled up my nose. "Why Tyler?"

"I thought maybe since you've been spending so much time together . . ."

"Tyler's just a friend. I'm back together with Nicholas."

She looked down and chipped the black paint off her fingernail. "I thought you hadn't heard from him in a while."

"I . . . I have," I said, suddenly feeling as though I needed to defend our relationship.

"Oh, really? When?" Sam straightened up and for once gave me her full attention.

"Last week . . ."

Her eyes widened. "And you didn't tell me? This is huge."

"He's been super busy with work." Maybe mentioning Nicholas wasn't such a good idea after all. "It was a letter. He's supposed to be back soon. But, since we were going to be close to his Dad's when we go to Disneyland, I was hoping we'd stop by. He's staying there right now." I'd have the perfect excuse—I was in town and wanted to invite him along.

"Oh . . ." she leaned in and whispered, "Top secret under cover stuff?"

"Yeah."

Sam bit her lip. "That sounds dangerous."

I took a deep breath and mashed my lips together. "You know, forget it. Maybe I shouldn't come at all." *And just go on my own to L.A. without you.*

"What? No. I want you there."

"Want Julia where?" Tyler asked, as he approached the table.

*Crap.* I froze, watching him take a seat, his aura brimming with curiosity.

"Nothing," I said and kicked Sam under the table.

"Ouch." She looked at me and frowned. "We're going to Disneyland. Didn't Jules tell you?"

Tyler squinted and cocked his head to the side. "No, she didn't."

"I didn't?" I shrugged and faked a laugh. "What did you get for lunch?"

Tyler's tray hit the table hard as Todd slid in next to Sam. Their sudden interest in each other masked the tension building between Tyler and me.

"You should come with us," Todd finally offered.

Tyler's aura teemed with suspicion. "When are you going?"

I opened my sack lunch and pulled out a bag of cheese curls. "These are so yummy. Have you tried them?" I held out the bag to Tyler.

He shot me a glare.

"Next week, after finals on Friday," Todd interrupted, as if he'd always been invited to go.

I glowered at Sam, my stomach clenching and unclenching. The more I thought about it, the more I didn't want to go. I could already see how the trip would unfold, starting with me getting stuck in the back seat and having to watch them be all lovey the entire drive.

I stood up, unable to take the pressure any longer. "Sam, can I talk to you in private?"

She looked startled, but nodded. "Yeah, sure."

I walked ahead of her out the double doors to the quad and turned to her once we got outside. Sam oozed dread. She knew exactly what was wrong.

"This was supposed to be our girl trip," I finally said.

Sam's eyes fell downward, her foot tracing a crack on the cement. "Yeah, but I didn't want him to feel left out . . ."

"Left out? You didn't even ask. I never get time alone with you anymore and I was counting on this. Now I'll be the third wheel."

"But what about Nicholas? You said he might come, too."

I inhaled and closed my eyes. "I'd never ditch you for a guy, Sam."

"Are you saying I'm ditching you?"

"No, but this just makes everything awkward now. I'm not even sure I want to go."

"What? Why?" Sam's mouth fell open. "You have to. I'm not going to stay at my aunt's alone. My mom thinks it's just us."

So that was it. I was the cover-up for her having a fun getaway with her boyfriend.

"So where's Todd staying?"

"He's got a friend down there . . ."

I crossed my arms. "You didn't think I'd be upset?"

"I'd hoped you'd understand," she said. "When Nicholas was around, I never complained when you two spent all your time together. I could have, easily. But to be honest, I never liked how he treated you and his convenient disappearances with his so-called job." She paused for a moment, mustering up her courage before she annihilated me with a hard stare. "Don't you see he's dangerous? But I didn't say anything and accepted your relationship out of respect, because you love him. And now that I'm in a serious relationship, I expect the same from you. It's just common courtesy. I love Todd and I—" she gulped and puffed out her chest in pride, "hope to marry him someday."

I couldn't believe my best friend, who's always been so sensible and sweet, was actually telling me this. What had Todd done to her? A million cruel things bounced around in my mind to say but I bit my tongue and blinked in disbelief. I quickly scanned her finger for a ring or something and found nothing.

I squeezed my arms tighter, partly due to the chill from the wind, but mostly because she'd chosen him over me.

"No, actually it's common courtesy when you plan a trip

with your best friend to not invite your boyfriend to come along, too. Behind my back."

Her pain flared and I clamped down my gift. We looked at one another for a moment and I swallowed hard. All I wanted was for her to tell me she'd uninvite him. She'd made a mistake. She was sorry.

"You're making this harder than it needs to be, Julia. Don't make me choose," she finally said and turned to rejoin Todd inside the cafeteria.

I stood outside, rejected and torn. How did this end so badly? And why, when I missed Nicholas so much, did I want comfort from Phil?

I gauged the interior before entering the kitchen door of Nicholas' house. Though I didn't think I'd go to Disneyland after all, I didn't want the group to give me a heaping dose of disapproval on top of my fight with Sam. The mood inside was the usual mishmash of Phil's boredom, Scarlett's annoyance, and Katie and Tyler's infatuation with one another. I wanted to vomit.

*Why do I come here?*

Phil's face lit up once he saw me. He vanished from the couch and reappeared at my side, taking my backpack from my shoulder before I could blink. "Hey, you . . . where you been?"

"School." *And taking my time.*

"Thank God there's only one more week of that. You stoked?" he asked with a mischievous grin.

I raised my eyebrow. "Maybe?"

"Big Senior on campus now."

"If I survive finals."

I glanced over at Tyler, who gave me a knowing look. Obviously, he hadn't ratted me out yet.

"And we'd be getting ready for Texas A&M," Katie purred while wrapping her arms around Tyler's waist. "You aren't still going, are you?"

"Well, yeah," Tyler said with a shrug. "I have a scholarship."

I chuckled at her mistake. Of course he'd go. He had a human life to live, after all.

A red puncture wound, just below his collar line, marred his neck—evidence of why he'd been ditzy as of late. I frowned at Katie. Though her sterile venom wouldn't make him a vampire, she wasn't supposed to be feeding on him, or any one for that matter. The unwritten tenant agreement for her to stay in Nicholas' house required her abstinence from drinking blood.

"Does that mean you're going to be hanging out here more often?" Phil said in my ear, while Katie begged Tyler to stay home.

"Yeah, I guess. I should try to get my job back."

I continued to eye Tyler's neck, sickened she'd break our most cardinal rule. The urge to confront them burned on my lips, but I refrained for fear Tyler would retaliate and tell everyone about Disneyland.

It didn't matter. Everything was about to change anyway. Once I reunited with Nicholas, they'd all need to move out. And whatever Katie decided to do from then on would be her own business. She probably would go to Texas with Tyler and move into his dorm room anyway.

Phil put his arm around me and pulled me into his shoulder.

"Whatcha thinking about, Parker?"

"Nothing. Just finals."

"Are you sure you're not thinking about your trip to *Disneyland* next week?" Katie asked, her voice sweet like honey, but cutting like acid.

All eyes fell on me. *Here we go.*

"Your what?" Phil asked.

"That's ill-advised," Scarlet interrupted.

Stunned, the group all turned to her in unison since she rarely spoke out loud. I ignored her and kept my glare on Katie. No one had claim over my comings and goings, especially not neck-biting Katie.

"Yes, that's on my mind as well, thank you very much for mentioning it. I need a vacation."

Scarlett inhaled deeply, while Phil's arms fell to his sides. Everyone's uncertainty laced the air around me, its tentacles looking for hearts to constrict.

"You're not welcome in Los Angeles. The line has been clearly drawn. If you are out at night for one instant, they'll find you," Scarlett said.

I smirked. "Have you forgotten the talisman? There's nothing those vamps can do to me."

"Physical harm, no. But psychologically . . ." Scarlet closed her eyes. "It's just not in the plan."

*The plan.*

She'd finally somewhat voiced her real purpose for being in our muddled group. Though everyone believed she liked heading up our coven, interested in our teenage drama and banter, I knew the truth. She only hung around to keep tabs on me so I'd fulfill my destiny, a fortune told to me by her deceased owner several months ago. Madame had read my palm and said I'd single-handedly wipe the earth clean of vampires, which ironically included her shape-shifting self. So of course, being in mixed company, the "plan" wasn't freely shared.

But because each vampire's lifeline depended on their maker being alive, in order to fulfill the prophecy, I'd have to kill Cain, the father of all vampires. Only then could they all be destroyed in one swoop. Though I hated the evil vampires of the world, and grieved daily the murder of my mother by one, I'd never do it, even if offered the chance. How could she even think I'd murder Nicholas, Phil, Katie and even herself?

"I'll be careful."

Phil shot me a pained look and opened his mouth, but closed it again. Guilt plunged into my stomach, but I kept my back stiff. I had to do this for me. If no one was willing to stand up against the vampires of L.A., then I'd go alone and use whatever guise it took.

"Chasing him is just going to backfire," Katie said.

I shot her a look. "What did you just say?"

"Honey, Nicholas obviously wants space. Going down there will just make you look desperate."

An ocean of feelings rippled through my chest, the biggest being anger. Katie of all people shouldn't be lecturing me on "chasing" guys. That had been her whole reason for living, prior to becoming a vampire. Only after her beauty was enhanced with vampiric juju, was Tyler unable to fend off her charm.

"You've got some freaking nerve," I finally said, my hands forming into fists.

Katie stood up and handed me a glare. "You just don't seem to care that there's more than just your concerns to consider in the Fab Five. As a group we decided a long time ago it would be best for you to stay here and wait for him to return. You can't just go flitting off to Disneyland and put everyone in jeopardy. It's stupid."

"Shut-up, Katie!" I exploded, adrenaline opening the floodgates behind my words. "You have no clue the sacrifices I've given you. A safe place to stay, and a coven for all intents and purposes. And all I've received in return is your snappy tongue. My boyfriend could be dead for all I know and no one here cares. And way back when, we decided we'd discuss it. Not that I'd wait forever."

"Well, the coven has spoken. Am I right?" She looked at everyone and when no one spoke up, she flipped her dark hair and turned her back on me. "For stuff like this, it's just how it needs to be. So deal."

The blood ripped through my veins like a freight train. Katie needed to understand who was really in charge here: me. And without my invitation, she'd be on her own, fending for shelter from the sun.

"I'm sick of waiting. I'm sick of everyone else deciding my future, sick of people disregarding my feelings. I won't have it anymore!" I punched my accusing finger in the air toward the front door. Freezing her ass in its place would finally give her the scare of her life, and force a healthy dose of respect for what I'd given her. "I want you out of here, Katie. Out of my boyfriend's house. You're no longer wanted here!"

The front door, which I thought was locked, popped open of its own accord, startling everyone. Phil and Katie ducked for cover, but Katie's body took flight in the air and moved toward the open doorway. She screamed and clawed her nails into the wood flooring. To my horror, the invisible vacuum sucked harder and pulled her body outside, dousing her in complete sunlight. Flames combusted off her skin before the door slammed shut.

# Chapter Four

Katie's screams trailed off into icy silence. Tyler ran to the door and opened it while Phil darted from behind the couch to the back part of the house, his arms smoldering.

"Shut the door!" Phil yelled.

"NO!" Tyler gasped. "What the Hell was that? Where's Katie?"

My eyes followed the deep grooves her fingernails had etched into the wood floor, their path leading directly to the smoldering pile on the doorstep. My throat constricted as I blinked in disbelief, then fell to my knees. Katie was only supposed to freeze in place, like Scarlett did the time I uninvited her. She'd just become frozen, unable to move, completely at my mercy. Not sucked out of the house! What had I done? I'd only meant to scare Katie, not . . . kill her.

"That wasn't supposed to happen." I shook my head and choked on the acrid odor of smoke that lingered in the air, horrified at the ash swirling at his feet. "I don't understand."

"What do you mean you didn't mean to? Where's Katie? This isn't funny!" Tyler yelled.

"Tyler," Scarlett said calmly, taking his hand and leading

him back inside, shutting the door. "You need to sit down."

"NO! This isn't funny anymore. Joke's over! Bring her back."

"She's gone." Scarlett grabbed Tyler by the arms and dragged him to the couch.

"What do you mean she's gone?"

Numbness deadened my thighs as everything played through my head like a bad horror flick. I didn't understand why Katie and Scarlett's uninvites worked so differently.

"I am so sorry." I looked up at him through my tears. How could he ever forgive me? How could I forgive myself?

Cold hands gripped my shoulders from behind, encouraging me to rise.

"Go talk with Phil," Scarlett whispered. "I'll handle things out here."

I couldn't move, let alone think over the sound of Katie's scream resonating inside my head, reminding me that I was responsible for her death. I looked helplessly at Scarlett as she motioned for Phil to come out of hiding and take me to the kitchen. Once we turned the corner, I collapsed into his arms.

"I didn't mean to," I sobbed.

He smoothed my hair and held me tightly against his chest. His body trembled against mine, rumbling out fear. "Shhh . . . it'll be alright, Parker. Don't be upset at yourself. We all know it was an accident."

"That's not what happened when I uninvited Scarlett. Katie was only supposed to freeze like a statue. Why? Why was she sucked outside like that?"

"You didn't know," he said, holding me tighter. "No one is blaming you."

I pushed off and wiped my nose with my sleeve. "I just wanted to teach her a lesson." My body shook, my legs morphing into rubbery strings of spaghetti.

He watched me with anxious, dark eyes, ones I couldn't believe I was looking into. Nicholas had killed Phil. I'd watched him die. Flashbacks of his death flooded over me.

"Wait. You came back. How? Tell me how!" I pounded my fists into his hard chest.

Phil creased his brow and firmly grasped my wrists. "I don't know. Alora did it. She never told me how."

I pushed him off and ran to the living room, catching Scarlett as she worked her mind powers on Tyler. His teary eyes were closed while he rested his head on the back of the couch.

"Phil—Phil was brought back. How, Scarlett? How did she do it?"

She took her gaze off Tyler and drew her eyes into thin slits. "I don't know." Anger trailed her words, clueing me in to the fact that even if she did know how to bring Katie back, she wouldn't share.

I swiveled around and plowed into Phil who'd appeared soundlessly behind me. "Phil, try to remember how she did it." In a frenzy, I gripped his shoulders and tried to shake him. He sighed, unmovable, and shrugged. I turned to Scarlett. "Search his memories. Find out what happened!"

"He'll only know what happened afterward, if that. It's useless, Julia, and not part of the plan."

Tyler, lost in shock, had reopened his eyes and gazed off into space, mumbling something incoherent. I wondered what Scarlett had done to him.

I regained my focus and glared at her. "No! We have to resurrect her. I'll go and ask Alora myself if I have to!"

Scarlett disappeared off the couch and reappeared in my face. "Come with me."

I allowed her to pull me into the kitchen when everything inside me wanted to strangle her neck instead. I had to make this right, no matter what and she'd comply—she had to.

"I don't understand," I said. "Why did that happen?"

"You uninvited her. What else did you expect?"

"Certainly not that! I expected her to react like you did when I uninvited you."

"I'm a half-vampire. My rules are different."

"Different?" I ran my hands through my hair. "Then you have to help me get her back."

"No, I do not," Scarlett said with a laugh. "What's happened is done. Her foolishness and disrespect to the human who gave her asylum was her undoing. Some lessons are hard to learn, especially for a fledgling. I'm glad to be rid of her immaturity and human *boyfriend*. They were only weighing us down. I've started to erase his memories so he can go back to his world, free of us. I can't allow you to lose sight of your destiny."

A nervous laugh bubbled out of my throat. "Everything is a business transaction with you, isn't it? You never give up. I've already told you, I'm not the one you and the Fortune Teller predict to solve this problem. And even if I am, do you realize what that means? I have to kill Nicholas." I pointed toward Phil, who'd appeared silently in the hall. "And Phil and *you*. Is that what you want?"

She smiled, sending a shiver down my spine. "That's how it all ends. I am ready."

Phil's eyes grew wide as his fear escalated. He moved into the room. "You really believe that, Scar?"

Scarlett turned, her aura filled with hope. "Yes. And it's what we want. The redemption we've been searching for."

He tilted his head. "How could sending me back to Hell be what I want?"

*Finally! Phil is seeing the light!*

I folded my arms in victory, celebrating to have an ally for once.

"But that's not where you'll go. Julia's the Seer and if we help her, we'll earn a place in Heaven."

Phil arched an eyebrow. "What are you talking about?"

"The ancient prophecies have foretold that when the deal was made with the snake and Cain, God made another deal as well. He bestowed gifts upon a Seer to search out and find Cain to destroy him. Julia is the Seer of this generation. If we help her fulfill God's calling, we'll be shown mercy."

Phil looked at her quizzically and frowned.

Scarlett started to pace, her anger rising when she failed to convince Phil. "I didn't believe Madame's prediction at first because I've never been able to find a Seer in all my years of looking. I was beginning to think the prophecy was a myth, but then Julia walked into our fortune teller shop. Now I don't believe it to be such a coincidence. Fate brought her to me. She's the one, and I must help her."

"What?" I moved between her and Phil. "What are you talking about?"

She glared at me, fire behind her eyes. "We are meant to work together, Julia. I'm to protect you from an early death so you can fulfill your calling."

I pulled my head backward and sucked in a deep breath.

"I'd never let anything happen to Julia." Phil appeared behind me and encircled his arms around my waist.

"Of course you wouldn't," Scarlett said. "But the Seers before Julia weren't as fortunate. Once Cain discovered the prophecy, he had the Seers sought out and killed. And eventually, through time, the prophecy was forgotten, though the gifts were still present. The Seer of the age wouldn't know why she was different. And without help, a vampire, naturally drawn to her, would find and kill her. But that doesn't have to be Julia's fate. With our help, we can find Cain and bring about the justice he deserves."

"I don't think so." I threw up my hands. "Other than this stupid empathy, there's nothing special about me. There's no way I'm this . . . so called Seer."

Scarlett lifted her brow. "Your empathy *is* one of the gifts. Why else would it be imperative you felt bloodlust?"

My mouth dropped open, my head spinning. Was this the purpose of our gift? Could my mother have been a Seer too? Did her empathy pass to me because of her death?

"No," I whispered.

Scarlett's face softened as she approached me. "You don't have to be afraid. We'll help you. Our death is not the end. There is life beyond this and everyone must choose whom they serve. Phil understands this. He's experienced *our* fate and received a second chance. Next time, things don't need to be the same for him."

Phil leaned his chin against the top of my head, radiating sadness and protection. He'd already been trying to make good with God on his own and working to avoid returning to Hell. But to assist in his own death? Though Scarlett's speech sounded logical, Phil and I could never actually follow through with it. I'd die first.

I pinched my eyes shut in an attempt to stop the insanity. "What you want is impossible. Why can't you see that?"

"Well, the prophecy states you'll save us innocently, so when the time comes, you won't have a choice. And the talisman will protect you so you can fulfill your task." Scarlett waved her hand over my neck and the talisman warmed against my skin as if in agreement to her words. "Until the day of reckoning with Cain, your safety is all that matters."

*No.* I touched the stone and glared at Scarlett. *No, you're both wrong.*

"So if the talisman is protecting me, I'm safe wherever I go. I can even go to L.A. alone."

She gripped the edge of a kitchen chair. "Julia, don't you see the danger of venturing into an area where vampires specifically want your death and can control your thoughts? We can't be there to intervene, to protect you. It's too risky. Especially for a vacation."

I shirked out of Phil's arms, tempted to scream in her face. "Disneyland? You think I still care about Disneyland after what just happened? No. I'm going to see Alora. Katie might have been annoying, but she was my friend and has been for a long time. I can't allow her to rot in Hell because of my mistake. Alora knows how to bring her back." *And I miss Nicholas and have to know what's going on.*

"It's unwise," she said plainly.

I formed my hands into balls and looked to Phil for help. He pursed his lips. He sided with Scarlett on this one.

"Katie can help. She can gain redemption, too. It's important I know how. What if someone else falls victim or there's another accident?"

"Nice try, but Katie had her chance," Scarlett said. "In time, none of this will matter. I only want the faithful by our side to help in the end."

"Stop it!" I yelled and pounded my fist on the counter.

"The greater good is what you need to remember, otherwise more will suffer. More mothers will be murdered, friends born to Satan's side, more destruction and death. We have a chance to do something honorable for all mankind."

"Brownie points with God." I laughed, "Are you insane?"

She bowed her head. "It's worth the sacrifice."

"No." I put my head in my hands. "I can't! I won't!"

I brushed past her and burst out of the kitchen door toward my car. With fingers gripped tightly on the steering wheel, I sped into town with no destination in mind. Everything was spinning out of control. Nothing made sense and I couldn't take it anymore. I hated the cosmos for giving me this stupid gift, Scarlett for being a thorn in my flesh, Nicholas for not being strong enough to fight his dark side, Sam for abandoning me, Phil for confusing me on a daily basis, Alora for ruining everything, Tyler for ratting me out, and Katie for dying. The frustration became words I shouted at the top of my lungs until my throat burned.

For once I actually wanted to talk directly to God. I wanted to know what to do. Laughter bubbled out of my throat as I turned on Highway 17 toward Los Angeles. At this point, nothing mattered but the truth. Screw finals.

My shoulders relaxed as I took in the view at the summit, the ocean in the distance over the tops of redwoods. The thought of being sucked dry and freed from the chaos seemed inviting. Maybe if I just stood in the middle of L.A. and screamed, the vampires would come get me. Maybe then, Nicholas would come to my rescue and stop this.

My phone vibrated with a text from Dad.

**- Come home. There's been an emergency.**

I pulled off to the side of the road, my hands shaking. Last emergency, Dad ended up in the hospital with heart issues. Was that happening again? My hands trembled as I dialed the phone.

"Dad?" I asked, afraid this time something horrible happened to Luke. "What's wrong?"

"Just come home, honey. Your mother's body has been found."

# Chapter Five

On the drive home Dad told me builders, in preparation for condos, unearthed Mom's resting place in L.A. on accident. Visions of the beautiful field where Nicholas had once planted all the flowers was now overrun with tractors and equipment, tearing up the mountainside. To my surprise, Dad wasn't as distraught as I expected. Instead, his heart was filled with anger and revenge as if he'd known all along, emotions too soon in the grief cycle. Luke completely fell apart, which ripped my insides to shreds.

Detectives did note the position of her body suggested respect, indicating someone who knew her had buried the body. That part hit Luke the worst, helplessness drowning him through silent tears. Dad said, other than a broken clavicle, they didn't find anything else showing how she was murdered. The truth, that a vampire killed her and Nicholas and Preston buried her, weighed heavily on my heart.

It was decided we'd go to L.A. as a family to bury Mom—and hopefully our demons as well. The Disneyland trip and my finals were postponed. Getting out of my obligation with Sam flooded me with relief. But, if I'd thought escaping to see

Nicholas with Sam in tow was going to be a challenge, there was no way under the dutiful watch of my dad I'd get that chance. I had to come up with another plan.

In my room, with my feelings blanket wrapped tightly over my psyche, deep-seated longing for Mom wiggled its way to the surface. Doubt, fear, and loss. I pulled out Nicholas' journal again, craving his words, hoping they'd fill the ache inside my soul. Only he and I knew the truth.

**May 25**

*Today has been the worst day of my life. My mistake cost my closest friend her life. I will never forgive myself. Her blood is on my hands and I'll never forget the look on her daughter's face when I took her home, alone. The poor girl. I will never let anything happen to her. Why didn't I go? Why didn't I listen to myself? Why did I let my dad talk me out of it? This damn curse . . . everyone I love dies.*

I gulped hard, swallowing down his guilt heavily scrawled across the pages. What would Mom say to all of this? She wouldn't have blamed Nicholas just because he was late to meet her at the park that night. The whole incident was poor timing. If Mom attracted vampires like I did, more run-ins would have been expected. But the set-up created a recipe for lifelong second-guessing for him.

Through my experiences, I'd come to realize bad things happen to good people—especially when vampires were involved. Some things couldn't be prevented. Unless he'd sworn himself to be her protector the day they'd met, but this still might have happened on a different day and I could have been a victim alongside her, or worse, his enemy as a newly sired vampire.

**May 30**

*I'm tormented by her eyes. I dream and I'm stuck, watching what happened and I can't stop it. Only when hunting them down do I feel any relief. Like I'm doing some good. Even though it's suicide, I'm having thoughts to hunt Cain myself and kill him. This has to stop. His death is the key to stopping all of it. Why am I such a coward?*

I sighed. All Nicholas wanted was to avenge the curse of the vampire, the destiny I ran from. What would he think if he knew I was the chosen one, the Seer? But now that we loved each other, would he want me to hunt down Cain and destroy him? Destroy us?

**June 1**

*I can't get this out of my mind. Something was strange about the vampire that bit AnneMarie. Before I finished him off, he acted drunk, delirious even. I'd never encountered a vampire that acted that way before . . .*

Phil's angst startled me. I shoved the journal into my backpack and pulled *Promise* off my nightstand.

"Parker," he whispered before opening up my window. "Can I come in?"

"Of course you can." I patted the carpet next to me. "Have a seat."

Now was as good a time as any to tell him I wasn't going back—that the Fab Five, down two members, was about to fall apart.

He sat down and took my hand. "We need to talk." His newfound happiness shocked me, especially after what happened earlier in Nicholas' kitchen.

"I have to tell you something, too."

"Wait. Me first." Relief snaked through us as he wrapped his arm around my waist. "Scar caved. She promised to find out how to resurrect vampires. So you don't need to go after all."

My jaw dropped. "She did? Why?"

Phil gave me his charming grin. "Because I just asked her to."

He said it so plainly like he'd asked her to pick up ice cream from the store. I knew better. His mischievous aura tipped me off something further transpired to get her to budge.

"And?"

"What do you mean 'and'?" He coughed to hide a snicker.

I put my hand on my hip. "She told me *emphatically* that she wouldn't."

"I gave her an offer she couldn't refuse," he said with an Italian accent.

"Like what?"

"My loyalty."

"You've got to be kidding me." I folded my arms over my chest.

"She needs me to be on her side and we both need you alive. So since you are determined, I showed her reason."

"You and your charm." I took a deep breath and collapsed into his chest. "But that doesn't mean she'll tell me once she does know."

"She's a pussycat. All meow, no bite. I'll get her to talk."

I knew he was fishing for a laugh to lighten me up, but I was in no mood. I closed my eyes instead and pouted up my lip. He couldn't even begin to fathom the depths of her manipulation. Lucky for Phil, I was too tired to lecture him about all the crap she'd been responsible for unleashing. There was an ulterior motive behind her change of mind, and I was sure I'd find out soon enough, whether or not I wanted to.

"So what's your big news?" he asked, interrupting my thoughts.

"Oh." I bit my lip, wanting to keep quiet. He deserved the

truth. And if Nicholas came back with me when we returned, he needed fair warning. "We found my mom."

"Your mom? I thought she was—she's alive?"

"No. They finally found her body."

"Holy . . . I am *so* sorry." He wove his hand into mine.

"In Los Angeles," I mumbled. "So, there will be a funeral . . ."

"You're kidding." Phil sighed and rested his head against the top of mine, oozing defeat. "After all that. And you're going to see Nick while you're there, aren't you?"

I cringed out of his view. "I'm going to try. I don't know, it'll be harder with my dad around. But I'm definitely leaving the Fab Five. I can't do this anymore, can't pretend we're together for some common good because Scarlett has a death wish—"

"Don't be mad at her," Phil interrupted.

I pushed off his chest and glared. *Traitor.* "What else did you bargain for?"

"Nothing. And you need to remember she's not the enemy. Did you know her mother was bitten when she was pregnant and died when Scarlett was born? And as an orphan, people rejected her because of her differences. The only rewarding relationship she's ever had was with that Fortune Teller who cared for her like her own. She just wants to fulfill her purpose—"

"Yeah, but—"

"Wait, I'm not done. Look at what happened to Katie, how easily . . . you know." He pulled a face and gritted his teeth together. "What if you get mad at me one day and you totally know you will. You could kick me out, too. The invitation clearly isn't permanent, even here. I could die tomorrow by accident and if that happens . . . I don't want to end up *there* by accident."

I stared into his nebulous eyes. "She's brainwashed you!"

"What she's saying makes sense and I've seen a side of life you haven't. Hell, fire, damnation! It's a real place, Parker. I'm willing to do whatever it takes to stay out of there."

I turned my back to him and folded my arms. Scarlett's fear tactics worked. She'd successfully coerced his cooperation against me.

"So I kill you and cross my fingers you all end up in Heaven? Do you hear what you're saying? I'm not going to do that. I think even if the two of you don't succeed in helping someone stop the vampires, you'll both be redeemed. What I remember from Sunday School isn't about what you do for God, but the condition of your heart . . . think about it. What could you possibly do that will earn you eternity? Nobody's perfect."

"Even still—"

"What about what you said before? About no one knowing their fate. Scarlett's reasoning is wacked." The tirade from earlier unleash my tongue. "Did she tell you she knew all along Alora was Nicholas' mom? Everyone thought Alora wanted to turn Nicholas in for the ransom, when in fact she just wanted her son back—" *And the necklace.* "Scarlett knew because she specifically asked me not to tip him off early. And by listening to her, she got what she wanted. Nicholas was turned to the dark side, against me, making my prediction easier to fulfill. I get that her life has been hard, but she's taking it out on me and fixated on this ridiculous prediction."

"Don't forget she did her best to try to resuscitate him."

"Yeah, right." I clucked my tongue. "She ended up getting bit and feeding him with super blood."

Phil took my hands. "Yes, she's an enigma, but she's fighting the battle, just like I am. She doesn't have to be good. In fact, she's technically the most badass half-vampire in the world with her mind-reading skills and persuasive abilities. She could have anything she wanted. But instead, she's chosen to do the right thing—to defend something that saves you and your kind."

When he said "your kind," it sounded like I was inferior to him and the cause of this whole mess. I pinched my eyes shut and shook my head, rejecting the logic. "Well, I have to go to L.A. and I'm going to take the opportunity to talk to Alora. It's my fault that Katie's dead and I have to bring her back."

Phil studied me, sad and defeated. "Alora won't tell you."

"Maybe she'll have compassion since Katie was her kin . . ." *in the loosest sense of the word.*

He remained stoic. "Compassion isn't in her vocabulary."

"Don't you care?"

"I do, but I care more about keeping you alive." Phil took ahold of my shoulders. "You have to promise me you'll stay inside at night."

Goosebumps of heat spread across my skin from where he touched me. "I'm sure if I stay with my family nothing will happen."

"No." He stared into my soul with his dark eyes, zinging electricity to the bottom of my feet. "Promise me!"

"Okay." I shrugged off his grip and darted my gaze away. I couldn't handle him looking at me like that—like I wasn't coming back. "I don't even think I can get away. So much will be happening. I'm not looking forward to it," I said as a consolation, so he'd stop being so worried and jealous.

He wrapped me up in a hug, radiating truckloads of helplessness and concern. "I'm here for you . . . until you cross the border into L.A, that is. I love you, darlin', but I've used up my nine lives."

I involuntarily snorted. "Are you trying to tell me you shape-shift into a cat now?"

"I've got my secrets," he said with a smile in his voice. "So, when do you leave?"

"Friday, I guess."

He paused for a moment and squeezed me tighter. "You'll get through this, Parker. You're strong. Just don't be stupid."

"Me? Stupid? Never," I said, trying to sound funny.

"Love can make you do dumb things."

*Like sit here and console me? You need to lecture yourself.*

Both of us had done stupid things in the past for love. But Phil topped them off, wearing his heart on his sleeve.

"Sorry," I said and held my breath, apologizing for everything that made our relationship difficult and convoluted. The last thing I ever wanted to do was hurt him. But he needed to face the reality I could be bringing Nicholas home with me. Everything *would* change.

"For?" He pulled back and rubbed his thumb over my cheek. "Don't feel sorry for me. You know what they say about karma."

"I hate to see you suffering because of me. You've sacrificed so much."

His lips spread into a grin. "You, my dear, have never been the source of my suffering. Though, I do think your blood would be very delicious."

"Stop it!" I nudged him in the side. I wanted to tell him that he'd find someone, that he'd be happy like Nicholas and I were. But selfishly I wanted him loyal to me, too, at least now when I needed someone in my corner.

Phil laughed generously and held up his hands, changing the subject. "No, seriously. Once you twist Alora's arm and figure out how to bring Katie back, you won't have to worry about her anymore. Hell's gonna take out all her spunk. And the timing might have been ideal. She was asking a lot of questions . . ."

"About?"

"About how to turn people into vampires, why she couldn't do it, and if I could. I think she was planning to bring Tyler over to the dark side."

"Oh, great." The memory of the fang marks on his neck came to mind. Fortunate for Tyler, the venom purchased to change Katie only made sterile vampires. Phil on the other hand, an accident, was sired directly from Alora which made his bite lethal if you survived. "Did Scarlett finish mind wiping him yet?"

"Yeah. Can't have him roaming around, practically crazed over her. Donors start having an unhealthy attachment to their donees. He wouldn't have been able to keep the secret very long. Hopefully he won't remember. You'll have to gauge it when you see him again."

"You knew Katie was drinking off of him?"

"Of course I did. She's never been one for restraint."

I leaned into his chest and sighed. A bad omen followed me, and everyone close to me ended up getting burned. Was I destined to be unhappy my entire life, like Scarlett? Would I ever be able to shake this and live a somewhat normal life?

"Do you believe in happily ever after?" The words popped out of my mouth of their own accord and my cheeks flushed after I said them.

"As in soul mates? Sure . . . I guess . . . maybe . . . I don't know. I suck when it comes to love," he said and touched the tip of my nose. "Don't make decisions to spare my feelings."

"But when Nicholas comes back, then what?"

He stiffened. "*If* Nicholas comes back."

I paused and shuddered, the weight of his statement hitting hard. I'd been denying that something could be wrong, that he might not come back. What if he didn't? How long would I wait? My stomach pinched. I had to find out for sure. I had to find a way to see him.

Phil took ahold of my waist and squeezed. "I'll always be here to pick up the pieces."

I sighed and dreaded that this might be one of our last tender moments together. His cocky carefree bring-it-on attitude always soothed me like a warm bubbly bathtub—such a nice break from life. Nicholas' fight against his dark side never allowed those kinds of feelings to appear. Responsibility first. What would he be like after the rehabilitation? Possibly worse. Who was my true soul mate now?

"Will you stay with me tonight?" I finally asked. "No strings attached."

"Of course," he said, smiling that toothy grin that melted my knees. "Whatever you need."

# Chapter Six

I pushed earbuds into my ears and cranked up my music so I could escape Luke's chatty banter as he drove my Acura towards the bustling city of L.A. Dad had flown down a day earlier to deal with details we didn't need to be involved in. The further we drove, the more I wished I flew down early, too. Luke's grief coping mechanism involved talking about everything under the sun, as if our trip was for fun and not to bury our mother. I struggled most of the ride to keep his pain at bay. At each wave of sadness, his pain flew through my force field and pelted me when I least expected it. Probably because my concentration suffered. All I could think about was Nicholas and how I'd get away to see him.

Once we went up and over the Grapevine, my pulse sped up; the reality Nicholas was so close yet so far from my vicinity rocked my body. The first opportunity I had, during the daylight of course, I'd jam over to his house. His dad's address was already programmed in my phone—612 Elm.

As we left the I-5 and hit the 405, butterflies tickled my stomach every time I saw signs for Beverly Hills. Would we be staying close? Once we turned off onto Wilshire Avenue, déjà vu set in.

"Where are we staying?"

"The Hilton."

My pulse sky-rocketed. "The Beverly Hills Hilton!?"

"Yeah, why?"

"Oh." I ran my hand through my hair, trying to remain calm, my gut pinching and swirling. "I've heard it's nice."

Luke let out a "pssht" like I was losing my mind.

As the hotel came into view, I turned away, the memories flooding in too fast—Nicholas playing the guitar in the enormous Penthouse suite while the fire roared in the fireplace and the view of the HOLLYWOOD sign loomed in the background. My eye caught the *Vampire Vineyards Tasting Room* across the street.

"A vampire tasting room? How funny," Luke said, catching me gawk at the peculiar business.

"Yeah, weird."

I held onto my talisman, then glanced in the air with a shiver, the irony too coincidental to deal with. Somewhere out there, the real vampires of L.A. were hiding, waiting for the perfect opportunity to inflict revenge. I'd escaped their clutches twice and knew their secret, something hated in their world. The talisman, finally working, would hide my scent this time. Could I come and go without them even noticing me?

We parked in the parking structure next to the hotel and walked inside. I kept my head down in case the girl who worked in the boutique or the guy at the counter would recognize me. All I needed was a "welcome back and where's Mr. Kendrick," to let Luke know that I'd been here, with a boy no less. Luckily all the faces I saw were new. Luke got the keys from the main lobby desk and we escaped to the elevator.

My eyes zeroed in on the 23rd floor, the Penthouse. My stomach angrily squeezed the burrito I'd eaten on the road. Then to my horror, Luke pressed the button as if it were our destination.

"What are you doing?" I said, pulling his hand away after nothing happened.

"Nothing. Chill." He retracted his arm from my claws with a frown. "Just checking if it would work."

I exhaled and faced forward, composing myself. "Only celebrities and presidents," *and lifesaving vampires,* "stay there. You need a special key."

Luke grunted and pressed the 18th floor button. "Man, Julia. Why are you all jumpy?"

I wiped my hands over my jeans. The rise in the cab made the butterflies in my stomach flit harder. "I'm not. I just don't like breaking hotel etiquette."

Luke grunted disapprovingly and we rode the rest of the way in silence. Once we got to our room, he called Dad and I excused myself to the bathroom. The three of us rooming together in a cramped hotel room was going to be torture. I could shut off everyone while awake, but once I fell asleep, anything they felt would infuse my dreams.

I took out Nicholas' journal.

**November 12**

*Dad and I were returning from Harry's when we saw some of the Chupacabra's harassing some guy in a suit. Bold of them to cross the border from Mexico into LA's territory. Heckling before the attack is the new thing. Seasons the blood with adrenaline I guess. Gave us a chance to try the new stakes Harry constructed from Dad's venom. After we dusted the vamps we found out the guy was none other than Barron Hilton. As a thank you, we're allowed to stay at the Hilton any time whenever there's a vacancy. Pretty generous of him. Of course, he has no clue who we are but I doubt he'll ever talk.*

I chuckled. Even in his own private journal entry, Nicholas remained humble. I started to read the next entry when a knock on the door, coupled with Luke's impatience, bombarded me.

"I'm busy!" I yelled.

"Dad won't be back 'til later so I'm outta here."

"What?" I said as I shoved the leather book back into my bag and opened up the door. "Not in my car you aren't."

Luke frowned as I reached for my keys. "If anyone is leaving, it's going to be me."

"Fine," he said with an eye roll, "let's go."

We rode the elevator down to the lobby and I kept watching, hoping I'd run into Nicholas somehow, like my presence here would serve as some sort of beacon and draw him to me. I knew, though, I'd never be so lucky.

The rest of the afternoon, I bided my time. We went to the grocery store to load up on snacks and drinks for our room and I suggested a movie. If I chose a chick flick, I could escape to Nicholas' for the two hours while Luke was preoccupied in another theater. But Luke had seen all the other movies.

We ended up back at the hotel a little after 4:00. Luke sprawled out on one bed with his Hot Cheetos and I ate my Red Vines on the other. He clicked on the TV. I scrolled through my phone, hitting Facebook and Twitter, then Farmville.

**- Sorry about everything.**

Sam's text interrupted my game.

**- Yeah. We'll do Disney another time.**

I lay there hoping she'd text back, but there was nothing else. I stared at the sprinkler system attached to the ceiling. Trapped and waiting. The sun would crest the skyline in a few hours and I'd have to wait another day. The thought burned me up inside.

A sudden snort disrupted my daydream. Luke rolled over and mumbled something under his breath; orange cheese dusted over his lips. My heart sped up. He'd fallen asleep. Quick as a flash, I wrote a note and slipped into the hall. My fingers fumbled the cold keys in my pocket as I watched the numbers count down to one on the elevator display. Within minutes I was in my car, zooming towards Beverly Hills.

My hands shook as my eyes locked onto the Elm street sign before I turned down it. I was here, finally here and going to see him within minutes. The manicured lawns and pristine houses filed by; much less ominous during the day than as I remembered. My pulse lumbered and sputtered for a beat when I spotted his house.

I parked and waited, noting the inside. Beyond sensing someone's impatience, all seemed well. I bit my lip and traversed the path up to the huge porch. A crow flew overhead, cawing out a warning as if to say, "don't go." I kept walking, amazed this was going to happen. My hand hovered in the air about to knock when the door opened.

I glanced up into big green eyes framed under tousled brown hair, my voice halting in my throat. Nicholas smiled, warm and inviting—the bloodlust completely gone. It took everything not to rush him and assault his neck with my arms.

"Yes?" he asked, confusion crossing his face. "Can I help you?"

My internal squealing party came to a screeching halt as Nicholas watched me as though I were a stranger.

"It's me, Nicholas. Julia."

On the outside, he appeared calm, but inside he warred with himself, wrought with confusion.

"Hi, Julia."

The air whooshed out of my mouth and stars sparkled across my vision, leaving me faint. How could he not know who I was?

"Who's here?" A female voice said, none other than the

*witch* Alora herself.

"Julia," Nicholas called out innocently.

"Oh?" Joy radiated forth, a kind I didn't think was for my benefit. "Well then, invite her in."

Nicholas' mystification drifted and he swept his arm out, filled with curiosity instead. "Come in."

I looked at him, then at the darkened interior of the house, wanting to bolt. My feet, numb and trembling, had different plans and crossed the threshold. I needed answers. He closed the door behind me. The soft sound screamed out finality like I'd be trapped there for eternity. Within the dim interior Alora appeared. Surprisingly, she'd shed her vixen getup for a sundress, like she wore in the photo Nicholas had of her on his dresser at home.

She smiled but oozed disdain. "Why, isn't this a surprise? I didn't think we'd be seeing you anytime soon." Her eyes zeroed in on my talisman. It warmed against my skin as if to recognize her. "As you can see, we've had a little *difficulty*."

"Who is this?" Nicholas asked.

"A friend of yours, sweetie. Someone you knew before your amnesia," she said then turned toward me with a sickening smile. "Come on in. Let's *chat*."

Amnesia? My fists formed into balls, tempted to knock her block off. She'd done this on purpose, taken my Nicholas away from me as revenge for not letting her keep the talisman that dark and dreary night on the beach. It took all my self-control to remain composed and not fall apart on the spot.

Nicholas, completely unknowing, smiled his warm smile I loved, but the emptiness behind it rolled my stomach over. There was nothing there. No love. No memory of us. Just a beautiful shell, watching me with interest.

"I believe Julia is here to return something of mine actually. Nicholas, darling, would you mind retrieving—"

I backed up and clutched the talisman to my chest, giving Nicholas an evil eye to stay away.

"Alora. I don't think that's a good idea," Preston said as he came around the corner. "That's something Nicholas gave to Julia a long time ago and belongs to her now." He glared at Alora for a moment. She frowned back.

I took a deep breath and studied Preston, a carbon copy of Nicholas but with dark eyes—both youthful and handsome. His heart no longer radiated the loneliness I'd felt when I visited before. Instead, kindness and empathy rolled out toward me.

"Let's reconvene in the living room and talk. I'm sure you've got questions," he said to me, a tiny hint of southern drawl in his voice.

Preston placed his hand on my back and led me into a room where two sofas faced one another. Antiques covered the lavishly decorated space, evidence of lifetimes of collecting, filling every possible inch in the room. I stood up straight and allowed him to lead me over to one of the couches, thankful for my ability to read emotions. No one was interested in tasting my blood today, though Alora brought with her a tall glass of something thick and red.

She took a large sip and the swirling happiness hit me hard before I could shield myself against it. Blood.

"Some habits are hard to break," she said, her canine teeth covered in red liquid.

"I see." I cringed and looked away.

Preston's calm infused my nerves as he signaled Nicholas to sit by me. He complied but kept an appropriate distance. I stared down at his hand between us, aching to entwine my fingers with his.

"Well," Preston began. "We were hoping for more progress before now, but during the memory treatments, Alora had a bit of trouble. She only wanted to go back as far as when the blood triggered his desire, but unfortunately his memories were difficult to trim, especially at the degree Nicholas was suffering. She'd need him to think about what happened, but when he was lucid, he wouldn't cooperate. So we sedated him, but then his past timeline would mesh together in an incoherent jumble.

"She did her best, but accidentally cut into most of his childhood. Once she realized what had happened, she started working to repair the fractured memories. It's a big puzzle with mostly snippets of intelligible information. Nicholas has had some breakthroughs recently though."

As Preston squeezed Alora's knee, she appeared grieved over the statement, such a competent actress. But I felt her smugness. "I feel horrible about it, Julia."

Could Preston not see through her lies? She didn't want Nicholas to remember me. Without our connection, she could get him to retrieve the necklace for her no problem. And if she could get her tentacles on Preston's past and press delete, she'd be golden. He was the only gatekeeper to the invincibility that dangled on my neck. And there was no way for me to stop her because if I staked her, Nicholas would die in the process as she was above him in the immortal bloodline.

I looked at Nicholas, noting the pain in his eyes, but not because he was hurting from lack of memory. He was apparently reflecting my own horror. I bit my lip to hold back the tears. I wouldn't give Alora the satisfaction.

"So we were friends? Here? In L.A?" he asked.

I gulped, embarrassed to mention we were way more than friends. "Scotts Valley, actually. That's where I live, where we met." My voice was horrifically shaky, sending a flush to my cheeks.

How would he ever love me again? Our relationship was built on the tragedy of my mother's death and if he didn't remember that, why would he care? Care that he'd vowed to protect my life because of that event? Without that ingredient, there wasn't any chemistry—no spark. I was just another plain girl sitting next to him, vying for his affection.

"I need to go," I said, quickly standing to my feet.

"No. Please." Preston placed his hand on my arm quick as a flash.

"I'm sorry." I pulled away, stumbling to the door. As soon as I opened it, the orange light from the setting sun cast its hue across the wooden floor. Both Preston and Alora disappeared, leaving Nicholas, lost and bewildered, watching me from the couch.

I don't remember how I got to the car or even if I shut the front door behind me, but I zoomed away, lost in a fit of tears. Everything I cared about melted out of my hands like a snowball on a hot day. He was the only semi-normal person who understood me, who fit the misshapen puzzle pieces of my life. He alone knew of my genetic malfunction, and loved me anyway. Alora had robbed me of that, too. She'd taken everything away.

I wanted to run back and blow up the house so the sun burned her into a million dusty pieces. Was this the final straw? How the prediction would play out? That I'd lose him in a way I couldn't repair? That I would be more consumed with Alora's death than anyone else's? Was this what Scarlett didn't want to tell me?

I needed to breathe, to drive, to get somewhere far away from the insanity. Heartsick and confused, I ended up back at the Beverly Hills Hilton. I ran into the room and locked myself in the bathroom.

"Julia? Julia!" Luke said outside the door, partly groggy from me waking him up from the slam.

I didn't want to deal with the pain, the sadness, the grief. All that was left of Nicholas was his memories written down in a journal. I wanted mine to go away, too—erased forever. And then it came to me. Scarlett could erase my past just like she'd done with Tyler. I could start my life over, never knowing what a wonderful guy he was. Maybe even right up to the point Phil became a vampire. She could erase Nicholas from my life and put Phil in his place. Phil would agree to it. He'd already offered to protect me emotionally and physically.

The stitching of my life would be easy, well, except I didn't want to erase this; the day I buried my mother and my family said our goodbyes.

Maybe Scarlett could be subjective. I just needed the pain to stop.

# Chapter Seven

The next day I pulled myself out of bed with strength I didn't know I had. The pain, so raw and close to the surface, made me want to crawl into a ball and sleep forever. Not only did Nicholas' amnesia mince me to pieces on the inside, I didn't get the resurrection ritual from Alora. I'd have to go home empty-handed and hope Scarlett would keep her promise to Phil in order to save Katie.

With very little conversation, the three of us got ready and drove to Westwood Memorial Park, Mom's new resting place. A small crowd of people dressed in black gathered at the mausoleum wall: friends she worked with, people from church, past neighbors, and relatives I didn't recognize.

When Mom's disappearance had been declared a cold case, the vicious rumor mill spun into action looking for someone to blame. Dad had always said we'd moved so Aunt Jo could help watch us when he traveled, but that wasn't the entire reason. Though he'd been removed as a suspect, his abrupt decision to leave raised suspicions of the family even more. Unable to handle the constant criticism, he eventually cut ties altogether.

The tension, which still floated thick in the air, should have settled when tests proved Dad's innocence. Even still, old grudges died hard.

I tried to be cordial to the lingering guests, but mostly focused on keeping up my shield. I was adrift, swimming in my own sea of loss, missing my mother and longing for Nicholas. One small misstep would send me crashing into the sharp rocks that were left of our relationship, our love. I had to keep it together. Just for today.

Luke sat next to me and whispered his guesses of who was who in the crowd when a taxi pulled up. Out stepped a woman with a purple fluff of hair—Grandma. I jumped from my seat and rushed her with a hug. Her tenderness encased my broken heart with a large bandage only she could give.

"Dear," she said, while pushing my hair off my wet cheeks. "It's so wonderful to see you again."

"I'm so sorry, Grandma. We just found out why—why I never got to see you."

"Oh, love. I never blamed your father. Please know that," she said with incredible sadness. "They loved each other deeply, as only we could know." A soft smile tugged at her lips but it didn't lighten her grief. "He shut me out. I should have tried harder."

She hugged me again and years of longing melted away, healing that place where we missed Mom, the real reason we were all joined together on a gloomy June day.

I escorted her to Luke who recognized her instantly. We joined into another group hug, during which Grandma reached out for Dad and pulled him into the circle.

"I'm sorry, Grace," he said, guilt swirling around us in a lazy looping circle.

Grandma tsked and, instead of bitterness, she drenched us in love. "That was a long time ago, Russell. And we are together again."

For that single sweet moment, we all breathed a collective sigh of relief and forgot the past. I marveled in Grandma's power to be able to encase us all with such forgiveness, mending everyone's soul—even Dad's.

Following the short ceremony led by Pastor Greene, people paid their respects and left flowers below my mother's new resting place in the wall. I left her wildflowers I'd found in a field behind the hotel—similar to the ones Nicholas had planted in her field. A token for him and me, something he would have brought, remembering she loved flowers so much if Alora hadn't snatched away his life.

The group reconvened at the home of Elizabeth Stanton's only a few miles away from the cemetery. She'd been Mom's best friend since childhood. We took Grandma in our car with us.

"You doing okay, Luke?" Dad asked as he parked.

"Yeah," he said, but I opened up my boundary a tiny bit to find his queasy tummy matched his green complexion.

"I have a few Tums in my purse," Grandma said, and Luke took them appreciatively.

The small, brick house reeked of Swedish meatballs and cheese fondue, two apparent favorite foods of my mother. The talk turned to nostalgic times, a conversation I couldn't really contribute to, so Grandma led me to a quiet place off the back patio.

"Where's that handsome beau of yours?" she finally asked, then felt guilt after my own feelings smashed over me and tears came from nowhere. "I'm sorry, dear."

"It's complicated, Grandma. I can't talk about it."

"Okay." She smiled and pushed peace my way, which I accepted. My heart rate slowly subsided.

I sat there, basking in the warmth she'd encased around us, trying hard to think of something other than Mom and Nicholas. All the questions about being a Seer and the real purpose of our gift ping-ponged around in my head instead. How could I ask her without revealing too much?

"Is there a way to help people remember the past with our gift?"

At my words Grandma's bubble burst, as if I'd intruded on something dark and painful in her life. She vanished on me again, hiding her feelings. "Not that I know of."

"Oh." I waited, unsure what to say. I had nothing cordial to offer to ease things for her.

"It's fine." She tapped my knee. "We all have our secret heartbreaks, right?"

"Yes." I faked a smile. Mine had Nicholas written all over it, and Grandma's had someone else she loved who couldn't be brought back as well.

She tilted her head and pulled herself together. "I came to L.A. because of my sister. We'd both lost our husbands and her mind had began to rapidly deteriorate. I didn't need care of a rest home, but Rose needed me, so we came together from South Dakota so she could go to this renowned mind clinic.

"They did what they could, but only after I'd worked with her did she ever show improvement. It never lasted long. I lost her this past summer."

"Oh, Grandma," I reached over and hugged her. "I'm so sorry."

"She's no longer suffering, so it's a good thing. I did what I could." She sighed as a tear glittered in her eye. "Did you already know about your mother?"

The details crowded my head in a fitful storm, every feeling visible for her to see. My strength crumbled, unable to hold the burden any longer. How would I tell her without freaking her out?

"You knew she had passed before they'd found her in the field, didn't you?" She placed her soft, withered hand on my arm. "You can trust me."

I gulped, unsure where to start. "Have you ever felt bloodlust before, Grandma?"

She grimaced and squeezed my arm slightly. "Hmmm . . . unfortunately, yes I have."

"Who feels those feelings?"

Darkness clouded her features as her eyes pierced through me. "There's only one unearthly monster that is capable of having those hideous feelings."

I took a deep breath and swallowed hard. "When Mom disappeared, I saw one of them. I saw what he did to her. I felt everything she felt. That's how I knew she'd . . . ."

Grandma choked back her tears and pounded her fist into the arm of the chair. "I told her never to go out after dark. That *they* were out there. That *they* were attracted to us, like a moth to a flame. But she'd already made up her mind we were here to stop them. That we could use our gift to seek them out and somehow destroy them."

The revelation startled me. How could Mom have possibly come to that conclusion?

I took another deep breath. "Did someone tell her that?"

Grandma wrinkled up her nose for a second, then shook her head. "Only after her gift presented itself in her early twenties did she finally get to see the creatures I'd warned her about. Then her obsession started and she went on a quest to figure out what they were and where they came from."

I already knew. They came from Cain after the serpent made a deal for immortality. What I couldn't get over was how Mom's Seer desires kicked in so naturally right after her empathy powers presented itself. Why didn't that happen to me? Was it because I was so young? Was it because for the most part vampires scared the crap out of me? Maybe the friendship between Nicholas and Mom wasn't an accident after all, like when I'd walked into the fortune tellers shop. Was Nicholas sent somehow to be her protector first?

"There, now," Grandma said, putting her arm over my shoulder, easing my confusion. "Today is a day we remember the goodness of your mother. And one day, we'll see her again. Death is not the end."

I studied Grandma's eyes to make sure someone wasn't messing with her mind, remembering something similar Scarlett had just said. She blinked back, her face shrouded in kindness. I scanned the shrubberies and trees just to be sure. Was she here, feeding my Grandma this baloney?

"You can't be serious. This isn't fair. My mother was murdered by a vampire because of our empathy. And now somehow this gift that attracts them has been passed onto me. This isn't a gift; it's a curse. It's why she died. Don't you think if we'd been given this 'vampire attracter,' we'd be given the tools to defend ourselves? It's insanity. It's not okay she died because she lingered too long outside at night. I need her. I've needed her every day of my life after *he* took her from me! And I witnessed it. It's horrible and cruel!"

The blame came spilling out of my aching heart in a messy heap. This vampire homicidal Seer cycle had been going on generation after generation and it had to stop. To only be warned not to go outside wasn't enough. Someone should have trained Mom in how to defend herself.

"Did Great-Grandma have this gift? What about her mother? And her mother? Why hasn't anyone taught anyone anything and just left me floundering? Shouldn't someone have told me to stay inside?" My chest heaved in controlled anger as I stopped myself just short of accusing her of Mom's death.

Grandma grabbed my shoulders and forced me into a hug as I broke down.

"You're right. It's all my fault. I should have been more insistent, firmer. We Londons have this terrible streak of stubbornness. There's a long line of early deaths of the women in our family. A sad but true fact.

"If I'd have known you had the gift so soon, I would have found you and taught you how to use it. Maybe you're different. Maybe you've been given the tools to defend yourself."

I cried softly on her shoulder.

"Tools? I don't think so. By luck Nicholas came into my life and he kept them away from me. And now he is gone, and Mom is gone, and I don't know what to do, let alone how to handle it. I don't want this *gift* anymore! I've never wanted it. It's cost me everything . . ."

"Dear, child." Grandma patted my back. "You carry the weight of the world on your shoulders. It's okay. I'm here."

I tried not to completely fall apart, keeping my shoulders stiff and holding most of my tears in. But Grandma had guessed right. The responsibility behind the prophecy haunted me any chance it got. I couldn't just live my life in peace and ignore it. The vampires would always be there, hunting me. And even worse, if I had a daughter . . . "I'm just so tired."

"I know. This is a very draining thing to deal with."

"Is there someone we can talk to about it? Anyone?

Grandma sighed. "Not that I know of, but it's not difficult to avoid danger, Julia. They can't get you when you're safe inside. They only come out at night."

*Such a ridiculous and impossible way to avoid them.* "Or if you invite them in," I added.

"Now why would you ever want to invite one in?" She handed me a coy smile.

I smiled back, her kindness finally breaking in and comforting me. If only she knew about Phil—that there were actually good vampires in the world. "Well, that's kind of impossible to avoid being out at night, don't you think?"

Grandma shook her head. "I've done if for over fifty years. People just think I'm scared of the dark."

*Killing them all off seems easier.*

She smiled mysteriously as if she'd read my mind just as Dad appeared on the porch, slightly worried.

"Sorry to interrupt," he said. "But Luke isn't feeling well, so I'm going to run him to the hotel. I'll be right back."

"Okay," I said, kind of wishing I could go, too. But the thought of Luke heaving and the small space we were staying in changed my mind.

"Oh, the poor boy," Grandma said. "I hope he feels better soon. I'll keep an eye on Julia."

I smiled as the talisman warmed on my skin. If anything, she needed me to watch over her.

As the day continued, Grandma filled me in on the missing pieces of Mom's life, stuff Dad never talked about. Mom and I were alike in so many ways, which thrilled and scared me at the same time. But the truth became evident. We were all basically the filet mignons amongst fast food hamburgers of society, tempting vamps much more than we should. So, the prophecy, highly flawed, didn't make sense. Other than empathy, there was nothing else present to assist when slaying vampires. Mom had become a victim, like anyone, like all the Seers before her. Maybe the talisman was the key. Thank God I had it so I could at least be outdoors at night.

The sun moved closer to the horizon, Grandma grew nervous. Dad still hadn't returned.

"I need to be getting home," she finally said. "Could you call me a taxi?"

"What? No. We could drive you. Let me just text Dad to see where he is."

After another thirty minutes, he finally returned—disheveled and smelling slightly of vomit. Luke must have lost his lunch multiple times and reeked up the joint. Something fun to look forward to.

As we drove, Grandma wrung her hands, her eyes glued to the sunset all the way to the Wilshire Rest Home. At the double doors, she hugged me tightly and whispered in my ear. "Get to your hotel quickly, you hear me? Don't tempt the devil."

"Yes," I whispered, then watched her walk inside.

Dad and I drove in silence, both of us completely exhausted.

"Sorry," he finally said.

I looked at him questioningly. "Dad, it's okay. Really."

"No. Somehow in the whole ordeal, I ended up hurting you kids."

His words were mostly truth. There was something underlying, another reason he kept us away from L.A. but especially after the trauma of the day, I didn't want to push things.

"Don't be too hard on yourself. It's in the past."

He groaned, seemingly at the red light, but I knew it was at himself. "I really hate this town. So many people."

*So do I.*

I bit my lip and leaned back in my seat. "Are we going home tomorrow?"

"The sooner the better," he said with an exhale.

*Good.*

I didn't want to ask about how Luke was doing, or what took Dad so long; I just hoped he'd be well enough to handle the drive home and not puke all over my car. At the hotel, I planned to bathe in anti-bacterial lotion to prevent catching whatever he had. My bout with the flu a few months ago was bad enough, thank you.

Once we pulled up to the hotel, Dad growled something under his breath as he slowed down and wove around clusters of excited girls in cheer uniforms. Due to a cheer competition, parking had become sparse.

"Here," he said, motioning to the curb. "Jump out and I'll go park the car."

"No," I said, noting a wave of bloodlust bouncing on the fringe of my detection zone, almost in tandem with the setting sun. My heart practically catapulted itself from my chest in fear. I couldn't let him walk outside unprotected, just in case. "Let's use valet."

"Oh, wait. I see one."

Before I could insist further, he zipped around the corner and parked in a dimly lit section behind the building. My heart continued to flounder like a fish out of water. Something lurked in the shadows and I didn't want to wait around to see who it could be.

"Come on, Dad," I said, pulling him by the hand.

"It's okay, Julia. You're with me," he said with a chivalrous tone in his voice.

I managed a smile, but still tried to coax him along faster toward safety. Once we approached the corner and the side door came into view, I felt confident we'd avoided disaster until the hair prickled on the back of my neck.

# Chapter Eight

"Why, isn't this a treat?"

The vampire's voice, etched forever in my mind from my last visit, scratched its nails down my spine. I turned and cringed. Slide, the vamp with the orange mohawk, smiled back in recognition. "Daring to trespass into lands you know you're not welcome."

My legs scrambled to bolt for the door when Dad swiveled around and pushed me into the wall, shielding me with his body. His fear escalated as he fumbled in his pockets for something.

*No! We need to run!*

"Dad," I whispered, tugging at his arm, my voice trembling as I watched Slide close the gap between us. Somewhere close by, more unseen lustful creatures lay waiting, excited at our predicament.

"I've got this, just close your eyes," he said, still heavily pursuing the item in his pocket—his wallet maybe?

Was he kidding? My extremities shook under the increased supply of adrenaline, wanting to run—now. These creatures weren't some gang members looking to rob us. They were vampires. Blood. Sucking. Vampires. I needed a weapon of some kind, maybe a pencil to stake it once and for all. Otherwise, Dad was going to follow in Mom's footsteps, right here behind the Beverly Hills Hilton.

"No, Dad. They don't want your wallet."

"Julia, don't argue with me."

I kept trying to inch us toward the door, pulling his sleeve to get him to move. For some stupid reason, he wouldn't budge. A cackle from above sent shivers up my legs.

"Please," I begged.

Dad finally found what he wanted and whipped out something that looked like a pen. He pointed it at Slide.

"Armed with a pen? Is that your stake?" Slide laughed and pounded his fist on his chest. "Be still my beating heart. Oh wait. You do know it needs to contain wood to do any damage. Who would have thought the old man and this shifty little sidekick knew each other? Family perhaps? And no protectors around. Interesting." He followed his statement by licking his teeth. "This is going to be fun."

Wooden or not, I wanted to grab the thing and chuck it at his heart anyway, knowing my aim would be aided by the talisman and could give us a few seconds to escape. But when I lunged for the pen, Dad pressed a red button and twisted his wrist. Red light beamed out and crisscrossed over Slide's chest in a big X. In awe, Slide stared down at his jacket as charred marks magically appeared behind the path of light. A huge chunk of leather fell onto the pavement at his feet.

Slide looked up, fury ripping through him. "Why you little—"

But Dad sliced the light across his throat and Slide's head lopped off his body onto the pavement with a thud. Slide looked at us from the ground and then over at his smoldering body; smoke poured out from his neck like a chimney. "Oh, crap." In unison his detached head and body burst into flames and turned to dust.

Dad continued to wave his magic wand around, into the sky and over the parking lot, making large swooping motions as he backed us toward the door.

Another scream brought down a man's body from the sky, which busted into a dust cloud upon contact with the asphalt before I could see if I recognized him—at least I thought it was a man. I gasped, but allowed Dad to kick open the door and lead me inside.

I clung to Dad's arm in shock. We'd survived. My eyes zeroed in on the ashes on the other side of the glass doors. Dad's focus lingered behind us, probably checking the lobby to see if anyone saw. Hyper girls' voices paired with nervous excitement was all that milled about. Somehow no one witnessed the carnage that had just happened outside. Together in relief, we watched the wind scatter the ashes away, wiping clean the evidence. Perfect timing as another pack of girls walked up from the parking lot ready to enter the lobby.

"Are you okay?" Dad asked.

I stared up into his hardened face. He'd been so tough the entire confrontation, but now that it was over, sheer terror looked back at me. I nodded my head, absolutely speechless. He took my hand to lead me into a corner, far away from prying eyes. We stared at one another some more in silence, riddled with shock.

"How did you know?" we asked each other in unison.

Dad splayed his hand on his forehead. "You know? How long—?"

"How long have *you* known?"

"Pretty much since your mom disappeared." His shoulders fell and he bowed his head. "And you?"

"Since this year."

"Was it that boy? The one who'd disappeared from school? Phil?"

I couldn't stop my eyes from wandering, looking everywhere but at the lines pressed in his face. "Yes."

"I knew it," Dad said, then grabbed my shoulders and shook me. "Why didn't you listen to me?"

I pulled away. "I did listen to you, but he hunted me down." Do I tell him about the mountain lion? Do I tell him about Nicholas? Or Scarlett? Or the prediction?

"They're dangerous, Julia. Nothing to toy with. If it wasn't for the fact he'd died in that fire, I would have moved us away. But now they definitely know that you know, which is the worst possible scenario. They hunt survivors down. That's why I have to travel so much. To keep them away from you kids."

He sat me down on one of the two love seats against the wall.

"Wait. You travel to protect us?"

"If I'm on the move and keep my private life separate, they don't have any information to blackmail me with. But now—"

"But you're a computer consultant."

"I do computer consulting, but for the government. For the ET unit. We investigate extraterrestrial activity."

"Like the *X-Files*?"

Dad laughed, which loosened him up a bit. "Something like that. But we can't stay around here anymore. We have to leave first thing in the morning. They're going to round up more numbers and come after us. They'll all know our scent. I need to call the office." Dad turned to me. "After Phil died, did you have any more problems? Any more sightings?"

I sucked in a deep breath, hating to lie, but he'd majorly freak if he knew how deeply entrenched I was with vampires. "No."

I wouldn't know where to begin to explain, let alone that Nicholas was a half-breed. But Dad didn't even seem to notice. He was lost someplace else, his mind whirling too fast with questions and fear.

"It doesn't matter. We'll leave your car here and sell it. Or get new plates. I'm going to have to take you with me when I travel to be safe, so I can keep watch over you. No. Better yet, we'll all go to the detention facility in Tulsa for the summer. Maybe we can fly out tomorrow. I can't have you kids wandering around unprotected. There's a training facility there. We'll get you inducted into the protection program. The VPP."

He jumped up and grabbed my hand, pulling me toward the elevators.

*Protection program? Training? Moving?*

"Whoa, Dad," I said, stopping him. "Sell my car?"

"They saw us. They can easily break into the mind of a DMV worker and get our address. Wait. I used the P.O Box for your car's registration. So, that'll be okay. We can keep the car."

He pressed the button to summon the elevator. I started to breathe faster. Dad was going overboard.

"Everything has been perfectly fine in Scotts Valley. They can't possibly discover where we live once we leave," *and never showed up when I was here the last time.*

The door opened and he ushered me inside. Once the doors shut, words flowed from his mouth about uncovering a huge operation where a rogue vamp was creating drones— sterile vamps. They were about to close in on the leader and now he would have to hand it off to someone else.

"Wait, you know about Cain?" I interrupted. "Where is he?"

Dad stopped; his eyes widened. "How do you know about that? That's top top TOP secret information, Julia. Did you find my room?"

"Room? What room?"

Dad grabbed my arm. "Tell me the truth. How do you know?"

"'Cause one told me. It's how they came into being. The serpent's bargain for his soul."

"Stop." Dad held his finger to his lips. "We shouldn't talk about this here. Does Phil know? Did he tell the others he told you? Never mind." When the doors opened on our floor, he took my hand.

I staggered to stay up with him, frustrated we had to stop talking. Drones? Sterile vamps? Did this have anything to do with the venom dealer?

"Later, I'll tell you everything. Let's get to the room and get some rest. We're leaving at daybreak."

He opened the door and left me standing in the hall. The vomit odor spilled out of the room, I staved off the urge to heave as Luke's snoring followed the sound of the bathroom door closing. I plugged my nose and entered the room, headed straight for my toiletries. I sprayed everything down with body spray and wiped my hands with anti-bacterial lotion. Dad's muffled voice could be heard through the wall, apparently talking to his boss.

I kicked off my shoes, put on my jammies, and crawled under the covers, everything hitting me hard. Sam hadn't texted at all and I just wanted to hear someone cared, anyone. I plugged in my earbuds and cranked on my trance music. Today was quite possibly the worst day of my life.

Luke and Dad slept the entire night while I lay awake, thinking. Every time I almost fell asleep, Alora's voice cackled in the recesses of my brain, haunting me that I hadn't gotten the resurrection instructions to save Katie and that she'd erased Nicholas's mind.

I couldn't believe Dad had known about vampires all along and had a job where he hunted them, of all things. But my troubles grew to insurmountable levels now that the L.A. fang gang had supposedly tagged me. Though the vamps could have smelled Dad's scent, with the talisman, they couldn't smell me. And I'd escaped before and they never followed me to Scotts Valley. But for my protection, Dad would insist I come with him to Tulsa. Somehow I had to convince him I was safe in Scotts Valley. Maybe if he knew about the talisman, he'd relax. I had to figure out something and quick.

If I left Scotts Valley, I could quite possibly lose Nicholas forever.

# Chapter Nine

On the ride home the next day, I watched Dad like he was a lit piece of dynamite. With my iPhone, I tracked our location to make sure he wasn't bolting for the airport and a flight to Oklahoma instead of home. He'd relaxed from the night before and his newfound calm scared me. What did his boss say on the phone exactly? Visions of the vamp protection guys dressed in black, snatching us out of our beds and stealing us away to Tulsa in the middle of the night riddled my thoughts. Would he do that to us without warning? He needed to be convinced beyond doubt there wasn't a vamp problem in Scotts Valley; that we could live there and not be afraid—all with Phil's excellent slaying skills of course.

Once I deemed we were on our way home, I popped in my earbuds and plotted my future as weedy fields zoomed by. Not only were there concerns of moving, but Nicholas' memories needed restoration, too. Yet again, something else I needed to beg Scarlett to help with. I could already hear her shutting me down, that he wasn't crucial to the final plan, just like Katie and everything else I needed or wanted.

For a quick moment, I peeked at Luke. He lay tucked in a ball on the back seat. I unblocked my feelings barrier just enough to see if he was improving, to slam it shut again before I lost my breakfast. Whatever racked his body fought with a vengeance against his immune system and didn't fight fair. I had a date with huge doses of vitamin C once we got home.

We finally hit Highway 1, cruising along the Pacific Ocean, and relief flooded me. Home. After this horrific and crazy weekend, we were finally home.

Dad pulled into the garage and helped Luke get out of the car. I took the silent cue to unpack and remain invisible if at all possible. I'd successfully created a leaning tower of suitcases in the living room when Dad walked down the stairs.

"I think Luke is finally improving," he said and motioned toward the garage. "I need to show you something."

He walked over to the workbench and pulled out a key from his pocket to unlock one of the workbench drawers; one I never really noticed was locked in the past. He opened it up and reached deep inside. Suddenly, the table top next to the drawer folded down on itself to reveal a metal door on the floor underneath. It slid open and gave way to stairs going down into what looked like a basement.

"What?" I asked breathlessly, my eyes practically bugging out of their sockets.

"Come on."

Cement stairs led down to a lit room below the garage. I followed closely behind Dad as fear and curiosity bristled down my legs. Once we reached the ground floor, he pressed a button on the stairwell that closed the hatch above us.

"What is this place?"

"It's my office," Dad said with pride.

My eyes scanned the humble room around us: an

immaculately clean desk, black armchair, up-to-date computer, and lamp adorned the work area.

Dad took a deep breath and swept out his hand, "behold. My work for the past fifteen years."

He flicked another switch and my eyes were drawn to several sliding doors that revealed a patchwork quilt of papers and pictures covering every panel. After a moment of visually dissecting the hodgepodge, I realized I was looking at some sort of collection of people. Pictures, dates, whereabouts, and current status—living or dead—were clearly notated along with a number. One panel contained a giant map of the world and little pins with numbers were scattered across the continents.

"Holy cannoli." My throat became dry when my eyes zeroed in on the guy with a number one next to his picture. Cain. This wasn't any grouping of people. We were looking at a vampire family tree.

Dad moved aside the panel to reveal another behind it. He located Slide and put a red X over his face before he moved him to a different panel with at least a hundred X'ed out vampires. Then he left a sticky note for the other dusted vamp with a big question mark.

"That's how I track the exterminated ones, which doesn't happen very often." Dad pointed to a cluster of X'ed out vamps. "You'd think with their mentality and lifestyle, they'd be fighting amongst themselves all the time, but they don't. Only one rogue hunter that we know of has been responsible for all these killings and these." He pointed to one grouping, then his finger lingered on faces I recognized. Justin from my high school, and the rest of Alora's coven: the twins: Angelina and Bettina, Toth, Adrian, Roland and Kim. I hadn't known their names before this. All deceased. Phil's picture was in the bunch.

"Phil," I breathlessly forced out.

Dad put his hand on my shoulder. "Yes, honey. We know who did it."

I swallowed and traced the red line over his tanned smiling face, thankful he wasn't being tracked on this wall anymore.

"Who did it?" My heart galloped in anticipation of the answer as I quickly scanned the rest of the faces. Nicholas wasn't on any of these lists.

"They call him Dirty Harry. Even his own kind can't seem to find him until it's too late. He never leaves survivors."

Dad pointed to a nighttime shot of a person with sunglasses peering out from a dark alleyway. The description underneath read, *Dirty Harry: brown hair, green or blue eyes, early to mid 20's. Believed to be responsible for large exterminations in California, New York, Florida, Montana, Texas, and Mexico. Possibly from Delagrecha faction II.*

I chewed the inside of my lip to hold back a smile. "So, he's a vampire, too?"

"He has to be. There's no other way to explain his powers. What's strange is why he'd work on our side. He has to know about the ET unit and our work. And ironically, since I've moved us here, most of the exterminations have happened right in this area. Vamps come north and never return home. Scotts Valley, until just recently, has been the safest vamp-free place to live. But the most recent issues with your classmates had us a little worried they'd captured Dirty Harry." Dad's hand swept back to Phil and Justin's faces.

I blinked hard. Nowhere in Nicholas' journal did he ever mention my father and his involvement with his extraterrestrial unit. His choice to live here was because of his commitment to protect me. Vampires flocked here in attraction to me. Maybe they were here to turn him in instead.

I slid Nicholas' panel aside and went back to Cain. Below

him were five vampires, all bearing a roman numeral and their special powers. These were the royals.

**I. Myhail Volynski:** genius, telepathic, telekinetic.

**II. Rachel Delagrecha:** blue-eyed females are stronger than males, shape-shifting, can fly, telepathic, memory tampering.

**III. Sapphira Fotenos (deceased):** element control, hypnosis.

**VI. Katherine Polkinghorn (deceased):** shape-shifting, visual illusions.

**V. Helena Goehring:** mind control.

My chest jolted when I spotted Preston's name directly under Rachel. He'd been sired directly by Rachel herself.

**Ia. Preston Kendrick:** born: unknown, birthed: unknown, whereabouts: unknown, status: docile. Married to human Alora Kendrick (Wright)—born: August 28, 1955, died: March 22, 1977, last known whereabouts: Dallas, Texas.

I closed my gaping mouth and regrouped. If he saw I recognized someone on this board other than Phil, he'd grill me big time.

"How did you get a picture of Cain?" I quickly asked.

Dad looked at me with apprehension. "How do you know about Cain actually?"

My eyes shot to Cain's picture again. "I asked where vampires came from and Phil said Cain. That it was a deal with the serpent for immortality."

"Hmmm . . ." Dad said. "Surprising he knows. Most don't."

I gulped, hating I'd lied and couldn't mention anything about Nicholas. I finally channeled him a little peace so he'd move on. His shoulders relaxed.

"We had an informant." He pointed to Darin Applegate.

**V22. Daren Applegate:** perpetually 22, dark hair, kind eyes, a red X over his handsome face.

I studied him for a moment, wondering how he met his maker. By Nicholas perhaps? Or by accident? He didn't appear evil in the slightest.

"Cain found out he was a human sympathizer and we've had trouble getting another ever since. It's difficult since Cain's a mind reader and only keeps his most trustworthy followers close to him."

A twinge of pity swept over me as I glanced at Darin's picture. There were more good vamps in the world than I'd realized. But as if someone poured ice water down my spine, my thoughts turned to what Cain would do should he ever get his hands on Nicholas. Was Nicholas still on the vampire most wanted list? I fought back a tear as I remembered his amnesia.

"So, who are they?" I asked to distract myself, while pointing to the next grouping—people who looked more average and not so model perfect. "More vampires?"

"That's our Recon, Undercover Ops, and Special Forces groups working around the globe to find and eradicate Cain."

"Oh," I gulped, wondering if he knew the secret. That Cain's death meant every last one of the vampires died, including my friends. "Why?"

"Because, Julia. All vampires must die."

"Oh," was all I could say as grief struck my heart. I didn't want to pry deeper for the real reason, in case he didn't know already. No use giving him extra fuel when I needed Cain to stay alive for Phil and Nicholas' sakes.

Maybe the fortuneteller had it wrong. Maybe Dad was the one who would end Cain's life, though he really didn't have any gifts that I knew of. The thought sent shockwaves through my trembling hands. First, Dad being in such tremendous danger, and second, the possibility of losing the vamps I loved. I couldn't let that happen. Sure, Dad's ET unit could kill off the younger trouble-making vamps and make the world a safer place like Nicholas had, but they couldn't be gunning for Cain. How, after his praise of Dirty Harry and Darin, could he turn on them and be so cruel? No. This couldn't happen and I had to stop them.

"You all right?" Dad put his hand on my shoulder, which infused me with concern.

"No," I said, using mind over matter to keep my knees from buckling.

The claustrophobia from being in such a small enclosure suddenly made breathing strenuous. Dad led me to the stairway and pressed the button. The breeze wafted down and I inhaled deeply before taking a step upwards.

"I think it's time to go. I've shown you too much as it is."

I made a mental note of the secret buttons' locations. Were there cameras? Would he know if I came in here without his permission? My glance swept across the interior once more before hauling myself up the stairs. No other way in or out other than the stairs. Quite the conundrum.

"Before your mom's accident, I'd worked as an IT administrator with the Feds." Dad pulled his lips in a straight line as he closed the hatch. "A friend in the Extra Terrestrial unit told me of a tip the local authorities couldn't follow up on. A woman, who remained anonymous, had called in and reported she witnessed a man apparently drinking blood from a woman's neck at the park. She described a child and the two other men who cleaned up the scene and took the child with them."

I gulped and looked away, the vision still hard to stomach. The two men were Nicholas and Preston.

Dad pulled me into a hug. "I was afraid to talk about it. I never wanted to hurt or scare you. Do you remember what happened?"

I shook my head. "Bits and pieces, but not much."

"I'm sorry I never said anything." He kissed the top of my head. "I worried for so long they'd hurt you, but once you started talking again, I thought it best not to bring up the bad memories. I have a friend at the ET you can talk to who fully understands."

"It's fine. I'm okay with it now."

He looked in my eyes and pursed his lips. "You've been so brave."

"I don't know about being brave . . ."

"You've encountered several vampires, lived to tell about it, and aren't cowering in the corner. That's the highest form of bravery I know of."

"Well." I faked a chuckle. "I was rescued when mom died and Phil wasn't just any vampire—" *neither is Nicholas.*

"We left L.A. immediately after I found out the truth. Scotts Valley just happened to have the lowest incidences of vampire crime and where your Aunt Josephine lived. That was the real reason we moved. AnneMarie's family said running showed my guilt, but L.A. was crawling with vamps. I had to get you out."

*I wish Grandma knew you knew. That might have changed a lot of things for me.*

"So now you're going to make us move again."

"Not yet. My boss thinks our run-in with Slide was a coincidence. He couldn't possibly have known you and I can't leave just yet. We're about to bust open another ring."

I almost smiled, filled with relief. We'd be sticking around. But mention of a new ring had me worried. Who were they and where did they fall in the vampire family tree?

"I'm glad we're staying. Who's behind this ring?"

"Nothing for you to worry about and I'm sorry. I wasn't sure how to talk to you about Mom. I didn't want to frighten you. Though that vamp got staked at the scene, we weren't sure if there were others around. I hired a detective specializing in the paranormal to keep watch over us, and for a whole year, nothing came looking for you. I figured you were safe."

I thought back to a journal entry Nicholas wrote where he'd mentioned an investigator watched the house. Nicholas thought he was there to keep tabs on Dad, not me. But Nicholas made his job easy by continuing to stake anything that came within a mile of me.

"After I'd learned about the existence of the paranormal, I transferred into the ET unit and kept a low profile by traveling a lot. There was a lot to do, locating and tracking them. But I felt fortunate. We never had any troubles in Scotts Valley, like Dirty Harry was here just for us. Well, at least until Phil showed up."

I looked into his withered eyes and shook my head. He'd held in so much to protect our family and I'd done nothing but give him grief. "Why are you telling me all this top secret stuff now?"

"Because, you deserve to know. And you'd find out eventually if you went through the VPP. It's a relief to tell you the truth. I've wanted to for a long time."

I gulped and shook my head. "But I don't want to leave."

"We're not. With Phil gone . . . we'll be okay."

I pinched my lips together to stop my smile. I was terribly relieved to come clean in some small stretch. And if he'd let me in on what the ETers would be doing, I could keep Nicholas, Sam, and Phil safe.

"So for now, you're going to have to be extra careful. Stay indoors at night if at all possible. Keep this on you—" he handed me a laser pen. "It's not your typical laser. It harnesses UV light under a powerful magnifying glass and it'll burn anything the light touches, not just vamps."

"Okay," I said, tempted to flick the pen on and test it out. If Phil thinks I'm a loaded gun now, wait until he gets a load of this.

"And I've made it a general habit to voice a general uninvite when I come home, just as a precaution."

"Uninvite?" My mouth went dry.

"Yeah, I assumed you knew about that. If you just say 'you're uninvited,' they'll have to vacate the premises immediately. Not that I think you two are inviting vamps in while I'm gone, you can never be too sure."

I swallowed hard the lump building in my throat, as visions of Katie being sucked out of the house and being burnt in the sun whipped around in my mind. Phil could have had the same fate here. I'd never put it together that Phil's "inviting" issues typically happened after Dad got home from a trip.

"I want to be open and honest with you but we can't talk freely in the house at night. We don't want to slip and have prying ears hear, or Luke . . . I think it's best if he's kept in the dark for now."

"Okay," I said as my phone vibrated with a text. I looked down, surprised to see it came from Sam.

**- Call me**

"You need to be discreet. And you can't tell anyone about this under any circumstances, no matter how bad you want to tell them. Understood? I can set you up an appointment with someone if you *have* to talk about it."

"Dad, it's okay, really. I've managed this entire time."

He inhaled forcefully. "Okay. Well, I've got work to do, but talk to me if you have questions or anything—and be safe."

I nodded.

# Chapter Ten

"Sam?" I paused and looked at the receiver when no one spoke right away. I knew someone was there—they breathed heavily on the line.

"Julia," she whispered.

My gut clenched and I yearned to read her emotions. "What's wrong?"

"You have to come over here. Something's not . . . right."

"What do you mean?"

"Please . . . just come over. My mom's at work. The key is under the flower pot."

"Okay." I began to freak out. She sounded either super sick or worse. "I'm on my way."

"Thanks." The phone went dead.

I raced over to Sam's house in my Acura, thankful Dad didn't decide to leave it in L.A., and ran through a stop sign in the process. Who knew what had her all upset, but if Todd had anything to do with it, he'd be answering to me. Upon running up the stone steps, I felt it. Bloodlust mixed with fear. Evil lurked in Sam's house.

*How did a vampire get inside?*

My hands clammed over with sweat as I fetched the key. The talisman flopped heavily against my skin as I stood up. Though it protected me, I couldn't go in unarmed. I scanned the newly manicured lawn for something I could use as a weapon, finding nothing. A low hanging tree branch caught my eye and I smiled—my only option.

When opening the door, sunlight poured into the darkened interior, leaving a large elongated shadow where I stood.

"Sam!" I yelled, holding the broken branch tight to my side. "I'm here. You don't need to be afraid anymore."

Something rustled upstairs, coupled with relief.

"Just say 'I uninvite you.'" I tried to stay calm, but could hear my voice rising in panic. Had Sam already been bitten or had she managed to hide from the unwanted guest?

Silence crept up my skin as slight restraint radiated from the creature watching me from the shadows. The vamp only needed me to move out of the direct sunlight in order to make me its next meal. Better me than Sam.

I held up the branch, my limbs trembling, and kicked the door shut.

"Come and get me, bloodsucker! I'm tasty and I'm here."

Before I could react, something pushed me off my feet and I flew backward, whacking my head against the wood floor. Stars flashed before my eyes as I struggled to suck in oxygen. My arms were pinned to the floor with strength I was no match for. Bracing for the attack, I closed my eyes and tensed, knowing full well the talisman would protect me. But the creature hesitated, warring with itself, like it actually didn't want to bite me, but couldn't help it—fixed on taking my blood. Then something grazed my neck. The hot sizzle of burning flesh and a blood-curdling scream told me the talisman had done its job as the vampire released me and fled to the adjoining room, leaving a trail of lingering smoke behind.

I rolled over with a moan and rubbed the large knot forming on the back of my head. The room tilted topsy-turvy as I sat up to catch my breath and get my bearings. Whimpers came from the other room—a soft, higher-pitched sound. A girl?

I crawled over to the wall to find the light switch. I waffled if I should find Sam first, or just kill the pathetic creature and be done with her. In the corner, the injured thing hid crouched in the dark, curled up under the desk, radiating pain. Pity took over.

"Who are you?" I asked, tiptoeing closer. I tightened my grip on the makeshift stake in case she decided to strike again. "And what did you do with Sam?"

She turned and hissed, her face hitting the light and a blanket of dark gossamer hair fell over her shoulders. "I am Sam."

I staggered backward, collapsing to the ground on my knees. Sam? There was no way the creature in front of me could be her. No. This was an evil, lying look-alike. My best friend couldn't possibly be a vampire.

"What are you? A demon?" She glared at me with crazed eyes, her tongue running over her blackened lips.

*Me the demon? No. You're the demon!*

"You just look like Sam. You aren't her!"

"I assure you I am." She stuck out her pinkie and smirked. "Pinkie swear. Double dare."

"No!" I wailed and brought my fists to my lips. "You can't."

She leered and swallowed hard, her fear and bloodlust spiking again.

I reached out my hand. "You don't have to be afraid. I know what's happening to you." I inched myself closer on my knees.

"Stop!" She put out her charred hand, wavering between revulsion and a grave desire to chomp down on my neck. "Don't get any closer. It's—you're too tempting. I don't want to get hurt again."

I backed away slowly and turned on another light instead. Her new beauty astounded me: glossy hair, delicate skin, dark sensuous eyes. "How—when did this happen?"

She stayed crouched down like a wounded animal and watched my every move.

"Todd's been bragging about this new doctor he's seeing who's been giving him blood transfusions to help with his stamina and energy for football. Anyway, he showed up here last night and he was absolutely gorgeous. His skin was flawless and his hair, so luminous. And his muscles were cut, even his stomach was this crazy six-pack. He'd been trying to get ripped for so long with workouts, protein powder, and weird diets. Anyway, he told me the doctor gave him this special *stuff* and that it wasn't steroids. He had an extra dose and wanted me to try it. He promised my acne would go away if I did."

She looked away and gulped. "Now, I realize how stupid that was, but I couldn't say no. Like he compelled me to do it."

"Stuff? Like in a syringe you inject in your arm?" The venom-drug pusher came into mind, the one Nicholas tried to scare, the one who sold Alora the venom she used to change Katie. Had Todd done the same? Acquired the venom from this so-called doctor?

"Lecture me later!" She clutched at her hair and whimpered as another wave of bloodlust washed over her. "I've learned my lesson. It's horrible. When does it stop?"

I slowly sat cross-legged on the carpet a few feet in front of her, trying hard not to make movements that would send my scent into the air unnecessarily. Her suffering grated my nerves, like fingernails down a chalkboard, and there wasn't anything I could do to help. Why wasn't the talisman blocking my scent from her?

"I think after a couple days it eventually goes away, if you don't give in."

"A couple days?" She dug her fingers into the carpet, ripping up two large handfuls of threads. "I'm going to die."

I bit my lip, imagining Sam's mom's reaction when she saw her shredded carpet. Then reality hit. This damage would be nothing compared to her broken heart over Sam's disappearance. Her only child. That's if Sam hadn't already done something to her before I got here.

"Where's your mom?"

"I didn't touch her, if you're asking. She's at work."

*Truth.*

"I'm not accusing you, it's just—"

"Look at me, Julia. I'm a . . . a . . . freak!" she screeched and began pulling out her hair in large clumps. Before I could beg her to stop, like magic the hair grew back. "What's happening to me?"

I wanted to jump up and hug her, then slaughter Todd for doing this to her.

"Sam," I said with an extra soft voice. "It's going to be okay. You injected venom into your body and now you're becoming a vampire. You're just craving blood. It will pass."

"Pass?" She full-body shivered. "I'm becoming a vampire? Are you freakin' crazy? He said it would make me beautiful." She moaned and wrung her hands.

"Well, look at yourself. You kind of are."

She pinched her eyes shut and shook her head. "I must have passed out from the pain. Once I came to, my throat ached so bad with thirst. I tore apart the fridge for something to drink. Nothing would stop it—not soda, water, or even milk. And then I saw the raw hamburger meat." Her embarrassment flared. "The juices helped."

"It's perfectly normal."

"Normal?" Sam slammed her fists down, adding crevices to the holes in the carpet. She briefly inspected her assault on the floor with large eyes and then her face wrinkled up in horror. "It's normal to want to bite your own mother? I could hear her blood pulsing in her veins and all I could dream of was sucking it all down, hot and sticky. That's disgusting! And you . . . I attacked you, my best friend. How did you burn me?"

I lifted up the talisman by the chain. "This protected me."

She traced her finger over her newly pink lips, eyeing the sapphire stone in fear. "You've known about this?" she waved her hands over her body, "and didn't tell me? How? When?"

"I—I just found out. Nicholas saved me from one and then he gave me this."

Sam swallowed hard. "He saved you from a vampire? How?" Her eyes glazed over. "He knows?"

I looked away, my cheeks burning hot. "Yes, he—he's been protecting me for a long time. Since my mom died."

"What do you mean?"

"A vampire attacked me and my mom when I was a kid and Nicholas rescued me. He's been my guardian ever since."

Sam ran her hands all over her face and neck, pressing and pulling, her raging appetite overcoming her ability to concentrate. "How is that even possible? He's our age."

"He's part vampire too. He doesn't age."

Sam's eyes widened. "You're dating a vampire? And yet he protects you from them—" She took several deep breaths, her eyes wild. "How does he protect you from them?"

"We can talk about that later. It's very complicated."

Her paranoia spiked as she eyed the front door. "Who else knows?"

"No one . . . Where's Todd?"

"I don't know where he is. He just left me." She folded her arms and cursed. "Left me here to rot and murder my best friend and mother. When I get my hands on him . . ."

I glanced at the time. Sam's mom would be coming home soon, but the sun wouldn't be down before then.

"We have to get you out of here. I have an idea," I said and slowly got to my feet. "I need some heavy blankets. I know someone who can help."

Once the sun set, I coaxed Phil outside to my car that stood parked in Nicholas' gravel driveway. With hesitation, I opened up the trunk. Sam unraveled herself from the blankets and looked up into Phil's face with shock.

Phil cursed under his breath. "For the love of all that is sacred."

"Phil?" Sam's eyes widened in awe and wonder. "You're alive?"

"You have to help her," I said, backing away. "I'm . . . uh . . . appetizing."

"And that you are." Phil gave me a quick eyebrow waggle before he helped her crawl out of the car, keeping a protective stance between the two of us. She stared up at him with hope in her eyes.

"It's okay, Sam. I'll get ya leveled out." He gently moved her hair from her eyes before he ushered her toward the house.

With a quick glance over his shoulder, he gave me a reassuring smile. I hoped he'd be able to bring Sam around to the sober way of life. He had to or I didn't know what I'd do.

I got in the car and drove home, aware Dad would probably be pacing the living room since it was after dark. Loneliness hit hard as a gentle rain danced on the windshield. Though I didn't want to go home, I had nowhere else to go, or anyone I could talk to about things.

Dad luckily only gave me a fatherly look when I walked in. I told him I was tired, overwhelmed, and needed to be alone. He gave me a sideways hug from the comfort of his La-Z-Boy, and went back to watching some war program on the history channel. I would have given anything to have him pry just a little, but went directly upstairs instead.

Tomorrow the bomb would drop. Tomorrow everyone would discover Sam was missing. Tomorrow the nightmare would begin again and the chasm between my two lives would grow even bigger.

All I could do was curl up in my bed with Nicholas' journal wrapped in my arms and sob.

# Chapter Eleven

"Well, look who finally decided to get out of bed," Dad remarked, looking over the top of his newspaper.

I stumbled into the kitchen and went directly for the coffee pot.

"You sleep okay?" he asked.

"Yes," I mumbled and poured myself a cup with extra sugar and cream.

"How are you handling everything?"

I shrugged. *As good as can be expected.*

"'Cause if you need to talk . . . "

"I'm fine, Dad." I gave him the "don't try to console me" look. Yesterday, I'd hoped to sit and finish where we left off, but not now—not after everything that happened last night.

"I contacted Connie at ET. She agreed to talk with you."

I huffed and cocked my head to the side. Though he flowed out an enormous dose of concern and I should have been grateful, he didn't have my permission to talk to Connie or anyone for that matter. He feigned an apologetic smile as I clenched my jaw before I wordlessly breezed past him and headed upstairs.

At the same time I heard a knock at the door. A wave of anxiety from the stranger struck me hard and stopped me midstride.

"Jules, will you get that?"

I gripped the railing, dread inching up my skin. "I'm in my pajamas."

Dad scuffed the chair against the floor when the knocking persisted. "Okay, okay."

I should have darted up the stairs but I couldn't make myself go. I had to know who was there. My heart almost stopped when my eyes met Sam's mom's.

"Please tell me Samantha is here." She stood on her tiptoes to peer over Dad's shoulder, her hair wild and eyes crazed. "Sam?" she called into our house.

"I don't think she's here, but please come in." Dad moved to the side. "Jules?"

I gulped and wished I could tell her anything to give her some hope.

"She's not here, Mrs. King."

Mrs. King's face blanched. "Did she call you? Do you know where or who she might be with?"

Dad squinted his eyes as my gaze ping-ponged between the two. I struggled to answer. "I haven't heard from her."

"Nancy, let's figure this out in the living room. I'm sure she's with a friend or boyfriend, and too embarrassed to call." He took her arm but she stayed frozen, her eyes—laden with dark circles—fixed on me.

My breathing accelerated as her suspicion clamped hard into my psyche, squeezing me like a vice. Did she know something? I cleaned up the best I could, minus the destroyed carpet. Under her stare, everything inside screamed to confess. Surely we could trust Sam's mom. I couldn't do this to her, take away her only child after she'd lost her husband to cancer ten years prior.

"It's that boy, Todd. Isn't it?" she asked, wringing her hands. "She's with him doing God knows what. She didn't leave in her car, or even take her phone. As far as I know, all her clothes are at home." She shook her head. "Where are they, Julia? Her text said to call you. You were the last to talk to her. Is she in trouble?"

My heart floundered in my chest. "I . . . I don't know," I stuttered out, unsure what else to say. "We didn't talk about anything important. She didn't say she was leaving. She was— home." My voice teetered up, hinting my lie.

Dad's curiosity spiked.

"Well, I'm going to Todd's parents after this. He took her somewhere and when I find out where, Heaven help him."

Visions of the interrogation at school with Principal Brewster and the fliers littering the halls when Phil was missing came back in a rush. I wanted to bury my head in a hole until the hysteria passed.

Mrs. King's agitation erupted. We didn't have the answers she came to find.

"Sorry to bother you. If she calls, please have her call me." She clutched her purse to her chest while she darted out of the door.

"Of course," Dad said, chasing after her and helping her into her car.

I watched from the doorway as she screeched her tires and tore off down the street. Dad returned, his brows pulled down, shadowing his eyes—what Luke and I called the infamous sleeper-wave eyebrows of death. "Do you have your pen?"

"Yeah." I snapped to attention at the directness of his question. "It's upstairs."

"When you see Sam, use it."

"Dad!" I gasped, amazed he'd ask me to zap her, no questions asked.

"And if she's okay, nothing will happen."

"And if she's not, it'll kill her."

"Yes." Dad looked grim.

"NO!"

I turned to run upstairs as he grabbed my arm. "You have to. I know you can't imagine this as a possibility, but if she's been turned, she won't be able to control herself. And honestly, Sam won't really be Sam anymore. The creature will look like her, but it will only want one thing from you and you'll have to protect yourself." He loosened his grip and pursed his lips, composing himself. "I'm sorry. I hope I'm wrong."

His exact interpretation of what really happened sent a quiver through my gut. In spite of all his warnings, without the talisman, I would have died yesterday. And instead of Sam's mom coming to our door, police would have informed him of my demise just now.

But the talisman did change everything. I'd been able to give Sam a second chance along with the rest of my vamp friends to choose a different life. The fact Dad would have zapped them on sight hurt. How could he be so cruel, especially since he knew civil vamps existed?

"You're wrong." I pulled my arm away. "You shouldn't be so quick to judge. You had good vampires that you worked with."

Dad laughed, the sound sadistic and mean. "Very few are civil, at best. And that's only after years of practice. They still need blood to survive and will do anything to get it. They don't keep humans as pets, just like you don't buy ice cream to admire it in the freezer."

He was misinformed. Vamps didn't need blood, they only craved it, and once they abstained the bloodlust decreased drastically and they could lead bloodless lives. "If my eating ice cream killed people, I'd quit."

"I'm not joking. For them it's not an option. They don't care if you were once friends. They kill to satisfy their overwhelming appetite. It's a simple fact."

*They can if they're given a chance.*

"But still," he said, "No going out after dark until we get a location on Sam. If she's been changed, she'll be lethal."

I rolled my eyes and huffed. "Hardly."

"Julia, this isn't something to mess with. She'll find you. You're familiar. She won't be able to help herself."

I wanted to scream that I had a vampire-warding talisman and that she couldn't harm me, but I wasn't sure if that was wise.

"So you're going to lock me up?"

"It's for your safety."

"Phil found me and nothing happened."

He pressed his lips together. "You were lucky."

"Lucky?" I snorted. "I thought you said I was brave."

"That too. You're just like your mother," he said, almost as an afterthought.

My throat hiccupped. "What do you mean?"

Grief hit hard as Dad sat on the chair in the foyer. He stared down at the floor. "Mom had an ability to sense the emotions of others. She once asked me what kind of person would ever crave blood. I thought she was joking and didn't take her comment seriously until it was too late."

I sat down on the stairs opposite him. "Why didn't you ever tell me Mom was an empath?"

Dad looked up, startled. "I—I don't know." His mouth froze, partly open as his skin paled. "Are you . . . are you one too?"

I looked away.

"That makes sense." He touched my arm. "I should have known; you've always been so aware."

"Freakishly so."

"Oh, don't think that," he said and stood up, pulling me into a hug. "You're special."

Who would have thought a vampire sighting would bring out everything I've ever wanted to talk about with my father, but couldn't? Well, almost everything. I peered deeply into his eyes, begging. He couldn't lock me up.

"So, since I sense them, they can't sneak up on me. That's how I knew Phil was around. So, I'm fine."

"I trust you, Julia. It's the vamps I don't trust. Do you not remember what happened to your mother? Your friendship with Sam might stop you from doing the right thing."

I sucked in a quick breath, tempted to challenge him. Could he kill his best friend? Luckily, the talisman saved me from ever having to make that choice. "I'm armed now, so I'll be careful. I promise."

"Even still, I'm taking your keys."

"What?"

"I'm sorry, pumpkin. I don't want you to be tempted."

There wasn't anywhere I needed to go, but handing them over seemed completely unfair. They hung on the wall in the kitchen and I couldn't snag them now without him knowing.

"This sucks."

"Just until we can locate her."

"Fine, whatever." I turned on my heels and marched upstairs, slamming my door.

# Chapter Twelve

$O$nce Dad disappeared into his basement office, I escaped outside to clear my head. He might have my keys, but a walk in pure daylight surely wasn't forbidden.

The ache inside for Nicholas and uncertainty with Phil and Sam drove daggers into my stomach. But Scarlett's disappearance angered me most. This wasn't the first time she'd gone missing in action. And now when I needed her most, she'd disappeared.

The giant redwoods creaked in time with the blue jays' happy song, as if they played a symphony together. I padded down the winding path with Nicholas' journal tucked under my arm. My destination: the place where fate had brought me and Nicholas together—our sacred spot.

I sat on the old familiar stump. Sunlight fought through the trees to illuminate the plants that needed the light, just like the depths of my heart, dying from the absence of everything I held dear. I didn't know what to do, where to turn, or how to cope.

A blast of overwhelming curiosity drew my attention away. I peered down the trail, meeting a pair of green effervescent eyes. His eyes. I gasped and stood. My hands instinctively wrapped around the talisman to protect it. The journal flopped open onto the trail.

"It's okay," Nicholas said, putting out his hand. "Don't be afraid."

"I'll scream," I said, retreating away, knowing his mother sent him here to find me and retrieve the necklace, far away from Preston's interference.

As I blinked, his shape blurred. Then his hand cupped over my mouth and his arm fastened my torso; his body pressing into me from behind.

"Shhh," he whispered in my ear. "I promise. I just want to talk."

Sincerity emanated from his being. Unable to help it, I melted into his arms, welcoming his touch. He smelled amazing and though he was there to take back what was his, all I wanted to do was kiss him.

"You won't scream?"

I nodded my head, tempted to jump into his arms. My body went slack as he loosened his grip.

"Here." He picked up the journal and handed it to me. "You dropped this."

I looked down at the journal and then back into his mesmerizing eyes. Our hands touched as I received the book. He gestured for us to sit down.

"I'm sorry I snuck up on you. I wasn't sure . . ."

He stopped and studied me, fascination lighting up his face, as if he admired what he saw. I looked away with a blush, my stomach dancing with butterflies.

"How did you find me?"

"After you left, I couldn't stop thinking about you. Preston and Alora wouldn't tell me much as usual, so I got in my car and drove. Once I arrived in town, I followed your scent."

"Oh," I covered my mouth with my hand and then let it drop down to touch the talisman. Though it warmed, I wondered again why it wasn't masking my scent. *Weird.* I shrugged the worry off, happy he'd been able to find me. Were his memories still there, just locked up somehow?

"You're calling your parents by their first names. Why?"

"They don't feel like my parents actually."

*Maybe not.*

He scooted a little closer. I fought back the urge to grab his neck and lay one on his lips.

"So, what do you want to know?"

"Everything, anything. How we met? The events that led to my memory being erased?"

"You don't remember anything?"

He shrugged.

"But you knew to come here?"

"You told me at the house."

"Oh, right." *Darn it.*

I looked away from his inquiring stare and my gaze ironically focused to the object on my lap. Everything he could possibly want to know was documented here, in his own words. A far better recollection than I could do. I gripped the leather bound book tighter, afraid of the consequences. What if he read what was inside and rejected me? But I couldn't keep it from him either.

My fingers trembled as I held out the journal. "You should start with this."

He touched the dagger cross on the cover, then the tattoo on his bicep.

My cheeks burned. "Yeah. It's yours and I took it. I'm sorry."

He opened the front cover and the photo he'd secretly taken of me slipped out onto his lap. The viridian flecks in his eyes sparkled as he picked it up and read the back. "I took this?"

"We have a long history, Nicholas. The only reason we are sitting here today, the only reason I'm alive, actually, is because of you."

His brow knitted together. "I'm all ears."

I sighed and touched his hand. "I don't even know where to begin."

He flipped his hand around and interlaced his fingers with mine. I squeezed back, his touch the lifesaving water I'd been dying to drink.

"Start at the beginning."

For several hours I breezed through the *Cliff Notes* of our crazy journey. I had to start with the significance of where we sat, the fact he'd pulled me off the cliff in front of us and staked the vamp he'd lied about, calling it a mountain lion, right on this spot. The details came out effortlessly from my mother to his mother and everything in between, except, of course, for the embarrassing parts of our relationship. I wouldn't dare tell him anything, for fear he might not feel the same for me again. Though he cared, his feelings were still platonic.

"What I don't understand is if Preston and Alora wouldn't tell you anything, why didn't you just talk to Harry?"

Nicholas' countenance dropped. "Harry died."

"He what?" My throat constricted as fat tears welled in my eyes. "When?"

"He had a heart attack shortly after my amnesia began."

"No," I whispered and felt the world sway.

Nicholas put his arm over my shoulder and shushed me. I wasn't sure what upset me more: the fact Nicholas wasn't more saddened or that Alora quite possibly murdered him. A tear slipped down my cheek as the grief washed over me. Not only for Harry, but everyone who'd been victimized over the vampire curse. If only there was a way to stop it without having to hurt anyone I loved.

Everything boiled down to Alora's never-ending quest to possess the talisman. She'd finally found the Achilles heel. By removing Harry and inciting amnesia on Nicholas, she could easily ask him to retrieve her heirloom.

"Why are you really here?" I gulped down the painful betrayal.

He clenched his jaw, hurt. "I told you already. For answers."

"Not to get the necklace?" My voice came out harder than I wanted.

"No." He pursed his lips and attempted to wipe a wayward tear from my cheek. I jerked away.

"I promise you, Julia. I'm here to find out about my past, which involves the necklace. There's obviously a good reason why I gave it to you and not her. And why you and Preston are so insistent she doesn't get it back."

My heart fluttered in surprise, melting my anger. "Yes, there is." The stone warmed, as if happy of that fact. "It wards off vampires. But in her hands, she'd become a day-walker and be invincible."

He clenched his jaw. "Then I made a good decision."

I studied his beautiful, kissable lips, yearning for him to just lean forward. "I think so."

An awkward pause filled the space as his fury and frustration flared then subsided. I'd indirectly told him his mother was a lying, conniving witch and he apparently connected the dots. His amnesia wasn't a mistake at all and now he finally knew it.

He shrugged off his anger and sighed. "So what do we normally do on days like these?"

A chuckle bounced out of my lips. Nothing about us was normal. "We could go to your house."

"I have a house?"

I laughed a little harder until I remembered Phil and I had turned it into a detox center for Sam. "Did you say you drove?"

He nodded. "Good. I have some people I want you to meet."

# Chapter Thirteen

The summer sun hung in the sky amongst a mound of soft fluffy clouds. I closed my eyes, basking in its warmth, happy I didn't have to get home quite yet. But just to be safe, I clicked my phone completely off to keep Dad's suspicions down. Hopefully he'd spent all afternoon worrying about locating Sam instead of my whereabouts.

As we drove, Nicholas remained quiet, his emotions flickering around like a pinwheel. And once he'd digested all the info I'd told him, the journal that lay on the console between us was ready to add more sustenance to his information overload.

I fidgeted, anxious to know what Phil and Sam were up to and wondered if popping in unexpectedly would be such a good idea. I'd also hoped Scarlett would be there to help unblock Nicholas' memories. One positive thing about the amnesia, Nicholas didn't remember he and Phil were sworn enemies. Otherwise, this reunion would have gone in a completely different direction.

"This is it," I said.

He hummed in acceptance, admiring his digs.

As we exited the car, I appraised the interior. A thick plume of bloodlust with a hint of desire exuded from inside. My body flushed as jealousy tangled its green fingers around my heart and squeezed. Was there something brewing between Phil and Sam? I trusted him to take care of Sam, not hook up with her, especially after he'd pretty much fallen in love with me.

"Ummm," I said, not sure exactly how to gauge what might be happening inside. "I hope you're not upset, but one of my friends was recently changed and she needed a place to hide until she could get a grip on her appetite. I didn't have anywhere for them to go, and your place was vacant, so . . ."

"Okay." He shrugged. "Let's go meet 'em then."

"Door!" I yelled, hoping not to singe someone who didn't move fast enough.

I braced myself as we entered the house, unsure of what I'd find. Nicholas' gaze trailed the claw marks Katie had left in the floor seconds before her untimely demise.

"Oh." I bit my lip, the guilt behind her death coming back to me in a big gust of remorse. "There was an accident. It's a long story. I'm sure we can fix it."

"Julia, you're here." Phil came around the corner, his hands firmly gripped onto Sam's shoulders as her bloodlust spiked. "And, Nick—"

Sam's screech startled everyone as she darted behind Phil.

I held up my hand and backed up against the door. "I didn't mean to interrupt," I said, as her pitch escalated. "I just wanted to see how things were going."

Phil tried unsuccessfully to pry her away from his back. "This is embarrassing. I swear we were doing much better than this." He grabbed Sam's hands and removed her nails from his shirt. "Sam. Chill."

"He's here to get me," she squealed.

Phil screwed up his face and followed her fearful gaze to Nicholas. "You two know each other?"

She started to hyperventilate. "I promise. I won't hurt anyone, please . . ."

Her reaction donned on me. She must have put two and two together from our talks at school and then at her house just now. That Nicholas hunted vampires for a living and not human criminals. "It's okay, Sam. Nicholas is not going to hurt you."

Phil mouthed an "O" and put his hand over her mouth. "Shhh . . ."

She yelped and wiggled, but he successfully calmed her down.

Taken aback, Nicholas took in the sight, his face darkened in concern. "Why is she acting like that?"

"Sorry," I said under my breath. "She thinks you're going to kill her."

Nicholas' eyebrows pinched together. "And why would she think that?"

I shrugged apologetically. "'Cause you've killed every vamp that you've ever run across." An important detail I'd somehow forgotten to mention. "I'll tell you more later."

Nicholas blinked at me in annoyance.

"So, you're home, Nick," Phil said with a half grin. "No hard feelings?"

"I need to explain," I interrupted. "Alora erased his memories, so he doesn't remember you. Actually, he doesn't remember anything."

Phil's eyebrows shot up as his glance fell on me, then at Nicholas. "Wow. I mean, Alora's cruel, but that's a shocker."

"Please don't start," I said. "Nicholas, this is Phil and Samantha. Samantha is the new vampire I was telling you about. Phil is trying to help her control herself. We're all *friends*."

"Hey," Nicholas said, seemingly uninterested in small talk.

He wandered over to the dresser, stopping to touch the photo of his mother.

Phil put up his hand to stop me when I moved to follow Nicholas. "Parker, you need to stay put. Tiger here is a having a rough time and you smell a little too delicious today."

Sam peered over Phil's shoulder, still watching Nicholas like a hawk, but keeping tabs on me, too, with a hungry gleam in her eye.

"Is Scarlett here?" I asked Phil.

He shook his head. "Haven't seen her since you went to L.A."

"Did she follow me there?"

"I'm not sure—"

Suddenly, a whir of bodies ended with Phil restraining Sam's arms against the wall, knocking a picture onto the floor with a crash. I gasped as Nicholas eyed the broken frame with pursed lips.

"Sorry," Phil said to Nicholas quickly.

Sam hissed, unaware of the damage she'd done. "I have to," she whined.

"No." Phil looked directly into her eyes. "Remember what I told you. The longer you withstand, the sooner it will go away."

Sam began to cry and sagged down.

Unable to handle her distress any longer, I headed for the door. "I'll be outside."

Nicholas turned to me with a nod.

I paced for a little while and decided to curl up in Nicholas' front seat. The journal fell open onto my lap to my favorite page.

**November 12**

*I finally told her how I feel. Overwhelmed with everything about her, her warmth, her scent, her laugh. She was curled up in my arms and it just slipped out. She froze and her beautiful eyes locked onto mine. She asked me to repeat myself. I wasn't sure if the timing was right. If it was too soon. If she'd say it back. So, I told her ... I love you. Her smile electrified her entire face and she cried and said she loved me. I've never been happier to hear those magical words. I constantly dream of holding her, to feel her warmth and every breath, to protect her. I hope I'm not taking risks I shouldn't. I just can't be without her. She's so special to me ... my everything ... my love.*

My heart swooned then swan dived into my shoes. What if he didn't feel the same way when he reread the pages? Could we honestly start where we left off with only a story to bridge our history together? Temptation to remove the page and keep it from him crossed my mind, but there wasn't enough time to take every page out where he'd sworn his love and devotion to me. I closed my eyes and prayed this would ignite a spark within him and he'd genuinely remember how things used to be.

Somehow, with the ease of knowing he'd returned, my mind quieted and exhaustion set in. Once the dream started, I knew I'd fallen asleep. Nicholas, Phil, Katie, Sam, Tyler, Todd, and I picnicked at the beach in full sun, the waves shushing in the background. We all were friends and happy, truly happy.

A dark shadow covered over us, like an eclipse. I turned just as Nicholas ripped the talisman from my neck. Then everyone bared fangs. I was to be the main dish. Before they pounced, I pulled open my eyes with a gasp.

But the bloodlust didn't evaporate like the nightmare had. Everywhere I looked, dark eyes peered at me through the windows of Nicholas' car.

"Look who's awake," one of them said. "Time to come outside and play."

A dark haired boy scrubbed his finger upward and the lock magically flipped up by itself. He popped the handle and opened the door. A rush of cold, clammy air flooded the interior of the car.

"You're not invited in here," I squealed, his motions happening too fast for me to catch the door.

I crab-crawled over the console onto the driver's side and mashed down the lock, holding it in place.

"Come on out," he said from the open door. Behind him others jockeyed for the closest position, faces I recognized. People from my high school.

"Nicholas!" I screamed, wondering why I was alone in the driveway inside a swarm of vampires. Did they go somewhere and leave me? Or was this a horrible nightmare? "Phil!"

"She's a breath of Heaven," a brunette girl said.

My mouth dropped open. "Rochelle? Rochelle Pierce?"

"Yes," she smiled, showing her canines. "Cool, isn't it?"

"No, not really." I wrinkled up my forehead. "Is the whole cheerleading squad vamps?"

She laughed and then looked over the roof of the car with sudden terror. I tried to see what scared her, but bodies and drooling mouths blocked my view. When I turned back to make sure I hadn't imagined her, she'd gone. Then, one-by-one vamps' chests began to explode with fire as something zinged through the air. Ash rained down, thickening the air. The sea of vamps parted and retreated to the shadows of the tree-line.

My view finally clear, I spotted Nicholas on the walkway staring down at his hand in wonder. He reached into his jacket, one he wasn't wearing earlier, and produced a stake. He pointed it towards the nest of human-like snakes hissing at him. I jumped from the car with spongy legs and ran to hide behind him.

"Where were you?" I asked, catching my breath.

"Phil and I were talking." He studied the symbol burned into the bottom of the stake, the one that matched his tattoo and the cover of his journal. "That was awesome. You say I do this all the time?"

I looked at him in surprise. "Yeah, and you made the stakes too."

"I found this jacket in the closet with the stakes hidden inside the lining." He held out the trench coat to show me and beamed like a kid in a candy store. I didn't have the heart to tell him Harry actually made most of them.

"We just want the girl," one of them screeched. "Give her up."

He chucked another stake at the voice and the vamp burst into flames. The others began to thin, their fear overpowering their lust for me.

Phil came outside with Sam still glued firmly to his side.

"Wow," he said. "It's a vamp fest. Are you advertising a blood drive, Parker?"

"Funny." I pulled a face.

Sam gasped, her eyes elsewhere. We followed her gaze and all of us turned at once. Todd stood out from the crowd in his vampire glory—mean and buff. I cowered momentarily. Nicholas flinched and I stayed his hand as he took out another stake, ready to eviscerate him. I wished I'd brought my laser so I could have the pleasure.

"Samantha," Todd twisted his face. "What are you doing here with . . . Phil?" His mouth froze partly open and then a revelation hit his eyes. "And Julia?" He arched an eyebrow at Sam. "Don't tell me you're protecting—a human?"

Phil squeezed Sam's hand. I channeled some courage her way as well.

"You have a lot of nerve showing up here." Sam's voice shook. "How dare you change me, then leave me alone. With my mother, no less! I had no clue what was happening to me. I almost murdered her and my best friend."

"You haven't fed yet?" He let out a gust of air. "What are you waiting for?"

"Of course I haven't. I've chosen to abstain."

Todd laughed a deep bellow that rumbled the ground. "No wonder." He clenched his jaw and turned his lecherous gaze on me, giving a once-over that creeped me out. "That won't last long, not with *her* around."

Sam gave a slight groan, her vampire side fighting painfully hard against what she was choosing to do. "You need to go, Todd."

"Do you know how much that venom cost? I didn't go through all the hassle to just lose you to some human-loving cause, Samantha. I don't have all night. Let's go."

"You took my humanity without permission." She gripped Phil's hand harder; her knuckles whitened. "There are consequences to what you're doing and I won't take part in it."

*Way to go, Sam.*

Todd's glaring eyes bounced from Sam, to me, to Phil, and landed on Nicholas' hand. I removed my grip to let him know he'd overstayed his welcome and Nicholas could stake him at any moment he chose.

"You heard her," Phil said, taunting him with a lift of his chin. "Hit the road, Jack."

"This isn't over," Todd said with a scowl right before he disappeared, along with the rest of the vamps.

Sam let out an exhale and gently collapsed into Phil's side. "Julia has to go, or we do. I can't take it anymore."

I opened myself up to feel her angst—overpowering and all consuming.

"We'll go." He kissed her on the forehead before he gave me an apologetic shrug. "She's right. You're exceptionally tasty right now." He launched the two of them into the air.

Tasty? How could that be with the talisman on? My insides crawled from the rejection as I watched them soar out of sight. That used to be us flying off together on some wild adventure and now, because I was tasty, I couldn't go.

*Why am I jealous?*

I sighed and turned to Nicholas for some form of comfort. In the olden days, he would have wrapped me up in his arms and kissed me. Instead he stared, waiting for me to lead.

"Do you smell me?" I asked, dejected.

"You are appealing." He turned up the corner of his lip. "So now what?"

I wanted to brainstorm what had changed with the talisman when reality hit and I freaked. Dad would be home, flipping out, especially since I shut off my phone and it was after dark.

"I have to go home."

"Let's go," he said and ushered me towards his ash-covered car.

# Chapter Fourteen

"Julia Katherine Parker! Where have you been?"

I sulked into the house under the scrutiny of Dad's sleeper-wave eyebrows as Nicholas drove away. He promised to come to my window later after Dad settled down, well, *if* Dad settled down.

"Sorry." I held my head low. "I was out with Nicholas. It's cool. I wasn't *outside* when it got dark."

"Cool?" Dad slammed the door, veins bulging from his forehead. "I told you to stay home! There's been a new outbreak of—" he made fang fingers to indicate the obvious, "and you're out gallivanting with—did you say Nicholas? I thought you two broke up. And why is your phone off?"

I inched closer to the stairs, hoping for a quick exit. "He just came back into town. Sorry, I forgot to text."

"Julia! You can't shut off your phone!" He pressed his hand onto his forehead and groaned. "It's after dark and dangerous. There hasn't been this many since, I don't know how long—" He sighed and shook his head. "I was worried sick."

"Dad, seriously. I was fine."

"No! You don't understand. The ET unit is coming here to set up camp. We need to find and stop the source. We're all in grave danger."

"What about Luke? Won't he get suspicious?"

I heard a flush and looked up as curiosity stood at the top of the stairs in the form of my brother with a horrendous case of bed head. "Grave danger?"

"Look who's up." Dad flipped his frown into a smile. "I was . . . quoting a movie. It's nothing. You finally feeling better?"

I followed with a fake laugh. Dad lied worse than I did.

"I think so," he said and coughed. "I'm going to take a shower."

"Good thing." I fanned the air with my hand as if I could smell his stink from there.

Luke didn't respond, only turned around, and headed for his room. I made a beeline for the stairs.

"Julia, we aren't finished. I *will* come talk to you later."

I didn't respond and ran the rest of the way up. After I closed the door, I turned *on* my phone, anxious for a text from Nicholas. Then I remembered I'd never asked if he'd reactivated his, or even knew he had a phone.

"Crap," I said as the phone vibrated with texts and messages, all from Dad.

I went to the window and looked out, unable to see the street. We hadn't worked out a time when he'd return. I'd merely informed him my window was on the second story in the back.

I curled up in my covers and found an old movie on the *Netflix* app on my iPhone to stay preoccupied. Halfway into the movie, another bout of bothersome bloodlust pounced upon the house. Though I knew I was completely safe, I pulled the covers up to my nose and watched the window.

Why did I suddenly smell extra delectable to vamps? I

looked to the talisman for support, noticing it hadn't changed temperature lately to signal danger like it had in the past. To my horror, white smoke swirled within the stone's blue depths. A dreadful thought crossed my mind. What if Nicholas' bloodlust had been triggered again? Was he going to will away the talisman from me? I clicked off my bedroom light and slid onto the floor, peeking over the side of my bed with my laser pen.

A tap on the window made me squeal. The dark haired vampire that tried to get me from Nicholas's car had returned and motioned with his finger to come outside. I smiled back, a little larger than I should, before zapping him with the laser. His smug expression faded to fear before he exploded to a crisp.

My breath bounded out of my lungs in tandem with my pulse, when another vamp appeared at my window. I blinked, astounded. Didn't they just see me blast the last vamp who tried to get me to come outside? I zapped him, too.

After the ridiculousness of zapping ten vamps in a row, I held down the button so the pen continually shot light out the window. The goons finally took a hint and stayed away. I shut them out of my radar as well, sickened by their disgusting love of blood—my blood.

Dad wasn't kidding when he said an onslaught of vampires had descended on the city. Did Todd sire our entire school? He said he'd bought the venom, but who would possibly want to dole out immortality so freely only for the money? There had to be at least twenty-five at Nicholas' and I'd killed over ten within fifteen minutes. None of it made sense.

I remembered what Nicholas had said about a vampire and their kin, about them all sharing the power equally. So the more in your family tree, the less powerful everyone was. It prevented any one vampire from siring armies of immortals. But these new vamps, though they didn't seem very smart, were actually quite strong and talented with special gifts, like mind-moving of objects. Whoever made them overcame the rules.

And with the talisman acting up, if there was ever a time I needed protection, it would be now. Actually, the whole town needed it. Where was Nicholas? I turned off the laser and looked out the window.

Hundreds of eyes peered out at me from the shadows. I screamed. Then the power went out.

# Chapter Fifteen

"Julia!" Dad yelled from down the hall. "I'm coming!"

He stumbled into the room and tripped over something, landing on the floor with a loud "oof."

"Where are you?" he asked frantically.

"Over here." I reached out to meet his hand. "The vamps. Where'd they all come from?"

"We're safe inside." He pulled me to my feet as we peered out into the scary darkness. They flitted across the lawn with jarring, blurred movements, like a swarm of bees. "I'm here."

Then the whispers started. "Julia, come outside."

"Dad," I squealed and put my hands over my ears. "Why are they after me?"

"I don't know, but let's get the power on."

"No! You can't go out there," I cried. Especially if he was only armed with a freaking laser pen.

"Don't worry. I've got a backup generator in the garage."

I swallowed hard. Together, with my nails firmly planted into his ribs, we filed down into the basement room. He flipped a switch and everything illuminated.

"I had one installed just in case," he said with a smile. "Now let's go laser some vamps so they don't wake up Luke."

I halfheartedly grinned at his excitement, but felt something change outside. The emotion game dominated earlier by the love of my blood was taking heavy hits against tremendous joy and fear. Someone had come to our rescue.

As we peered outside the living room window, I braced myself for what we'd see. Three pairs of vamp eyes appeared and gawked back. Before Dad could laser them, something zinged through the air and hit them with a thunk. Fire crackled out of their torsos in unison, puffing them into smoke and ash.

"Oh." I bit my lip, moved by Nicholas' amazing physique as he performed ninja moves in our yard; a duffle bag filled with stakes sat at his feet. No use in hiding the obvious now.

"Your boyfriend is a vampire hunter? *Dirty Harry*?" Dad's anger ignited. "And you knew this all along and didn't tell me?"

My mouth wouldn't work, caught in a lie and afraid to tell him the real truth. This was going completely in the wrong direction.

"It was to protect him," I finally spit out.

"Protect him from whom? We're the good side."

"Yeah, but . . ." I pushed my sweaty bangs out of my eyes. "He asked me not to. I couldn't betray his identity. And if I told you, the entire agency would find out. Besides, there's stuff about him you don't understand."

"Like what? What could be more important than telling me?"

My shoulders sagged. "I was respecting his right to anonymity."

"Anonymity? Jules, it's about getting rid of the bloodsuckers. Something we all want—"

"It's not that black and white."

Dad huffed in apparent disappointment with me and continued to watch as Nicholas remembered his abilities of speed and agility. "Well, no wonder we couldn't find him. He's obviously not a vampire after all. I mean, I've seen him come get you in plain daylight. I'm impressed. How can he do all of those moves?"

I bit my knuckle and willed Nicholas to at least slow down a little. "He's into martial arts."

"I'm impressed. He must wear something that keeps the vamps from biting him."

*A venom drenched undershirt and not to mention, reflexes of a cobra.*

I didn't answer and eventually, the incoming vamps got a clue and stayed away. He went back to his car and leaned against the hood. He had something in his hands—the journal. My throat hiccupped.

"Is he guarding our house?" My dad looked dumbfounded.

"Uh, you think?" I held out my hand and smirked.

"You don't have to be smart with me, young lady," Dad said.

His double-standard angered me. His loathing hate for the vampires was understandable, but he'd unfairly lumped them all in the same category, even civil vampires, like Darren. What if Dad knew Nicholas was a half-vampire, would he think him the enemy? Would he allow me to date him? I didn't think he'd accept Nicholas because of his bloodline, though he didn't have a choice who his parents were. So unfair, especially since he clearly fought on our side.

Dad's scratched his stubble on his cheek. "Do you think he'd talk to me?"

"He won't know anything. He's suffering from a case of amnesia."

Dad's composure dropped. I fought back a smug smile.

"I told you it was complicated."

He grunted something under his breath, growing bored.

I took the cue and moved to the stairs for a quick exit. "So, I guess I'll be going to bed now, since the drama seems to be over."

"Please promise me you'll stay inside," Dad asked, his eyes beseeching.

"I will, but I want you to know something," I said as a gust of courage bolstered my nerves. I pointed to my talisman. "Nicholas gave me this. It's an amulet to protect me from vampires and makes biting me impossible."

Dad squinted. "What?"

"This." I held the glowing stone away from my chest.

"Julia. Are you sure?" His concern bounced around us. "I've seen those same trinkets in vending machines. How could it possibly protect you?"

"What?" My mouth parched as I looked down at the stone and back at him.

Did he not see the twenty-five carats of beauty practically singing in my hand? Something Nicholas had said about the talisman only being attractive to the beholder came to mind; that it cloaked itself.

"Was that before or after his amnesia?" Dad asked in concern.

My pride insisted I go outside just to show him just how awesome the necklace worked, but I knew the perceived danger could aggravate his heart problem. I decided to stop pressing the issue. Otherwise he'd duct tape me on an ET psychiatrist's couch in Tulsa, far away from my friends and Nicholas.

"Before, but never mind. I've got the pen you gave me and it works great."

"Oh?" His eyebrows shot up.

"The vamps were stalking me outside my window before the power cut out. Good night." I hurried up the stairs, leaving him gawking in the foyer.

Dad didn't go to bed until almost daybreak. His anxiety traipsed often through my bedroom door before he checked on me, keeping me awake. I briefly considered setting up the blond wig under my covers again so I could visit Nicholas outside, but I'd promised I wouldn't. And after everything that happened tonight, I didn't want to push Dad's heart over the edge. Somehow, I eventually fell asleep.

Morning came and I awoke to the sunlight dancing across my closed eyelids. I pried them open a little after 9:00 A.M.

Disappointment twisted my stomach until I felt Nicholas' sweet aura close by. He sat outside the window, staring at the trees with a new sense of awareness. I slid out of bed, snuck into the bathroom to brush my teeth, and pulled my hair up into a ponytail before going to the window. I covered the holey Mt. Hermon Ponderosa Camp T-shirt I wore with a sweatshirt.

"Been out here long?" I asked, while sliding up the glass.

He looked at me with awe, as if I were someone else, an angel perhaps. Not a girl with disheveled hair in a wrinkled sweatshirt and flannel pants.

"You're finally up."

I ran my hand through my tousled bangs. "Sorry and I'm a mess."

"You're beautiful."

I gulped, my heart doing flips in glee. He smiled and held me in his gaze for a moment before producing the journal.

"I read the entire thing."

I bit my lip, anticipating his reaction, but before I knew it, he was there, kneeling down, his warm breath wafting over my face. "How have you been so strong? All of this must have been so difficult."

I wanted to say "you have no idea," but my voice solidified in my throat.

He pressed his hands to my cheeks and caressed my face. "My words don't do you justice."

My legs sunk into the carpet as his eyes searched deep within my soul, reading everything I'd kept locked away from him while I waited for his return. Then his lips were on mine, sweet and gentle, like he didn't want to frighten me, but couldn't wait and ask permission first. I kissed him back harder, aching and happy at the same time, weaving my hands into his soft hair.

And just like that, everything slammed back together, a wheel turning in a well-worn groove, almost as if we'd never been apart. I crawled as he lifted me out onto the ledge, lips locked and pulling in each other's essences through our breaths. The bliss sucked out all the worries I'd stored deep within my muscles, healing me. He was here. Together with me. Tears of joy trickled down my cheeks.

"You remember us?" I asked with a sniffle.

"Not entirely," he said, while placing a wayward lock of hair behind my ear. "But that just gave me the general idea."

I curled into his lap as we sat on the ledge. There wasn't anywhere I'd rather be, especially after losing him and gaining him back. I planned to stay there all day, rekindling the past if he'd let me. Activity on the patio interrupted our reunion.

I leaned over to try to listen to the commotion.

"They're here to investigate a disturbance in the force," Nicholas whispered, a hint of concern in his voice.

"The what?" I rolled my eyes. Dad and his ET geeks. "They're just a bunch of—"

"Investigators looking for my kind. Once the sun came up, hoards of cars showed up with tons of equipment. That's why I moved around to the back of the house. Am I safe here?"

"Of course you are. They don't have trackers or anything. But that means I'm definitely trapped," I said with a sigh.

"In more ways than one." He tightened his grip and nuzzled his nose against my ear, sniffing and kissing my neck. Goose bumps shot down my arms.

I giggled, slightly self-conscious 'cause I hadn't taken a shower.

"Maybe you can overhear and find out where the vamps came from."

He tilted his head. "From Doctor Evil."

"Who's that?"

"You haven't seen *Austin Powers?*"

I nudged him in the arm. "Yes, but I highly doubt that's who they mean . . . it's code."

"You ruin all my fun." He wove his finger over my back, making designs. "A very old vamp who likes to do experiments on human blood. He'd been classified as docile in the past, but now he's making an army."

"Why?"

Nicholas pinched his eyes shut. "A war, maybe. They aren't sure."

"A war. Here? In Scott's Valley?" I shivered and Nicholas gripped me tighter.

"I have to hand it to them, they're brave geeks if they think they can stop it. And your Dad wants to recruit me. I've actually been the talk of the morning."

"Oh, no." I pressed my hands to my eyes. "He saw you last night and freaked. You're kind of a legend. They call you *Dirty Harry.*"

I hoped the nickname would trigger a memory, or sorrow for his Godfather. To my disappointment, nothing but curiosity wafted from him.

"Why would they give me that name?"

I gulped down the truth, too raw to tell. "Who knows? Better than *Boba Fett.*"

Nicholas laughed. "It's weird. I can't remember facts about my own life, but I remember movie trivia. Go ahead. Ask me anything."

I took a deep breath. Though we joked, the gravity of a vampire war didn't sit right. How convenient for everything to come together in my town of all places. Scarlett had to be orchestrating it. Was this her attempt to make me intervene and kill off everyone? I could barely hold my own with my attractive scent. Without the talisman and a laser pen, I'd have been drained dry already.

"I just don't get why the talisman isn't working right. Technically, the vamps shouldn't be able to smell me, yet they can. Almost like it's amplifying my smell."

"That's not movie trivia." He took a dramatic sniff right at my collarbone before kissing it. "I'm not complaining."

I chuckled. "I'm thrilled I smell good to you, especially since I haven't showered, but I'm not happy I've become a five-star chum basket that incites feeding frenzies. One or two wayward vampires might have been the norm before, but dozens?" I bit my lip. "Why couldn't you have written something in the journal about it?"

"Preston probably knows," he said as an afterthought and squeezed me tighter.

I wiggled out of his grasp and turned to face him. "You think? Could you ask him?"

"And leave you here unprotected? Never."

I squealed on the inside, thrilled he'd be staying for good. "Can't you just call him?"

"Preston who?" He pulled me into his arms and nibbled on my ear.

I laughed. "I'm serious. You once said his number was in your phone. Let me see it."

"Phone?" He shifted slightly. "What else do I have that you're not telling me about? Don't tell me I have a motorcycle."

"Um . . . I don't think so," I said with a big smile. "But you'll need to reinstate the service on your phone."

"Why do I get the feeling you want to take care of this now?"

I pressed my lips together. "I just want to know what we're up against, that's all."

He sighed and rested his chin on my shoulder. "Five more minutes, please?"

I leaned into him and kissed his forehead. How could I resist? After another round of kisses and snuggles, he reluctantly let me go. I crawled into my room and finally took a shower.

# Chapter Sixteen

Nicholas hadn't been kidding when he said lots of people with stuff had invaded our house. Wires and cables lined the floors as geeks took up every inch possible of our tiny abode.

"Hey," Dad said, his insides chiming with pride as I walked into the kitchen. He'd created a buffet of food for the welcomed guests. "Everyone, this is my daughter, Julia. She's wise to the force." Dad touched his nose.

A few looked up from their laptops, giving me their fake names. I almost spit out my coffee when I met Boba Fett. No one really cared I was Russell's' daughter, which was fine with me. I didn't plan on making friends and hoped they wouldn't stay long.

"I'm going to go out with Nicholas this afternoon, if that's okay with you."

The room quieted, the occupants snapping to attention and all eyes falling on me.

Dad raised a brow. "Sure, but be home *before* dark."

"Oh-okay," I said and turned around.

The lingering quiet continued as I topped off my coffee and slathered jam on my toast. You'd have thought royalty pranced through the kitchen from the awe beaming forth. The girl who not only knew, but dated the slayer. I almost turned around and offered to sign autographs, but grabbed my bag and headed out the door instead.

I ran smack into Sam's mom.

"Julia," she said, out of breath. "Is your father home?"

I glanced over my shoulder into the house, then back to her worried face. How would he explain the geek assault inside?

"Yeah," I said. "Let me get him."

She paced on the porch as I wove through the maze to the kitchen. "Sam's mom is here."

"She is? Okay." He cleaned off his hands on a dishtowel and motioned I lead the way. "Did Sam show up yet?" He whispered behind me.

*What do I say? Yes?*

I trusted my gut and pinched my eyes shut. "She's a vamp, Dad."

He stopped midstride. "Oh no." He put his hand on my shoulder. "I'll handle this."

I braced myself before he opened the door. "Mrs. King, nice to see you again. How can I help you?"

Her sudden anger practically slapped me in the face. "You can start by having Julia explain this!" She held out two empty syringes, each labeled in a different language with a symbol that resembled a pitchfork. "Are you two doing drugs?"

"No, of course not," I said with a gasp as Dad's eyes zeroed in on the vials.

"Can I see those?" He rolled them over in his hand and hummed, ruffling out sadness. "Where did you find them?"

"In Sam's room. Where else? She hasn't come home and apparently you haven't heard from her either." She looked at me in desperation then grabbed my shoulders. "Where is she, Julia? Answer me!"

"Hold on, Nancy." Dad removed her hands from me. "Why don't you come inside and we'll figure this out. I've got a friend who's a detective investigating a lot of these disappearances. Let's call him."

She stood firm, nailing me with eye daggers. Again, I wanted to confess. Why couldn't she know? I beseeched my father with my eyes, begging to come clean.

"Mrs. King. I—"

Dad grabbed my hand and gave me "the look."

"What, Julia?" she asked, her voice anxious.

"I'm sorry." My eyes hit the floor.

Dad patted me on the back and walked Mrs. King inside.

"I've got this," Dad whispered. "Go ahead with Nicholas. We'll talk later."

He closed the door and left me on the porch, speechless. My heart ached. I turned to see Nicholas down the street, leaning against his car, his hands hooked in his jeans pockets.

I walked over to him and wrapped my arms around his torso. He kissed me on the head. "Bad news?"

"That was Sam's mom."

He squeezed me tighter. "I see."

Wordlessly and filled with empathy, he opened the car door for me. The car hummed to life and we left it all behind.

I swallowed back a tear. "It's always the same. I have to lie and tell parents I don't know where their kids have gone. And now, with this venom dealer, her mom just accused me of doing drugs."

"Venom dealer?"

"Oh, right. I keep forgetting what you and your old self know. Wish you would have written down your thoughts about him."

He shrugged. "Yeah."

"You were worried about information getting into the wrong hands. I can't believe you kept a journal anyway, but one time when we were driving, you smelled him, or the venom, and pulled over to confiscate his stuff. You jumped out of the car and totally freaked me out."

"I did?" Nicholas asked with a chuckle and laced his fingers between mine.

"One of your more random moments, but maybe if we drive by the spot, you might remember something."

"You'd think after making out with you on the roof, I'd remember *something*," he said, a playful smile on his lips.

With a blush, I tucked my head down. Though I'd kissed him tons of times, the experience on the roof ledge hit totally different levels.

I pressed my lips together to stifle my urge to attack his lips once again and suggest we forgo vamp hunting for the day. "Turn here."

The empty alley didn't provide the answers I'd hoped for. Who was I kidding to think the guy might be there, just waiting for us to rough him up for answers. Actually, all the streets were peculiarly empty. We drove a little farther and a window of a dilapidated brick building caught my eye. The same symbol I'd seen on the vials decorated the glass.

"That's it. Right there." I pointed to the window of Dr. Volynski's clinic.

Nicholas abruptly stopped. "What's here? Do you see him?"

"No. Keep driving." I turned to study the building through the back window as Nicholas cruised by. "It's the symbol on the vials."

"That's the Ukrainian coat of arms."

I shot him a look of astonishment. He remembered the coat of arms but not our astounding kisses?

"What?" he said with a shrug.

"Never mind." I smiled. "Weird. Maybe he's *him*. The doctor vampire who's giving out immortality."

"Do you want to go back and check?"

"No," I said and chewed on the corner of my lip. "I think I'll just tell my dad."

We continued on to the cell phone store and Nicholas had to practically give them the promise of his first child to get them to turn on his cell phone again. I sat in the waiting area and noticed the newspaper on the chair next to me. A picture of a clean-cut guy in a suit holding a sign that said "The End Is Near, Repent" caught my eye. I studied it momentarily, then tucked it under my arm as Nicholas approached.

"All ready?" I asked.

He nodded and we headed for the car.

"Did you see this?" I asked, producing the paper.

I read the article out loud as we drove back to his house. Authorities were trying to figure out why and where hundreds of college and high school students had disappeared to from the local schools. They'd enacted another county-wide curfew, like they had last September, and people were advised to keep tabs on their children at all times, especially after dark. Unexplainable stories of people being taken right before their eyes sickened my stomach and I barely could finish the article.

I stared out the window and watched the trees zip by. "We have to do something."

"Like?" His blasé attitude didn't sit well with me.

"I don't know. Stop the venom distribution at the source. Something."

"Isn't that what your Dad's unit is here to do?"

"Yeah, but . . ." I studied his scowl, confused where the disdain stemmed from. "That was your passion once. You were 'Dirty Harry' and took care of things before they got out of hand."

"Hmmm . . ." he said and stared out the front windshield. "Didn't I do that last night?"

He had, but his anger towards the innocent being changed or murdered wasn't as strong as before. His past relegated to mere words on paper that didn't touch his heart, robbed from his memory by his mother all for a power grab. I hated her for it.

"You don't care?"

"I do," he turned to me, pained. "But after living in the dark for months, I finally found where I feel whole. And that's with you, so I'm not leaving your side. I can't lose you. Last night was grizzly, let me tell you. Night of the living dead."

I looked at the floorboard. "Okay." He gripped my hand like a lifeline, like I'd slip away from him if he let go. How could I complain? He cared most about me.

❦

We arrived at his house and I still felt the tremendous bloodlust coming from inside. Sam, only three days sober, still wasn't handling things well.

"I guess I'll wait out here," I said as Nicholas disappeared into the house to fetch his phone.

I ached to tell Phil everything and also let Sam know her mom was going crazy with worry over her. Well, maybe that wouldn't be such a good thing to tell a blood-sick vampire right now. I leaned against the car and remembered the night before. Todd looked right through me like I was a piece of meat. And then running into Rochelle and the other guys from the football team. Who else would he change?

Nicholas came back quickly and frowned. "It needs to charge."

"Oh." *Of course.*

What would Preston say once Nicholas called? Would he even care? We were in the middle of a practical apocalypse with a failing talisman, a forgetful guardian, a deadly best friend, a distracted ex-love interest, a missing accomplice, a fretful father, a sickly brother and a house full of ET geeks who specialized in paralleling their work to *Star Wars*. I was in huge trouble.

We had all day to plan a counter offensive, but Nicholas, mesmerizing me with his green glacial eyes only wanted to relax and spend time with me romantically. And I couldn't fight it. If this was it, the time I'd accomplish my goal, the time I'd murder everyone I loved, I wanted to spend my last day on the beach with him, snuggled in his arms far away from the panic, listening to the waves crash and smelling the salty air.

"Okay," I said. "You win."

Nicholas ticked his head to the side. "What do you mean?"

"I have a place I need to show you. A special place and we'll block out the world for today. Sound good?"

"Should we bring lunch?"

I smiled. Some things I guess are ingrained, like good movies and the Ukrainian coat of arms.

# Chapter Seventeen

The awe in Nicholas' face made surprising him with our own private beach even more exciting. We stood in the mouth of the sea cave once again and experienced the rush from the wind and the waves. Then he insisted we build a gigantic sandcastle using the shells we'd collected as decorations. While he built up the sand into a huge mound at lightning speed, I giggled, unsure which Nicholas I enjoyed more. The carefree one before me was much more relaxed and able to enjoy life, more so than his prior self.

When we finished, Nicholas built me a huge bonfire and we collapsed in exhaustion to admire our handiwork—our dream castle where we'd live happily ever after. I snuggled up against his chest and snacked on treats, watching the fog dissolve into fluffy filaments just offshore.

I couldn't imagine a more perfect afternoon. Unfortunately, once we slowed our pace, my nagging conscience ran into overdrive with different plans. Nicholas didn't seem to have a problem letting everything go, but I did. The coincidence of the insignia on the doctor's office and the vials was too huge to ignore. Not to mention, we needed to find Todd and, though I didn't want to do it, stake him before he used venom on anyone else. Something told me the dealer and the doctor were one and the same. I couldn't leave all that responsibility in the hands of Dad's ET unit.

"What are you worried about?" Nicholas asked, while pushing my damp bangs off my forehead. "You've got a little vessel bulging out here that says you're thinking too hard." His touch launched a ripple of luscious electricity down my spine.

"Stuff."

"Why do I have this feeling that the old Nicholas wouldn't be lounging here on the beach making sandcastles today?"

I gave a sly smile.

"Then what would I be doing?"

My smile faded. "Probably breaking into the doctor's office."

"Ah," he said with a head tilt. "Would it make you happier if we did?"

"I don't know. Maybe." I pushed the sand around and buried my toes. "There's something weird about that place and I think we should check it out."

"If it will calm your fears, then let's go. We'll come back and finish our sand city later."

I smiled half-heartily. "Okay."

❦

Once we drove closer to the building, I doubted the brilliance of my plan. Who were we to just waltz right inside? What would we say? And what kind of doctor did people think he was anyway? Was this Todd's doctor? No doubt sensing my fear, Nicholas laced his hand with mine and squeezed.

We parked and walked around to the front of the building. I peered through the window; the waiting room looked normal and empty. But, lingering bloodlust hinted there were vampires nearby, possibly underground. I hesitated at the door, unsure how to warn Nicholas.

He rested his hand on my shoulder. "It's okay. I'm right here with you."

The entrance connected a long windowless corridor to a door at the opposite end. But strangely, there wasn't a door to the waiting room on our right. Was the room through the window a trick to make the office look like an actual clinic?

I spun around to stop our procession. My *spidey senses* were going off in my head as the door clicked closed behind us, extinguishing all the sunlight. Weak florescent lights flickered in the creepy hallway, tinting a green pallor over Nicholas' face. My heart sped up. Why did I insist we come here?

"I've changed my mind," I whispered as I reached around his torso and pulled on the door leading outside. Locked.

"Can I help you?" a woman's voice said through the intercom from the other end of the hall.

"Um," I said, tempted to say we got lost when a strong desire to tell the truth rushed through me instead. "We're here to see Dr. Volynski."

"Do you have an appointment?"

I frowned and looked to Nicholas for help. "No . . . we were just in the area." He continued to exude a calmness I climbed under for security.

We waited for a long quiet minute.

"Come in," she said with a chipper voice. The door ahead of us clicked open.

Against my better judgment, I opened the door. The waiting room inside wasn't decorated like your typical doctor's office. Rich crimson paint covered the walls to match the velvet couches and gold tapestries hung over darkened windows.

"Welcome," a beautiful girl with long black hair at the dark mahogany desk said. Her sweet voice melted my fears. "Are you here to give blood?"

I gulped and crossed my arms over my chest. "Actually, I just want to see the doctor."

Her brow rose. She typed with long black nails into the computer. "We don't have any openings today, but I can schedule an appointment for tomorrow. Who referred you?"

"Todd McMullan." His name popped out without a thought.

She radiated surprise, and then quickly became stoic as she studied the computer screen. I marveled at the convenience of hosting a blood bank. The perfect disguise for vampires to acquire the sustenance they needed with little to no attention. The fake storefront suddenly made sense. But did she know Todd? Had he warned her about the possibility of our arrival?

"Hmmm . . . He's not in our computer, but that doesn't surprise me."

She touched an earpiece in her ear and a light illuminated on the top. "Yes, right away."

"Here." She pushed a clipboard toward me. "Fill this out. And we'll need a blood sample."

"A blood sample?" I backed up, knocking into Nicholas' chest.

Her lips curled up auspiciously. "Why, yes. You're here to have your blood analyzed, correct?"

I squinted. "Oh. I think there's been a mistake."

"There's no mistake." She pressed a green button on the desk and the door opened to the left. Another pretty girl with white blonde hair snapped a latex glove on her hand, a not-so-nice vampire.

"I'll take your sample," she purred.

My instincts screamed to run and hide, but I scrambled backward instead. "Um . . . I forgot to eat. I can't."

"You can't leave without us procuring a sample," the desk girl said with a shrug.

More vamps appeared, all ready to take my sample. Their growing feeding frenzy became deathly palatable. Someone screamed for Nicholas. Me. He cracked a chair to pieces and broke off the legs just as the blur of vampires jumped us. One fried from grazing my necklace and Nicholas finished off another with a chair leg. I flashed on the laser and waved my hand in a fast arc.

The blonde and the brunette sliced in half, along with a few others, and fell to the floor with a squeal for their lives. Smoke quickly filled the small room. I coughed, no longer able to breathe. A warm hand cupped mine and tugged me towards the closed door. Nicholas butted his shoulder hard against the wood, knocking it down, and I sailed behind him as he demolished the next set of doors. Sunlight poured through the permanently opened doorway and nabbed another poorly placed vamp.

We ran down the street to the car. I pulled in a cleansing breath to purge my lungs of dead vamp remains.

"What was that?" I squealed, daring to look back as Nicholas dragged me forward by the hand.

"I think we found the secret hideout." Nicholas lead me to in the front seat and latched the seatbelt.

As we drove off, I worked hard to catch my breath. "Holy crap. I can't believe I did that."

Nicholas shook his head. "Me neither. Now what?"

"I don't know. You usually know what to do. We need to alert someone. Do something." I chewed on my fingernail. "We can't let them get away."

Nicholas slowed the car down and parked alongside the road. "Should we go back?"

"No. We aren't prepared. We need weapons. Did you bring any?"

He reached over and warmed my shoulder with his hand. "My coat is at the house."

"Should we talk to Phil? Maybe Sam—" I sucked the air between my teeth. "It's not safe. We all need armor. And I don't know if she's cool with me or not."

I mashed my lips together. From what I could feel, after the fight broke out, a lot of vamps were about to come to the rescue. We'd barely escaped alive. Best bet would be to go at sunset and stake them when they tried to leave, from a distance. Then Sam and Phil could join us after dark and finish off any that were hiding inside.

"What's going on in that head of yours? The vein is back."

I smiled and interlaced my hand with his. "Why don't you take me home so I can check in with my dad and then call me so I can conference call with Sam and Phil. We need to come up with a plan because this is way over our heads."

Nicholas hummed in agreement and drove me home.

# Chapter Eighteen

"Julia Katherine Parker!" Dad barked, his famous sleeper wave eyebrows pinning me to where I sat on the edge of my bed, far away from ET ears. "I didn't say go find the venom dealers. You killed eight of their people."

I gaped at Dad. "How do you know already?"

"We've got the whole place under surveillance. Now they're all in a panic and probably ready to leave tonight." Dad paced the floor.

"How the heck was I supposed to know? I just saw the sign and walked in."

He splayed his hand over his forehead and mumbled. "What am I going to do? We have to hurry and get everyone assembled to go in before sundown. We can't risk losing *him* again." He turned and pointed his finger. "You, young lady, will stay home until this is handled."

"What?" I flopped back on my bed.

"It's for your safety." He headed for the door. "I'm telling the rest of the unit. They'll know you can't leave the house, no exceptions. Don't disobey me."

*What am I, like five?*

"Ooooh!" I balled my hands into fists and watched him close the door. It took all my strength to keep from knocking all my books from the shelf onto the floor and screaming bloody murder.

The phone rang from my pocket. Nicholas.

"Hey," I said and slumped back onto the floor with a huff.

"What's wrong?"

All I wanted to do was crawl into the phone and disappear to the other end, far away from everyone and everything. Why didn't we just stay on the beach today?

"Our visit to the clinic ruined everything. Apparently the ETers have been staking out the place for some time. They're packing up right now to ambush the doctor."

"Parker!" I heard called jovially in the background. "Come over!"

Sam giggled shortly after. "I promise to keep my teeth to myself."

It was so refreshing to hear my happy friend again.

"Hmmm," Nicholas said somberly. "So, you're in trouble?"

"You could say that. Grounded 'til I'm dead."

"Dude, let me put it on speaker," Phil interrupted.

Suddenly everything sounded louder.

"I heard you tazered 'em! That's so awesome."

I let out a rush of breath in a chuckle. "Yeah . . . well."

"Fab four!" he called out. "Ain't no other vamp fighting machine."

I laughed. "You guys are definitely more my type."

I could imagine them, all lounging around on the leather couches in Nicholas' place, laughing together like a family.

"I'm stuck here tonight, though," I said in disappointment. "Sorry."

"What? And you're going to let that stop you?" Phil purred.

True. He knew me. Maybe a little too well.

"My dad is on to me. I can't." I lay back and closed my eyes, pretending I was there. "So, you guys have to get in there and handle things."

"I'd like to stake Todd first," Sam said, her voice suddenly sharp. "He's already replaced me with Rochelle."

"Oh." *That was quick.* "Did you run into him again?"

"Yeah, last night. There's a whole group of them from school all hanging out at the docks."

"What are they planning to do?"

"Who knows? Make more? Take over the city?" she said in disgust. "They need to be careful because it's going to become an epidemic and raise attention. Having Todd for a leader clearly isn't the brightest move."

"I say we bust into the doctor's office, stakes blazing. Take no prisoners," Phil said.

Phil was getting a little carried away in his bravado. Then the cardinal rule in vampiring 101 hit me like a ton of bricks. If your maker dies, you and all their kin die too.

"Wait. I just remembered. We can't kill off the doctor, or else . . ." Someone's gasp finished my statement. I heard Sam ask "what" and then shriek. "Crap. My dad and his unit are going to clean house in a few hours. You have to save the doctor, otherwise Sam . . . ." I couldn't bear to voice my biggest fear— her death.

The sudden silence screamed over the line. "You still there?"

"Yeah," Nicholas said. "I think we need to come up with a different plan. I'll keep you in the loop. I also need to call Preston."

"Okay," I said and hung up.

Part of me really wanted to end the call by telling him I loved him, but felt the sentiment was too soon. We'd only made out the one time on the roof in this newly budding relationship. But to consult with Phil? The old Nicholas would never have allowed him to take charge, let alone agreed to work with him on an attack. He liked to work alone. Could they actually be friends in this new paradigm?

I looked around my room, lost and bewildered. Phil's carefree attitude and Nicholas' ignorance was a blueprint for disaster. They wouldn't be able to do this without me. I crept down the hall, trying to catch word of the upcoming operation, hoping to leak back intel.

"Hey," I heard Luke say with a scratchy voice from his room. "What's going on down there?"

"Look who's alive." I swirled around and rested my arm against his doorframe, mindful of his germs. "Meeting of the geeks apparently. They're all going to some conference tonight."

"Yeah, I know that part. Dad made me stay upstairs. Germ-a-phobes."

I arched my eyebrow. They had every right to be leery. Whatever he had was lethal. "Feeling better?"

He coughed and I stepped back. "Yeah."

"Well," I said, making my fingers into a cross, "I'm still not taking my chances."

"Ha-ha. Very funny."

I went back to the hall and hung my body over the railing as far as I could without the occupants below spotting me.

"At least you could get me some food," Luke called out, watching me curiously.

Food. Just the excuse I needed.

I snuck downstairs and walked past two people covered head to toe in black hazmat suits. One touched the other and the fabric glowed a bright red light. I squinted at the brightness.

"Hey!" someone called behind me. "Don't look at that."

He rotated me around and I looked up into a handsome face not much older than my own. "Is that a laser suit?"

"Uh, I can't tell you that." He scowled over my head and the two behind me scurried into the garage. "It's top secret."

I pouted my bottom lip out. This geek was actually rather cute. But if that suit was what I thought it was, I was impressed.

"Cool," I whispered.

"Yeah, well." His cheeks flushed and he let go of my shoulders, exuding attraction. "Don't look at it or you'll go blind."

*He likes me.*

"Sure thing." I winked to toy with him. "I'm Julia."

"I know. Just be careful."

I may be on house arrest, but that didn't mean I couldn't flirt with the guards. They might let me out early for good behavior.

Pizza boxes littered the kitchen counters and I found a few slices for Luke. Dad wasn't anywhere close that I could sense so I lingered longer than normal on my way back to the stairs, hoping someone would say something, to no avail. This would be an excellent time to have Phil's hawk hearing.

Luke found a movie on the TV in his room and I slunk to the floor, eating a piece with mushrooms and olives myself, sitting with half my body in the hall. My phone remained silent in my pocket.

After an hour passed, I lost all patience.

**- Call me.**

I'd already given Nicholas the rules of not texting anything incriminating. The phone finally rang and I bolted to my room.

"So?"

"We have to tip them off," Nicholas said.

I chewed on my lip. "Really?"

"There's no other way. We have to protect the doctor and we don't really know who he is, so we really can't kill anyone. Later we can knock them off one by one."

I groaned. Such an impossible task. Maybe if I sat in an open field with a laser suit on, then all the vamps would come to me like a moth to a flame. Phil, Sam, and Nicholas could take the stragglers out, well, hopefully without hitting me by accident. "Can we capture the doctor somehow?

"And hold him in what?"

I knew where this conversation was headed, somewhere way over our heads. "You knew how to make special weapons and armor before," I said, trying to keep my voice calm. Remembering Harry made my chest ache. "There were special metal cages reinforced with venom at the beach. Phil knows where."

The task suddenly overwhelmed me. Killing the bad guys was one thing, but becoming the vampire judge and jury? We were talking about keeping a prisoner. Who were we to put him in shackles forever so Sam could live and others wouldn't die—noble, yes, but feasible? But if we didn't do something, Cain would be forced to stop the problem without any mercy. So the doctor's capture was really our only option.

"We have to for Sam," I whispered. If I ever saw Todd again, he'd be fried in a nanosecond for doing this to my best friend. "What did Preston say?"

"He believes that the collection of newborns is causing the necklace to weaken. Too much bloodlust in one place."

You could say that again. I touched the talisman, happy that I at least knew it still worked where it counted—stopping a vamp from biting me. "Is he upset you left?"

"Hmmm," Nicholas said. "Slightly, but he understands."

"Did he offer any advice?"

"I didn't tell him anything. None of his business as far as I'm concerned."

"Good idea." Who needed him or Alora involved when we already had enough problems with my own father. Preston typically didn't get involved anyway unless Nicholas' life was in jeopardy. But maybe he'd be concerned once news hit the tabloids and papers. The deaths and disappearances were bound to make national headlines.

"And no Scarlett either?"

"Um," Nicholas said, sounding confused. "I don't think so."

They obviously hadn't had a chance to meet yet which was odd. Would my end-of-the-world cheerleader who vowed to protect me at all costs miss my first battle? Where the heck was she?

"So what's the plan?"

"I'm going now to find Dr. V, and Phil and Sam will meet up with me later. They can swing by and get you once it's dark, since you're grounded. Sam is cool to be around you now."

I chuckled, not only at Phil's obvious influence in nicknames, but the fact Nicholas wanted me to come along, courtesy of Phil. He definitely hadn't gleaned from his journal that I should stay far away from the vamps, especially Phil. "Just be careful."

"I will. I should go. I'll keep in touch."

I hung up and felt the anxiety heighten with the activity downstairs. The geeks were ramping up for the task, like kids waiting to go trick-or-treating or something. Hopefully Nicholas could get to the doctor before they did. If not, he'd be getting the resurrection directions from Alora post-haste so I could bring back Sam and Katie.

I looked under my bed for the blond wig to stage up my bed, when Dad knocked on the door.

"Yeah?" I said, hiding the evidence and grabbing *Promise* as though I'd been reading the entire time.

"I just want you to know that I've talked to your brother and he's been instructed to do whatever it takes to make sure you don't leave the house tonight. If you purposefully defy me, Luke's Blazer will become mine and I won't return it."

"What?" I said and slid off my bed to my feet. "You don't trust me?"

"Frankly, no. I think this is too tempting for you. And your boyfriend should stay clear as well. We don't need his or your help tonight. If you want to invite him over here instead, you can. But it's for your own good. I can't do my job and worry about your safety at the same time. Once we get this coven handled, I'll remove all the restrictions and give you back your keys. You just have to trust me and stay put."

I didn't know what to say. Dad had thought of everything this time, beyond using duct tape to fasten me to a chair. But I didn't like how the bottom line put Sam's life in such jeopardy.

"Fine," I said and flopped down on my bed. "Nicholas managed just fine before your group showed up, so I don't know what you're so worried about."

"Was that before or after his amnesia? Because I think an experienced vampire hunter wouldn't have ever taken his girlfriend into a known vampire lair."

My voice hitched in my throat. Dad was smarter than I gave him credit.

"I'm warning you, Julia. I'll take your car permanently, too. Don't leave the house tonight."

He closed the door, taking all my thunder with him.

# Chapter Nineteen

The geek squad packed up and left, leaving my bewildered brother and me in their wake. Evil thoughts to drug him with sleep aids crossed my mind once or twice. My conscience stopped that in a jiff. I paced the floor like a caged lion, waiting to hear word before combing through the freezer to find some ETer ate the last of my Ben and Jerry's ice cream.

"We have to go to the store," I begged Luke.

"You think I'm going to let you leave the house after Dad said he'd take my keys?" Luke popped his feet up in the La-Z-Boy and clicked on the TV. "There's a box of brownies in the pantry. Make them."

"I don't want brownies." I clenched my jaw and stared at my phone again. What was happening? Why wasn't Nicholas texting me?

The sweet auras of two happy-go-lucky people graced the rooftop—my flying carpet ready for takeoff. I darted upstairs to my bedroom.

Phil peered inside, white teeth gleaming. He propped his hand in the air like a mime, stuck outside of some invisible box.

"The invite wore off again?" he asked.

"Yeah," I shot back sarcastically. "My dad might be behind that."

Both Sam and Phil's eyes grew wide, signaling this was all news to them.

"Nicholas didn't tell you my dad is part of a vampire hunting unit in the government?"

"Uh, no," Phil said, his tone just as sarcastic.

"No way, Jules. This whole time? And you didn't know?"

I looked at Sam and admired her newfound sense of control.

"Not until Slide from the fang gang in L.A. tried to dine on us for dinner and my dad came to the rescue, laser pens flashing and all."

Phil pulled a face. "Parker, you've been holding out on me. And why are you wearing pajamas? Where's that tight, black get-up of yours?" He produced a dingy T-shirt I could only assume had been drenched in venom. "Put this on."

Sam wrinkled up her nose and pulled out a corner of her shirt for me to see. "Stinks a little, but it's supposed to protect me from stakes."

I bit my lip. "What? I don't need that."

"If there's a wayward stake or something, you'll be protected," Phil said with sincerity.

A wave of anxiety burned through me. Though I couldn't go, at least they'd remembered to wear homemade armor. I crawled out onto the ledge and sat on the windowsill in a heap.

"Thanks, but I can't go with you tonight. Luke's been instructed to keep track of me; we'll both be grounded for the rest of our lives if I leave. I bet he comes up here in a few minutes to make sure I'm still home."

At my comment, nosiness began to poke his nappy bed-head into my disappearance.

"Julia!" he yelled. "You better be here, or I'm going to kill you."

"Yeah, I'm here," I yelled back. "Just reading. Go away." I looked at Phil and Sam with a shake of my head. "See what I mean?"

"Come downstairs where I can see you!"

I rolled my eyes and crawled back inside. "I have to pee. Give me a minute!"

"Hmmm," Phil said, "I'd say you've got problems. Don't worry. We've got a plan." He looked sweetly into Sam's eyes and she smiled.

I crinkled up my lips and wondered exactly what that plan involved. My impatience got the better of me. "Stop wasting time and go. Make sure my boyfriend isn't in over his head and make him text me."

Phil shot me his tummy-tickling grin and took Sam's hand. They were gone before I could say goodbye.

"I'm taking a bath, if you'd like to watch," I said over the railing in an effort to disgust him.

Disdain floated up from the ground floor and I smiled.

"Pound your foot against the tub every few minutes or I will."

I huffed and returned to my room. Knowing him, he would. I shut down my feelings radar and ran the water. Maybe a bath would be the ticket to calm my nerves. The bubbles popped around my ears, reminding me of the amazing tub experience in the Penthouse Suite in Beverly Hills.

Though the new Nicholas was more fun, I was beginning to miss the old one. Now, he frequently needed assistance, which took away from the magic we once had. And his naïveté worried me constantly, especially now.

After a few minutes, I drained the water and hopped out. The bath idea was a bust and I wouldn't indulge Luke's worries by banging my foot on the tub. While blowing my hair dry, I thought of all the things that could go wrong, including something bad happening to Dad. My gut kept telling me I needed to be there.

I finally broke down and sent Nicholas a "hi" text. He didn't respond. In a nervous rush, I threw my jammies back on and trudged downstairs, determined to make the brownies after all when I noticed Luke standing at the door.

I released the hold on my radar to sense his overwhelming lust of someone I couldn't see. Someone with deep-seated anger and desire for power. My blood froze in my veins.

"Hello, Julia," Alora said.

"Step back, Luke," I cautioned and ran to the door, getting between the two of them. "You're not invited here." I eyeballed the threshold as she continued to smile, her lips imparting that sweet sticky grin.

"Now, let's not be rude." She glanced at the talisman, her envy tripling. "I'm only here for Nicholas. Is he here?"

"Sure you are," I glowered. "Go home, Alora. You're not welcomed here." I calmly began to close the door, tempted to slam it in her face.

"Wait," she said, her fear escalating all of a sudden. "If you care for him, tell him he has to leave this town immediately."

"And why would I do that?"

"Because Cain is coming and if he finds Nicholas here, he'll kill him."

All my blood instantly felt like it sloshed down to my feet. "Cain? Here? When?"

"Soon," she said and looked again at the talisman.

Ice spread out from the stone and chilled my neck. I tried to catch my breath. Things were going from bad to worse fast. The new Nicholas, naive to dangerous vampire matters, didn't know his lifesaving mantra—kill all survivors. We'd let Todd go. Did Todd turn him in?

"How do you know?"

"Easy." Alora smiled. "The talisman told me."

"The what? How?"

"Look at it." Red bloody tendrils of smoke wove over the stone, covering up the blue. "It's Cain's, you stupid girl, and he's calling for it. You can't mask it from him because you're human and don't have the power."

My throat felt thick, making breathing difficult. Luke grabbed my arm.

"Are you okay?" he asked me, then turned to Alora. "I think you need to go now."

But I couldn't concentrate. His? I was wearing Cain's talisman? Was that what the prophecy was going to be over? Cain coming and reclaiming his jewelry and I'd stake him to keep it? Could he take it from me? I was afraid to ask, gripping the door for strength.

"Was this your doing? Did you tell him? Did you bring him here?"

"Never," she said adamantly. "I can't stand the man."

*"I did,"* Scarlett's ethereal voice echoed in my mind.

I closed my eyes, my legs weakening. *"Of course you did."*

"You brought him here?" Alora screeched, her voice morphing into a cat scream as she shape-shifted out of human form.

"Did you hear that?" Luke let out a gasp. "Holy—"

Scarlett didn't only speak to me apparently. I swiveled around and closed the door as the cat fight erupted. He fought me to reopen it.

"That woman . . . she turned into a cat!"

The screeching outside faded and I hoped Alora was smart enough to keep her ground against Scarlett. Her death would take Nicholas' life. This confirmed even more that we needed to go rescue Dad.

"I know. Listen. We have to save Dad."

Luke's eyes remained wide. "We have to catch her. She's

some crazy freak thing."

"Deadly!" I grabbed Luke's shoulders so he'd look at me. "A vampire and if we don't leave, Dad won't be coming home. Murdered like Mom."

Luke oozed disbelief. "Is this a joke? Am I getting punked?"

"Where are your car keys?"

Luke went to the window and looked out. "'Cause that was the most realistic thing I've ever seen. How'd you do it?"

"I'm serious!" I yelled. "This isn't a joke. It's very real."

Luke laughed.

"We need to leave. Now!" I looked down at my attire. Black flannel pants with pink poodles weren't going to fit the bill. "I'm changing first. If you want to come, you can, but you can't stop me from leaving."

No matter what I said, he laughed. I stamped my foot. A wave of bloodlust stopped my tirade.

"Okay," I said, throwing open the door. "How about this?"

I stepped outside and fanned the air around my neck. Within seconds a ravenous vampire came from nowhere and tried to pin me against the side of the house. Once he hit the talisman, he recoiled, his hands and face burning like always. I whipped out the laser and zig-zagged the guy to dust.

Luke's mouth dropped open. "What the—?"

"Real vampires." I stood with my hands on my hips. Another was close by and too hungry to learn from his predecessor. He got dusted before he could touch me. "Any questions?"

Luke backed into the house. "This isn't funny anymore, Julia."

I walked in after him and shut the door as more bloodlust came on the scene. "I know. I'm not laughing. We have to save Dad."

"Where is he?"

"Those geeks are out using their new toys to stop this

growing coven."

Luke staggered backward. "He's fighting those *things*?"

I raised an eyebrow. "Yes."

He pulled his hand through his greasy hair. "Is he insane?"

"No. It's his job."

"Job?" Luke collapsed on the chair in the foyer. "Are werewolves real, too?"

I chuckled. "Not that I know of." I sat on the step opposite Luke. "Vampires have been around since the beginning of time. They are more like snake people."

"Did she mean Cain from the Bible?"

I nodded. "Yes."

"Wow." He took a moment to digest everything. "And how long have you known?"

"Since Nicholas saved me off the cliff, from a vampire."

He blinked back at me. "How did you not freak out and tell everyone?"

"Would you have believed me?"

He shrank away from the window when two vampires showed up and drooled on the glass. "No, probably not."

I waved my magic wand and exterminated them. "So, where are your keys?"

Luke didn't move, exuding fear. "How come I've never seen them before?"

"I don't know. They only come out at night. The sunlight kills them."

"Why aren't they coming in here?"

I exhaled heavily. "They have to be invited."

"Julia, how are you so calm? I'm seriously freaked."

"I'm not. We have to get Dad."

Sudden happiness sliced through my psyche as the door opened. Boba Fett and the cute guy from earlier were strutting their stuff, hair slicked back from sweat and smiles plastered across their faces.

I got to my feet. "Where's my dad?"

"Back there," Cute Guy said, motioning behind him.

My body collapsed in relief and I ran outside to find his car. A few others drove up and the entourage filed past me, way too happy for my liking, but not Dad. Luke stayed inside, staring out at me with terror in his eyes.

In a panic, I grabbed the arm of the closest geek. "What happened?"

He smiled wide. "We got him."

"We killed a *Royal*," his buddy said next to him.

I worked hard to hide my horror, but felt my heart drop like a stone. Sam, my best friend, was gone now. Why hadn't anyone texted me?

"No," I whispered and took out my phone to text Nicholas.

**- call me NOW!**

This couldn't be happening.

I pivoted in a circle and staggered into the street. "Alora! Scarlett!"

The disaster, leveling me in my spot, urged me to beg my enemies for help. I'd do anything at this point. With no answer, I ran into the house and rifled through the drawers, looking for keys, any keys. One of the geeks left a set to a Toyota on the table, I hovered my hand over the top, tempted to steal them.

"What are you doing?" Luke asked.

I yanked my hand back and pulled him aside. "Something is wrong. Dad's not back. I'm going."

"Going where?"

"Downtown. I know where the sting operation went down."

"Dad said to stay here."

I looked him dead in the eye. "Something is wrong, I know it."

"I'll just call him."

"Then do it." I held out my phone.

Just like I thought, Dad's phone rolled over to voicemail and he didn't respond to our texts.

"See?"

Luke grabbed the nearest geek by the arm. "Where's my dad?"

He furrowed his brow. "He's not back yet? Let me check."

I watched as the ambiance of the room flipped from excitement to confusion. Somehow, Dad didn't make it back with the rest of them.

"What do you mean you don't know where he is?" I barked. "Who's in charge of this operation?"

Boba Fett wiped his brow. "Russell, your dad is."

"Great." I slapped my hands against my thighs. "So who's driving? We need to go find your *illustrious* leader."

# Chapter Twenty

Quiet anxiety filled the car on the ride downtown and rightfully so. Rule number one: you don't bust open a vampire ring and leave your leader behind. Someone's head was going to roll, if not all of them.

Luke, who wouldn't stay home alone and insisted on going, sat behind me, shook up and scared. They'd made him put on a suit and armed him with a laser. I only took the special glasses so my eyes wouldn't fry if I looked at the light.

We parked out front on the eerily quiet street. I stepped from the vehicle and a chill of evil settled heavily over my bones. Smoke still lingered in the air, reminding me of what Nicholas and I did earlier. I gulped and confirmed with Luke he wanted to go through with this. He nodded.

Boba Fett and the cute guy, who I found out was Austin, put on their bulbous helmets and flanked me as we walked inside. *Great, escorted by the bug patrol.* We moved through the double sets of broken doors Nicholas had destroyed earlier, into a back room, and filed down a set of stairs leading underground. The air changed, weaving its icy fingers over my skin as we traversed each step. Flashlights from the crew illuminated the corridors. I reached out to feel Dad's presence inside the oversized tomb and couldn't find him. Dread clenched my stomach.

Creepy laughter echoed from deep within the belly of the structure as bloodlust imprinted it's ugliness on my psyche.

"There are vampires down here," I said to Austin. "You didn't finish."

"Impossible." He made some signal with his fingers and a few of the geeks branched off.

I grabbed Luke's arm with one hand and gripped the laser with the other, finger on the button. I didn't trust the geeks in the slightest to protect him.

*Nicholas, where are you?*

My hysteria made encapsulating the bloodlust impossible, completely masking any other weaker feelings I might have sensed. But the task might have been useless anyway. If he was unconscious, void of feeling, I'd have nothing to detect.

"Where did you see him last?" I demanded.

"Here," Austin said as we stopped at a room that looked like a laboratory with a wall of freezers lined across one side and a metal counter on the other. Foggy air leaked from a busted glass door and billowed over hundreds of broken vials of what I assumed to be venom.

"Together we found Doctor Evi—Volynski here," Austin said, motioning to the pile of dust on the floor. "Everything happened quickly. There wasn't much of a fight."

"When?"

"About two hours ago."

I pursed my lips. Right before the ETers arrived, two of the doctor's newborns had attacked me. How could that be? Were they not the doctor's kin?

"How did you know it was him?"

"Looked like him." He stood with his legs wide and hands on his hips, like a hunter showing off his kill. "And he wore a lab coat with his name on it."

I choked back my tears as I analyzed the remains of the doctor on the floor. Austin hadn't a clue they'd also murdered my best friend at the same time. Somewhere else, Phil was probably going nuts over a matching pile of ashes, scattering in the wind like Katie's had not too long ago. I fought an overwhelming desire to grab his collar and tell him what a moron he was.

"So what happened to my dad?" I asked openly. "Did anyone see where he went?"

I was met with blank stares and questioning faces.

"Well then what are you all standing here for? Find him!"

The group scattered and finally someone found the lights.

"I'm sorry, Julia." Austin touched my arm.

I shrugged him off and bore daggers into his face. "Don't you have a protocol for this? Don't you have a boss somewhere you need to report to? My dad is missing and we need to find him!"

Austin gulped and stared at the floor. "We went in unauthorized. Russ said it would be a quick in and out. We'd get the doctor and worry about the other stuff later. Easy."

*Easy?* I laughed hatefully. "I can't believe this."

My arms fell to my sides. This was nothing more than a revenge mission orchestrated by Dad. Austin, some genius who lacked street smarts to realize the danger, was only his subordinate. And Dad had the audacity to get on *me* for being dangerous.

I put my nose inches from his. "Stop apologizing and call whoever's in charge. I don't care who gets in trouble. We need help to find my dad."

Austin's hands shook as he took out his phone and dialed.

I adjusted my glasses and left the room to give him privacy. Luke, still in shock and utterly confused, stuck to my side as we walked farther down the hall. I planned to search every inch of the place if it took me all night.

The more distance I put between the ETers, and us the easier it was to concentrate, except for Luke's overwhelming fear and agitation. The monotony of the rooms drilled holes into my already aching brain—large metal tables, stainless steel sinks, more refrigerators, and cabinets. My father wasn't in any of them.

"Was that doctor one of them?" Luke asked.

"A vampire? Yeah."

Luke shuddered at the mention of the word "vampire." "Why was Dad after him?"

I took a deep breath. "Long story."

We pushed on, deeper down to stairs leading back up to the ground floor. From the outside, the building above didn't seem as vast.

"Can anyone bust these doors open?" I yelled. My voice was greeted with a return echo followed by unnatural laughter.

"No," the faceless vampire whispered. "You're trapped."

"As if," I called back, knowing the bloodsucker was near. "Come and get me."

I was so ready to fry some vamp butt; I only needed a target.

"Don't do that," Luke whimpered behind me.

"What? Taunt them? I have to, or it's going to stop us from finding Dad."

Suddenly, I was ripped backward into a darkened room, my pen yanked out of my hand. I went to scream when fingers covered my mouth.

"Shhh," a soft, warm breath tickled my ear. My body melted like taffy once I recognized Phil's voice. "Don't scream."

I agreed and he let me go. "Have you been here the whole time? Where's Sam?"

"Here," she said behind me in the dark.

"What?" I swiveled around and ran for her voice. My arms squeezed around her neck upon contact. "You're alive."

"Get your brother in here," Phil said in earnest. "Quick."

Luke hysterically called for me in the hall, followed by a high-pitched wail. I ran out of the room to find him.

"It's okay, Luke."

He jolted around. The smoldering arms of a vampire were attached to his suit. "It's not okay!"

I pulled off the crispy appendages and led him into the room, closing the door behind me. The exit sign illuminated a disturbing green glow over his wide eyes. His breath puffed in and out in quick succession.

"It's okay. Just breathe."

"It's not okay," he yelped. "You left me out there with that *thing*. Where's the lights?"

"Take the pen from him," Phil whispered.

"Who's here?!" Luke stumbled backward and hit his fist against the wall.

The bright florescent lights assaulted the room. Sam and Phil hid next to a set of cabinets. I lunged for Luke's extended arm and knocked the activated pen from his hand just in time.

"Damn, that hurt!" Phil nursed a spot on his leg where the laser nicked him.

Luke fell to the floor to seize the pen. I kicked it away and grabbed his shoulder, igniting a burst of red hot light.

"Argh," I yelled and let go. "They aren't going to hurt you. Calm down!"

He backed up against the wall, trying the door I'd closed behind us. I stopped it with my foot and grabbed his hands. He fought me and canvassed the room, his eyes wide. "Sam? What happened to you?"

She shrugged and smiled, a little too large, flashing her canines.

Luke panicked again and pushed me hard against the wall.

"They aren't going to hurt us. Just take off that suit before you hurt me again, or someone else for that matter."

He shook his head and eyeballed Phil, terror exploding off of him in an invisible fireworks display. "No. They're *them*!"

I moved to block his view of Sam and Phil. "They are not going to hurt you. Please stop freaking out."

His fragile psyche bordered on hysteria. I looked to Phil for help.

"Luke. It's all cool, dude." He held up his hands. "I'm not like them and neither is Sam."

She locked eyes with him and walked up slowly, taking his hand. Peace bounded from her invisibly. Luke's shoulders relaxed.

Phil appeared behind me. "I think I gave her some mindreading juju like what Alora's got."

"What?" I swirled around.

"I had to ensure she wouldn't die, so I . . . you know," he cocked an eyebrow and smiled, waving his hand to highlight the puncture wound on her neck.

"You bit her?"

"Well, yeah."

My mouth perched open. "You sucked her blood?"

"No," Phil said adamantly. "I did not. You would have been proud of me. I just didn't have any other way to inject her directly."

He gave a weak smile as I contemplated what happened. He'd infused her existing venom with his. Ingenious.

"Is that why she didn't die?"

"Die?" he asked. "Why would she die? I'm confused."

"The doctor. They got him. I saw the ashes."

"They did?" Phil's brows creased. "It's not Dr. V. We took him to the storage building at the boardwalk like you asked. Nick's with him."

"I'm so confused." I pressed my hand to my forehead. "Then who did they kill inside?"

Phil shrugged. "Beats me. We got here. Nick had Dr. V, so we transported him via sky D'Elia to the boardwalk like you wanted."

"You captured Dr. V?"

"Well," Phil curled up the corners of his lips. "Sorta. Nick actually did."

I sobered up immediately at the thought of the doctor being locked up in a cage, the same cage I was in not too long ago. "And my dad?"

"What about your dad?"

"You didn't see him?"

"I'm kinda avoiding vampire hunters," Phil snorted, looking to Sam for confirmation. "I don't think there's anyone *human* here, besides those freaks in the suits and you two. There aren't even that many vamps."

Sam let go of Luke, who took a deep cleansing breath and dropped his shoulders. "We only came back to get Todd and once I see him, he's going to get it." Sam slammed her hand into her palm.

"So, do you think he might be here?" I questioned "Did some vamps escape? Could he have been captured by Todd's coven? Where would they take him?"

Phil held his hands up in surrender. "I don't know."

"Why then didn't Nicholas text me or call me and tell me? I've been worried sick."

"Dude doesn't know how to use the phone. I've had to show him every time," Phil said, his smile a little too bright. "His amnesia is deep, let me tell ya."

I shook my head, overwhelmed with decisions and details. A wave of bloodlust hit, warning me more vampires were clued in on our location.

"I guess we should go to the storage facility and decide what to do with the doctor."

Phil shrugged. "It's your call. We don't really need him around anymore."

"True." I shifted my weight. Something about executing Dr. Volynski apart from the heat of battle didn't feel right. I threw my hands up in the air. "Fine then, let's get out of here."

Phil gestured toward Luke. "Not until he takes off that vamp smokin' suit. I don't trust him."

I turned to Luke. "You have to take it off."

"No." He folded his arms across his chest. A red glow emanated from his biceps.

I put my hand on my hip. "Then you're going to have to stay with the ETers. I'm leaving with Phil and Sam to find Dad. And the way we're traveling, you can't wear that coat."

"How are we going to travel?" Luke said, curiosity piqued.

# Chapter Twenty-One

"You didn't say we'd be flying!" Luke screamed, clawing onto Sam like a cat about to be given a bath.

I laughed as Phil and I flew together just a few feet away.

"This is awesome!" I yelled into the night sky. The cold air whipped my hair around my face, bringing back fond memories.

"I've missed this," Phil whispered in my ear.

"Me, too." I squeezed his hand that rested firmly against my stomach. "You've been a little too busy to cart me around these days."

He hummed and my heart warmed at his nostalgia. Even in the midst of chaos, his presence made me feel safe and whole with his body pressed against mine, his arm around me. I'd always cherish him as one of my closest friends.

"Lucky for me Nick lost his memories, huh?" he teased. "Or that reunion might have turned out really ugly"

"Yeah." I smiled as he chuckled.

Out of the corner of my eye, though, I caught him watching Sam. A feeling of admiration and attraction stirred from within him, surprising me.

I tried to shake it off and rested my head against his cheek.

"So after all this, you gonna stick around? Or run off somewhere? There's nothing really keeping you here." A twinge of sadness gripped my heart at the thought of him leaving, but things wouldn't remain like this if Nicholas regained his memories.

"I guess I could travel the world. See stuff. Maybe Sam will want to come along." I stopped the gasp in my throat before it escaped. "What about you and Nick? The fab four could travel together."

His suggestion gripped my stomach. He and Sam? Together? I wasn't so sure I was on board with this.

"Ummm. I do need to finish high school," I spit out.

"You could join the dark side and quit like me," he suggested, his voice brimming with husky sexiness that made saying no difficult.

"No. I could not. That wouldn't go over well especially with my dad and his line of work."

The thought of my dad made my stomach somersault. We shouldn't be talking about the future. We should be focused on finding him before it's too late.

"It's fun, Parker," Phil sing-songed. "You know you want to and I've got plenty of venom to share."

"Let's just find my dad first, deal with Dr. Evil, and—" I gasped, completely forgetting about the real news, about Cain coming to town.

"What? What's wrong?" Phil gripped me tighter.

"I got a visit from Alora tonight. And Scarlett. They had a big cat fight in my front yard. Alora said the necklace was his and he was coming to get it. We have to hide. If he finds Nicholas, or any of us, we're all dead meat."

"Whoa. Slow down. What are you talking about?"

"Cain! He's coming here! We're all in a lot of trouble."

I explained what happened at the house and Phil didn't say much more, but the great deal of protectiveness he exuded spoke volumes. I crawled underneath it to feel secure until we arrived at the boardwalk.

Down below, the Ferris wheel spun empty. The apocalypse was upon us, ready to rip our world apart. Good thing tourists knew and stayed far away. Phil swooped me down just outside the storage structure.

Sam did the same and Luke lay down and kissed the sand. "Firm ground."

"Come on," I said and pulled his hand to help him to his feet. His adrenaline rush fed my desire to get to Nicholas.

As we opened the door, memories of being captured here not too long ago worked a heaping dose of guilt as I stared into the doctor's eyes. He was quite a bit older than I imagined.

Nicholas got to his feet with his cell phone in hand. Frustration that could register on the Richter scale rolled off him in abundant loads. "I don't know how to work this thing."

I ran over to him and hugged his neck, noting he was more roughed up than normal. He kissed me on the forehead and wrapped his arm around my waist.

All of us stood and stared into the cage at the old man, feeble and scared. On the inside he was much more confident than I would have liked, though.

"Please," he begged, his Ukrainian accent very prominent. "Please don't kill me. I will do anything."

*Lies.*

"I think you've done enough. Actually, we should just do everyone a favor and stake you right now," I suggested.

"Please. I am not your enemy. The epidemic wasn't my fault. My partner, he stole my research and began to create an army behind my back. He wanted to take over and rule."

His act, tremendously convincing, softened everyone but me. I read through his perfect lies.

"Nice try." I turned to Luke and held out my hand. "Give me your pen."

"No." The calculating hardness of the doctor's voice gave away the coldness inside him. "That would be disadvantageous, especially to Samantha."

Sam moved closer into Phil's side.

"We've taken care of that. She's no longer *yours,* but thanks for caring." I clicked the pen on and pointed the light just above his cage.

The doctor ducked. "Mixing venom I see. Tricky business, playing with physiology you know so little about."

*Truth.*

I moved the light a little closer to his head, tempted to singe a few of the hairs on top.

"And if you kill me, I can't fix your mistakes if something goes wrong. All the secrets die with me."

I clicked off the pen and raised a brow, trying to remain visibly strong. "What do you mean?"

"Depending on the venom line, it could strengthen or be of a detriment to the subject. How are you feeling, Samantha?"

"How do you know my name?" she asked softly.

"You're my child. Why wouldn't I know you?"

I took a deep breath and looked at Phil. He remained stoic though inside he was as terrified as was Sam. Luke and Nicholas stood motionless, both waiting for me to make a move. Problem was I didn't know what to bargain with anymore.

I pulled my eyes into slits. "Then I guess we have no choice but to hold you hostage."

The doctor smugly settled in on the floor as if he was there by choice. "Well, until my men find me, which they will because you absolutely smell divine." He inhaled in. "I guess we'll be getting to know one another."

*Unlikely.* I gritted my teeth and looked to Nicholas. "I need to talk to you."

He ticked his head towards the door and held out his hand as a guide. Once outside, I grabbed him and hugged hard. "This has been the worst day ever. My dad is missing. Please tell me you saw him."

"He is?" He caressed my shoulders. "I didn't. Sorry. It was quite chaotic. I grabbed the doctor and the others went after a decoy."

The tears seeped out from my weakened exterior and I bit my lip to stop them. I wanted to scream. I wanted to hit something. I wanted my Nicholas back so he could tell me what to do.

"We'll find him," Phil said from behind me. "I'll fly Nick so we're faster. Sam can stay here with you and Luke as a guard. We'll regroup before sunrise and move Dr. V. to the house where Sam and I can watch him. No one's going to come for him during the day."

I looked questioningly into Nicholas' face.

An encouraging smile pressed across his lips. "We'll find your dad. Don't worry."

I reached up and cupped my palm under his chin. He kissed me sweetly and relief washed over me. We finally had a plan. "Just text me and give me updates, please."

Nicholas arched a brow and looked to Phil.

I shook my head. "Okay, have Phil give me updates."

"Sam already knows," Phil said, urgency in his voice. "Be safe and don't let that fool trick you into anything."

I winked at Phil. "You've already schooled me well on how to handle that."

Phil laughed, cleansing my soul.

"You'll need this." Nicholas dropped a tiny key in my hand. It thudded hard against my palm, the weight of it shocking me.

Nicholas smirked. "Must be made with venom, too."

"I'd say." I raised a brow, wondering why on earth the key needed to be infused. But before we could discuss it, Phil had latched one hand on Nicholas' shoulder and they soared up into the dark night. I clutched the talisman for a moment and hoped I'd made a good decision.

When I returned inside alone, the three occupants quietly stared at one another.

"Interesting change of the guard," the doctor said and folded his arms. "Where'd your boyfriends go?"

"I think there are other things you should be concerned with, like your accommodations." I pointed to the large holes between the beams on the ceiling. Morning would come, along with the unforgiving sun. He didn't need to know that I hadn't planned on letting him die, at least not yet.

"So brave running this show all alone. We'll know soon enough if the venom transfusion worked or not." He ogled Sam as she shifted nervously in the shadows.

Luke had found a seat next to some netting, his eyes heavy-lidded. Sleep sounded incredibly appealing to me as well.

"What I don't understand is why you would give out all those vials and weaken your power?" I asked.

"You know quite a lot, my dear, for a *human*. It's fairly easy. If the vampire is unable to sire, then there isn't a power shift, no matter how many I allow to be created. It's as if they are all one being." He looked dreamily into the sky, in awe of his discovery.

"Really?" I creased my brow. "But why so many?"

"Attention." He smiled broadly, revealing his canines. "Sometimes, one must use fire to flush out big game."

*Cain. He's trying to get Cain to come here.* I shook my head and clamped my lips shut. He wanted me to talk, to tell him what I knew. Instead, I leaned up against Luke's shoulder and relaxed, the exhaustion catching up to me.

"You would make an excellent addition to my coven."

I laughed. "Tempting, but I've already had other offers and their powers are much more impressive than your run-of-the-mill variety."

"Oh." He tsked and turned his head, appearing offended. But he still radiated confidence, like he was waiting for the perfect moment to reveal his secrets.

I couldn't care less. We were going to be there a long time and the bars were infused with venom so he couldn't pry them open. I snuggled up next to Luke who'd fallen asleep and closed my eyes. Maybe now he'd be quiet and I could rest. Sam would warn us if we had visitors.

"I thought you'd want to keep the venom in the family," he said softly.

"What?" I sat up and stared into the cage. A shot of adrenaline pumped into my veins.

His eyes cut into me with a hard look, evil brewing deep inside. "Eye for an eye, Julia. My men will do whatever it takes to keep me safe."

My heart dropped like a stone. Did keeping the venom in the family mean they'd change Dad into a vampire just so I'd spare the doctor's life? How could they have known I'd captured the doctor?

I stood before the cage. "Do you have my father?"

He smiled, but remained quiet. I needed him to answer me so I could emphatically know for certain.

"Answer me!" I screamed and shook the bars.

"You will let me go," he said calmly. "Or he will be executed."

I felt something fuzzy try to cloud over my judgment and I backed away from the cage. "You'll be executed if anything happens to him, I promise you that."

I reached in my pocket to find my phone, when Sam groaned in the corner and doubled over. She began to cough up blood.

"Oh my gosh, Sam!" I ran to her and tried to hold her up.

"No." She pushed me away, her bloodlust suddenly heightened. "I need to go outside."

The doctor snickered from his cage. "That would be a good idea, Samantha. Never nice to bite your friends."

"Shut-up!" I yelled. "This isn't helping your predicament."

"Isn't it? Let me go. I know how to save your friend."

*Truth.*

"Then do it!"

"Alas. I don't have my tools. They're at my home, probably the same place your father is right now."

I couldn't tell if he bluffed about whether or not he had my dad, all of his statements true but contradicting. Would it be too dangerous to incinerate him and be done with his snippy remarks? But then Sam might die, her DNA infused with half of his venom. I heard her retch again outside and felt her pain— like her insides were ripping apart. I wasn't sure what was the right thing to do.

"I don't trust you," I finally said.

"Your plan is falling apart."

"NO!" I pulled out my phone to text Nicholas when it sailed out of my hands between the bars right into the doctor's. "What?" The pen followed shortly after.

Something began to vibrate against my hip like a tuning fork. I looked down and plunged my hand into my pocket, curling my fingers over the key. The metal burned to the touch, but I wouldn't let go. Vessels bulged from the doctor's neck as a grunt escaped from his lips. We stood off, his face contorted, his eyes staring directly at the key's hiding place.

"It's mine," I said, my fist growing tired.

He finally gave up and glared at me. The key chilled and quieted in my palm.

"It doesn't matter." He smiled right before he dropped my phone and the pen on the ground and crushed them under his foot. "Now we are even. You don't have your tools and neither do I."

My legs wobbled underneath me and I closed my gaping mouth. My breath came out quick. I had to hide the key somehow. The answer came to me. I bent over and tucked it deep within my shoe so he couldn't take it when I wasn't paying attention.

My exterior crumbled as the broken useless plastic pieces of my phone lay dead on the cement. I had no way to contact the boys now. We were here, somewhat unprotected, and his men could show up at any moment.

And when I thought things couldn't get any worse, the doctor's face lit up in a huge grin and then I felt her. The lust for power and blood.

Alora was headed for the building.

# Chapter Twenty-Two

"Why Myhail, how did you get yourself into this predicament?" Alora asked sweetly, surveying the surroundings.

I took a deep breath and positioned myself in front of Luke to protect him. I should have never left the laser suit at the clinic.

"Alora, darling. Will you please—?" the doctor motioned toward the lock in earnest. "It's iron clad, as you know."

When the doctor stood, his appearance morphed from that of an old decrepit man into a younger man in his 40's, handsome and strong. I blinked hard to make sure my eyes didn't trick me.

"Taking a hostage?" She turned to me and frowned. "You're in way over your head, Julia."

The doctor clucked in surprise. "You know one another?"

"Yes, unfortunately." Alora sighed. "Give me the key, Julia."

I shuddered, trapped. Either of them could hurt Luke whether I cooperated or not. Would they have pity if I didn't put up a fight and gave up the key willingly?

"We can do this the hard way, or the easy way." She combed her fingers forward, palm upward. "Let me get you out of this mess."

Though totally annoyed, for once she wanted to help. There was something for her to gain by keeping us alive. Without much of a choice, I agreed unwillingly.

"It's always the hard way with you," I said, my tone biting.

She smiled in victory. "You, my dear, are of no consequence. There are other things of greater importance about to happen, isn't that right, Myhail?"

"Yes," he said with an extended hiss on the "s." "But I've yet to find a queen to rule with me." His admiration spiked.

"Yes, such a shame." She smiled coyly.

"The invitation is still open, Alora."

Alora winked at the doctor while my jaw dropped. I couldn't believe this flirtatious banter was happening in front of me. They knew each other? And that closely? What about Preston? Bile rose in the back of my throat in dread of the punishment we'd receive after they finished flirting. Would he make an example of Luke? Would he attack me?

"Give me the key." She stepped closer and pinned me with her glare. "Now," she whispered.

With sweaty palms, I removed my shoe and took out what she wanted, praying for a miracle. Within seconds the doctor was freed.

"Thank you." He took Alora's hand and kissed it. "Maybe I should look into switching to combination locks."

"It's a testament to how brilliant you are with your—" she held up the key, "inventions."

They chuckled and then grew silent, obviously exchanging information telepathically. My heart thumped wildly in my chest while I watched, wanting to run for it. He was the weapons dealer after all and knew about the strength of vampire venom. He must not have been able to snatch the key.

I held my breath during their quiet, joyful exchange. Luke

didn't move, frozen in fear alongside me. I could no longer feel Sam's presence. We didn't have a chance.

"It's too bad you didn't take up my offer earlier, Julia," the doctor said with a sickening smile, hope glimmering out through his eyes. "Mankind is about to have a wake-up call. Vampires will no longer hide in the shadows. We'll rightfully take our place and rule over all. You'll serve or you'll die."

"I'll die before I serve you," I said in a rash statement, hoping he'd attack me only to get the zap of his life. Maybe then he'd avoid Luke, thinking he might have the same power.

"So be it." He gave Alora a nod as if to signal something and disappeared out of the room with immortal speed.

I stood in shock at his abrupt exit. He wasn't going to harm us?

Alora faced me, the ice queen once again. She pulled back her gossamer curtain of red hair and gracefully pushed it behind her ear with a smile. "Your brother still lives because of me. Give me the necklace and I'll see you both home safely. Then after we take over, I'll spare your family."

*Checkmate.*

I shifted my weight; my legs felt heavier than usual. "After you take over?"

"Cain is coming to discipline Myhail and stop him from making anymore vampires. Their reunion will be all but pleasant. Myhail has a *surprise* for him, though. Not only will mankind suffer, but the vampire world will have a change in commander-in-chief as well."

"How?" I gulped down the panic rising from my stomach. "If he kills Cain, he'll be committing suicide."

"He's not going to kill him, you imp. It'll be more like a permanent coma."

I clutched at my throat. He had the power to incapacitate

a vampire without bondage? Could that really be possible? We could put the bad vamps to sleep and the madness could stop without me having to hurt anyone.

Alora moved forward, butting in on my daydream. "But if Cain claims his necklace before that happens, things will not turn out so nicely. Nicholas has incurred the worst crimes against our kind, punishable by death."

The talisman chilled on my neck like ice; so cold, I had to move it away from my skin.

Alora arched an eyebrow and eyed the stone with envy. "Already it's not masking your scent or itself for that matter. Once it turns completely white, it will no longer belong to you. Cain will kill you for it and take your beloved Nicholas' life. I can protect him and you if you give it to me."

*Lies.*

Luke stirred behind me, filled with trepidation. "Just give it to her," he whispered.

Sorrow glossed over me. She would spare us, yes, but she'd be indestructible with the talisman on. Her asking me to give it to her yet again revealed her true intentions. And what was to stop her once she tired of Myhail? Reigning as supreme ruler alone, as a day-walker and unable to be staked was more her style.

I could never give up the necklace, regardless the cost. It might be the only thing to save Nicholas' life if he ever faced Cain. He needed it far more than me.

"I can't," I whispered, saddened I couldn't tell him why.

Alora's face hardened. "I see."

Her gaze flickered to Luke, then back at me, her hateful decision made. Within fractions of a second, he was within her grasp, his neck bent to the side unnaturally by her long spindly fingers.

"Give it to me or he dies."

Her words hung in the air, slicing through me like a Samurai sword, slitting my heart with one cold precise movement. I couldn't breathe or think, all I saw was Luke's giant blue pools staring at me, washed over me in terror. An explosion of rage ripped through me as my hands fumbled with the chain and refused to maneuver the delicate clasp. How dare she blackmail me. How dare she even think she'd won. Somehow, someway, I vowed, even with my dying breath, she'd pay for this. Though I'd have rather died, for Luke's life, I succumbed and handed over the talisman.

Joy ricocheted off the walls, assaulting my psyche as she put the jewel on her neck. The stone illuminated a brilliant white, like a diamond.

"But you said . . ." I choked out, surprised at the color.

She laughed heinously. "It's considering me to be as powerful as Cain. This shall be my greatest hour."

She turned and headed for the door in haste.

"Wait," I said. "You promised to get us home safely."

She looked back; the corner of her lip turned up. "It's always darkest before the dawn, Julia. Good luck."

Her words sent chills up my spine as she vanished. I slumped to the floor, lost and beaten. She'd taken the key so we couldn't even lock ourselves safely inside and wait until morning. We were free lunch to any vampire that happened upon us.

Then I remembered Sam.

Luke followed me as I ran outside. Blood tainted the ground next to a long groove that ended abruptly. Only her body wasn't at the end of the indentation.

I looked around at the other footprints that marred the sand, then into the sky. Did the doctor take her? Did she fly away to safety?

"Sam!" I yelled.

Luke stood close behind me, antsy and anxious. I scanned the surrounding trees. We needed to get moving if we wanted to make it home in one piece.

I bit my lip and looked toward the road. The *Gas and Go* was just beyond the row of summer rentals. If we could just get there, I could call Nicholas to come get us. Maybe we'd be lucky. So far there weren't any vamps around.

"We need to run."

# Chapter Twenty-Three

As Luke and I sprinted with all our might to the *Gas and Go,* all the tragedy I'd caused tumbled down upon me, crushing my spirit. First Katie's death, then Dad's and Sam's abduction, and now quite possibly Phil and Nicholas' capture; all of them suffered needlessly because of me. I'd even put Luke in harm's way by allowing him to come along tonight. Everything had become a complete mess because of my decisions, because of my stupidity, and now, when Nicholas needed the talisman the most, I'd lost it to his mother. And though she promised to protect him, I knew from the past when it came down to her needs or his, she picked herself first—even if it meant Nicholas' death.

I moaned at the gravity of it all. If only I'd told everyone the truth from the beginning, then we could have worked together to conquer this. But instead, in my stubbornness and efforts to keep secrets, I'd thrown everyone into harm's way. After Myhail and Alora put Cain in a coma, they'd rule with a relentless army, forcing humanity into slavery for whatever bidding they desired.

Maybe I should consider the prophesy. Maybe I should embrace my fate. Maybe I should beg Scarlett's help and usher

her, Phil and Nicholas into Heaven, after all. Everyone would be better off. Who cares if it would crush me.

If it weren't for the fact we ran for our lives, I would have insisted Scarlett take me to Cain right away.

Luke saw the sign. "We made it!"

I sighed and slowed down. A tear of thankfulness fell softly down my cheek. First thing we'd do once the guys showed up was take Luke home. But we celebrated too soon.

Twenty-five feet from our goal, a wall of vampires, all dressed in black, appeared from nowhere, blocking our path. We stopped short.

"Are they *them*?" Luke whispered, out of breath.

"Yes," I mumbled, throwing up a shield against the overpowering bloodlust they radiated, making me want to puke.

"What do we do?"

"Pray for a miracle."

A droplet of sweat ran down my cheek as I searched for somewhere to escape.

*Nicholas! Phil! Scarlett! Please! Where are you?*

"It's a little late for a walk," one of them heckled, a voice I recognized—Jackson from the football team.

They all laughed as Todd stepped forward, the light catching his luminous face. "Julia?"

My hands clenched into fists at my sides. If only I could land a punch right in his smug vampire face and break his nose.

"Where are your bodyguards?" he asked, blatantly checking out the surroundings.

"They'll be here any second." I tried to keep my voice calm as my chest heaved in huge waves of panic. "So I'd be careful, if I were you."

A collective "ooh" came from the group. Todd shushed them, growing impatient. "Where's Sam?"

I shrugged and noted his new honey wasn't at as his side. "Probably staking Rochelle. Or is she not your girlfriend anymore?"

Laughter echoed from the guys.

"How is that any of your business?" he asked with a scowl.

"How is Sam's whereabouts any of yours?"

He cocked his head to the side. "Because she's my girlfriend."

"Not from what I've heard."

Another "ooh" followed Todd's laugh. He shook his head. "You have a lot of nerve, which is quite impressive since you're about to die."

I smirked. "Maybe you haven't heard what happens to vampires when they mess with me." I hoped somehow my reputation preceded me. "But then again they don't really live to talk about it."

They responded with a hiss.

"What are you doing?" Luke demanded quietly, writhing in fear on the inside, as he stood ridged next to me.

"Stalling," I breathed and continued to pray between insults.

Luke followed my lead as I took a step backward. The temptation to run twitched my muscle fibers, willing me to pick either fight or flight. Neither would get us very far. Todd's patience grew weary with each insult and without a miracle, the football team would happily devour my overly delicious blood in seconds.

"So, if you're done asking questions," I suggested, "we'll be on our way."

I motioned for Luke to cross the street opposite the drooling group of leeches when he was whisked away before my eyes. I reached out and grabbed thin air in a panic. My scream rang through the night as jealousy and confusion billowed out from the advancing group.

"I said to wait," Todd barked and the group slowed, stopping a few feet from me.

"Where's my brother?" I wailed, tempted by a brief wave of insanity to rush him and squeeze his neck. Instead I moved backward, keeping my cool. "I promise you all will die if he's hurt!"

Baffled, Todd scanned the horizon and then at all of his lackeys, wearing a frown. I searched, too, but for feelings of pain and euphoria from the hidden vampire downing his blood. But I sensed nothing.

"My boyfriend is the slayer," I yelled. "He'll hunt each of you down and send you all to Hell if you hurt Luke!"

Not even a blip of fear hit the radar at my threat like it had with the L.A. fang gang. Only bewilderment crossed their pasty faces. Nicholas' reputation must not have had a chance to run through their rumor mill yet—all newly changed.

Todd smiled hugely. "How would he ever know?"

Hate and evil poured out from his dark eyes, practically choking me. The vampire inside had erased anything remotely virtuous inside him, if there was anything there in the first place. Quickly, I picked up a broken branch from the gutter and clutched it in my hand. He could try to take me, but I'd go down fighting.

The faces of people I loved flashed before me, especially Luke's. This was it, the end, and I would never get to make things right. After everything, Scarlett's plans backfired. In her haste to get things moving by soliciting Cain here to Scotts Valley, she'd abandoned me. And now I had no clue where Luke was and Todd's goons were about to slaughter me. I'd follow in the footsteps of all the Seers before me. The urge to pound someone in the face for giving me such a stupid wimpy body pressed into me.

I curled my fingers forward, tempting fate. I'd at least send Todd to Hell for siring Sam and allowing my brother to be taken. "Come on. Give me your worst."

His eyes flashed bright and he was gone.

"Oh, no, you don't," a girl said, and suddenly I was airborne by someone in tremendous pain. I wiggled around and looked up into her saddened face—Sam.

"You're here! You're okay." I clung to her arm and watched the football team run around like confused and angry ants below.

"Get on my back, it's easier," she said, her voice raspy.

I maneuvered myself onto her back as she cruised in a low circle. "Hold on," she called out over the wind. "I've got something I need to do."

"Hey, jackass," she yelled, gaining Todd's attention.

He looked up and fear washed over him as his eyes zeroed in on the stake rushing towards his chest. Heat warmed the air as we flew through the burst of flames from the impact. The guys next to him wailed, accidentally catching on fire. They all scattered.

My mouth fell open. "Holy crap."

"Much better," she said sullenly, her body going slack as she took one last look, then coasted away from the scene toward home. "I can't believe I wanted to marry him."

I expected her to feel more joy, or some sort of exuberance in staking him. Only relief flowed out, which was quickly replaced by exhaustion. Astonishment stunned me as I watched the fiery blaze disappear behind the naked trees and buildings. I'd lived after all and Sam just staked the love of her life—totally without remorse.

"Wait! We have to go back! Luke!"

"It's okay," Sam said. "He's fine. I knew you'd be okay with that necklace, so I got him out first."

The air whooshed in and out of my chest rapidly. What if she was a minute later? What if she was too tired to come back for me? "Thank you," I said breathlessly.

I didn't have the heart to tell her Alora had the necklace now.

"Anytime." Sam's pain accosted me again.

I focused my energy and tried to push healing and hope her way. She relaxed a tiny bit, but slowed as we neared my house.

We landed on the lawn and Luke attacked me with a hug, knocking me off her back. "You're alive."

Tears trickled down my cheeks as I buried myself into his shoulder. Our relief twisted around us, healing our souls. "I thought they got you."

"Sam came and pulled me out of there," he said. "I told her to hurry back and get you, because—" He glanced at my barren neck.

"I know." I continued to hold onto his arm tightly.

"Come on." He pulled me across the lawn toward the house, sudden urgency in his voice.

I reached back to grab Sam's hand, finding her slumped in a ball on the lawn. "No!"

Luke scooped her up into his arms and charged toward the house. I mumbled an invite under my breath as we crossed the threshold so she could be taken inside. Her head lulled around on the crook of his arm. She opened her eyes and searched for me.

"Please tell my mom the truth," she whispered. "Tell her I didn't run away with Todd. That I didn't have a choice—"

"No," I smoothed back her hair from her face as Luke laid her on the couch. "You're going to live."

"It's too late. I'm dying." She lay completely still, staring at the ceiling with glassy eyes, already looking like a corpse.

"Here," I said, offering her my wrist. "Take some of my blood. You need a transfusion."

She pinched her eyes shut and rolled her head away, curling into a ball. "No. Just leave me be."

My hands trembled as I placed them on her body and imagined the conflicting venoms working together symbiotically to heal her, to stop fighting. She only writhed more. I switched back to hope and healing and she relaxed, but her suffering was still increasing.

"We need to get her to the doctor." I looked to Luke for help.

Austin, Dad's main guy from the ET unit, stood in the darkened hall, his face ashen. "You're a sympathizer," he said, his eyes filled with shock. "You told them. You're the one who ruined the mission."

In his hand was his laser, ready to shoot. I flipped around and held out my arms to shield Sam. "Don't you dare!"

"That's how they knew we were coming. They created a decoy and took Russell in revenge. I thought I lost you as well, but someone said they saw you both leaving with the bloodsuckers willingly. I didn't believe it." His cheeks reddened as if he'd been slapped. "Your father's abduction wasn't my fault, but yours."

I stood up and signaled for Luke to keep Sam covered. "Don't pin this on me. You told me you went in unauthorized and you left the scene without him."

"No." Austin walked toward me, hatred in his eyes. "He was with us and we all left together. His car never made it back here, though. That's because they snatched him en route. Because of you."

"Look," I said, my hands shaking. "I know things you don't. Vampires are not all bad. I've been rescued countless times by them. Sam in fact just did that for us."

He laughed nervously and pointed his finger at me. "They'll sweet talk you just enough to break down your defenses. Now it makes sense why you refused a bodysuit. Are you one of them? Part vampire?" He aimed the light at me and crisscrossed the beam over my torso.

"Stop that!" I said, feeling the burn from the light through my clothing.

"Or are you in love with one of them? Are you a donor?" He pulled back the corner of my shirt and examined my neck. "Are you sleeping with one of them?"

"Don't touch me!" I slapped his hand away. "I lost my mother to a vampire so you can save your judgment. But as we stand here and argue, I could lose my father as well. Don't you people have trackers on your bodies? You're dealing with killers!"

He squinted his eyes, radiating distrust.

"You do! Where's my dad?" I wasn't sure if I should mention that he'd most likely be at the doctor's hide-out. "Tell me, Austin. He's my father!"

"We already looked for him. The phone had been tossed in a field. He's not there."

"You only use your phones?" I grabbed his collar. "What field? Where?"

"In the middle of nowhere." He pushed me away. "It's useless. They've won and you helped them."

"I didn't." I staggered backward. "Where are the other ETers?"

He lowered his head and sat down. "Do you see anyone here? They are all gone." He bent over and pressed his palms into his forehead.

I fell to the ground to get at eye level and took his hands away. "I have to go to the spot you found the phone. Please tell me where?"

He smiled, crazy behind his eyes. "Bonny Doons Road."

"And the suits? Where are they?"

"All gone," he said, with a sick and twisted laugh. "It doesn't matter. They know how to disarm them. Did you give them Luke's suit? Traitor?"

My eye twitched. "I'm no traitor."

I let go and stood up. We were wasting precious time. I needed transportation to the field.

"Luke, where's the keys to my car?"

The horror in his eyes hit me like a slap. "You're not going back out there?"

"I have to save Dad."

He shook his head.

"Please, Luke," I begged. "Dad is out there. I need to find him before it's too late. This problem isn't going away. You heard the doctor and his plans. And I have to do whatever I can to save Sam."

He gulped, wavering inside. Sam moaned softly behind him. Luke's eyes flicked to Dad's office door, betraying the secret location. Then the lights dimmed. We all looked up.

"They've already killed the cell network," Austin said sarcastically. "It's just a matter of time before they cut the power, too. If I survive the night, I'm leaving in the morning. Good luck."

I swallowed and left the room to pilfer through Dad's desk. The keys were hidden in the back of a drawer.

I came back just in time to feel Austin's hatred flaring.

"Are you going to leave *it* here?" he asked Luke, not knowing I was behind him.

"Not with you," I said and knocked into his shoulder as I walked past, snatching his laser pen out of his front pocket. "She was infected against her will."

"Aren't they all?"

I made a face and withheld punching him in the nose, appalled at myself for flirting with him earlier.

"We need to put her in my car," I said to Luke. "Can you carry her?"

"No," she whispered. "Just put me out of my misery."

Austin snickered. "I'll do it."

"Shut-up!" I screamed.

I turned to her and touched her skin—cold, icy cold. My soul crumbled at her request. "Please, let me try to help you. I owe you this."

"I'm going with you," Luke said. "You need help."

I inhaled deeply. "No," I said adamantly. I'd put him in enough danger for one night.

Scarlett would have to show up and help me fulfill my Seer duties. If not, I planned to beg Sam's life from the doctor and pledge my allegiance if it saved her and my father's life. And somehow in there, find Phil and Nicholas. At this point, remaining human didn't seem feasible and together as a united vampire front, we could do more good anyway.

"No. I'm going and that's final." Luke stood as his courage abounded. "Give me a pen, too."

# Chapter Twenty-Four

My mind spun, heavy with snippets of the night's events as I drove down the winding road. Eucalyptus trees created a barrier from the fog billowing in from the ocean, softening the surroundings into an ethereal light. Something about maneuvering the car through the clouds didn't feel real, like I'd been dreaming. I beamed out my radar like a beacon searching for Dad. Could I be so lucky as to find him out here? I figured I'd keep driving until I felt him or the vamps since Austin, the douche, wouldn't tell me where exactly they'd found the phone.

Luke's concern and Sam's pain rubbed raw against my nerve endings. I channeled some comfort their way and hoped for a quick rescue somehow or just that this trip wouldn't be in vain. Though getting in and out without a fight would be a miracle, I had to hope. Because as soon as we were done, we'd need to get out of town, far away from Cain, the doctor and all-powerful Alora.

I turned down a gravel road out in the middle of nowhere and stopped. A barren field surrounded us, covered with bushes and weeds poking out of the fine mist. The naked eye would assume the land to be uninhabited, but I knew differently. They were here. Hundreds of them.

My head swayed with the overwhelming lust as the hornets' nest thrummed all around me. The insanity of showing up here unannounced was by far the worst decision ever. I was about to stick my foot right in the nest. But I'd do anything to save Dad and Sam.

"Is this it?" Luke whispered from the backseat.

I gripped the steering wheel for support. "Yeah," *most definitely.*

The moonlight broke through the clouds, tinting the surroundings a peculiar cerulean hue. I killed the engine and shut off the lights.

"How can you be sure?"

I ignored the question and tossed Luke the keys, grabbing my jacket. "Don't open the door. I don't care what you see or what they say. Close your eyes and hum if you have to. You're safe inside here."

"You're not going out there, are you?" Fear and disbelief emanated from him, punching me in the gut.

"I have to."

"No, Julia." His angst rushed over me, a cold errant wave. "Not without me."

"I'm just going to check it out and will be right back." I faked a smile like everything was okay, knowing full well I could be ambushed. "Stay with Sam. Just flash the laser if you see anything or need anything."

I stepped outside before he could argue further and shut the door. The salt hit my nose and cold chilled my bones as I pulled on my coat. Nothing could be heard but the ocean waves in the distance. My legs trembled as I moved forward through the brush, the bloodlust vibrating all around me. They had to be underground, the reason I couldn't see them.

An entrance must be close by. The probability I could find it, let alone enter, not having immortal powers, would be zero to none. But I'd still try.

I closed my eyes and focused hard. As Grandma had instructed me, I began to weed through all the bloodlust, encapsulating their feelings far away from me. Then I felt him. A lone person: frightened, hungry and tired.

*Dad.*

I ran to the spot where the feelings emanated the strongest and put my hands on the ground. He couldn't be that far below if I could sense him. I began to dig into the soft sand, focused on reaching him.

"Dad," I whispered. "I'm coming."

Arms came from nowhere and enveloped me. I squealed and went into hysterics, trying to wiggle free from my assailant. The laser fell from my pocket. "Let me go!"

"Shhh," he said. "Or they'll hear you."

He wrapped his hand around my chin and made me look up at him.

"Phil?"

His lips curved into that charming smile I loved and he loosened his grip. I collapsed into his chest, fat tears pouring down my cheeks. "Where have you been?"

He crinkled up his lip. "Here. Trying to get in."

I blinked in disbelief. "You can't find the entrance?"

"We can't get in. Nicholas went around to the other side by the cliffs to see what he could do. I already told him that without an invite, we're screwed. He still wanted to try."

"You let him go alone?" My mouth fell open.

"Yeah, I'm sure he's fine. I've been watching the entrance and staying downwind so they don't smell me." He pointed to a cave opening hidden on the ridge. "Hey? Who's minding the doc? Sam?"

"He got away." I slumped into the side of the log we hid behind. "Sam had a reaction to the venom transfusion, then Alora showed up and—"

"What do you mean *reaction*?"

"She's dying, Phil."

Panic spread across his beautiful face. "Where is she?"

"She's with Luke." I motioned behind me toward the car.

"I need to get to her."

"No!" I grabbed his hand as he attempted to leave. My body yanked up and hung beneath him as he flew toward the car. "Stop! Only the doctor can save her. He's got an antidote."

Phil's agitation flared as he landed on the trail. "Then we have to get inside. I can't let her die."

"Duck down, will ya? My brother has a laser." I pointed over to the car.

Hiding together behind a rock, I quickly explained everything that happened. There was more than just Sam to consider: that Alora had threatened Luke so I had to give her the talisman. We had to get Dad and clear out fast before Cain showed up.

Phil cussed. "Without an invite, I don't see how I can."

"Can I walk in?"

"Hell no!" His endearing protectiveness skyrocketed as he closed his eyes momentarily and pulled me into his side. "You smell way too delectable first off and it's too dangerous. I don't see how they aren't all out here right now trying to steal a sip as it is."

I scrunched up my face. "I don't get that. How come I'm so much tastier than anyone else?"

"I don't know, but you need to get somewhere safe

downwind so I can con a vamp to get me inside the place."

I was about to begin another round of begging when the love for power assaulted me. I swirled around as Alora morphed into a human, too late to warn Phil. Her cold hands grasped our shoulders at the same time.

"By all means, let me escort you."

"Alora?" Phil choked out, covering his surprise with a smile. "You're here?"

"What happened to *my queen*?"

"Of course, My Queen." He bowed his head. "I thought you were in L.A."

"I was." Her gaze flickered to me. "But certain events brought me back to this God forsaken city."

*Whatever, witch.*

She pierced me with an insufferable glare. The stone glowed from within her cleavage, burning my eyes with its light. An urge to grab it and run for the car coursed through me.

*"You wish,"* she hissed.

I glared back.

"If you can get me inside, that would be cool." Phil inclined his head toward the cave opening.

I glanced over Alora's shoulder at the car, now shrouded in fog. If Luke went ballistic with the laser now, he could kill Phil accidentally and most likely Alora wouldn't be scathed.

"And what about her?" Alora pinned me with a scowl.

Phil pulled a face as if I were of no importance to him. "Leave her out here. She's—" he curled his lip to show his teeth, "distracting."

"Yes. I know what you mean."

"Don't talk as if I'm not here." I shrugged off her grip.

Alora studied Phil, her hand still on his shoulder. "Will you have her?"

"She's—difficult. I've chosen another."

"Oh?" Alora cocked an brow. "Your new fledgling, perhaps? Where is she? You haven't left her alone, have you?"

"No." His eyes fell to the ground. "I didn't have time to ask. Her maker was under attack by a group of slayers. To save her life, I mixed her venom."

Alora gasped and gave me a sideways glance. "That's forbidden and dangerous."

"That would have been nice to know ahead of time," he snapped. A grim expression crossed his face. "The doctor has a cure. I need to get inside to get it, to save her."

"Oh, does he?" She mussed with the front of his hair. "Where's Nicholas?"

Phil shrugged. "Don't know."

"I'll find him," I said and moved backward.

Alora snatched my wrist. "You should come inside. I told Myhail I'd take care of you and we don't want to disappoint him."

*"Nicholas will hate you if you hurt me."*

*"He'll never know, my sweet Julia,"* Alora said.

*"He'll know. He came for me after all."*

She looked beyond me, contemplating something. I hated that the talisman shielded her feelings from me as an expression I couldn't read briefly crossed her face. Could I be the weak link in their faltering relationship?

"I have an idea. She could be an offering." Alora smiled a little too large. "To Cain when he comes."

I pulled against her grip. "I don't think so."

"Good idea," Phil chimed in, his eyes electric. "She's kind of a delicacy."

*What? Good idea? A delicacy?* Phil's act was a little too convincing.

*"If you cooperate, I'll see that you live. Otherwise, you'll follow*

*the footsteps of your father."*

My throat constricted. "What?"

"Come."

She pulled me to the opening of the cave and mumbled an invite.

*"What's happened to my father? Tell me now!"*

*"Shhh."* She pushed me inside. Her smile over my suffering pitched my stomach into a fit.

*"I swear to you, if something's happened to him—"*

*"You'll what? Sic your cat on me? Get Nicholas to kill his own mother, thus himself? I think not. You're mine, Julia."*

*Never.*

As they moved inhumanly fast, dragging me down what felt like a hundred slippery steps, the fire inside me snuffed out. She was right. There wasn't anything I could do without the talisman. And yet for some sick reason, instead of killing me, she spared me—like she enjoyed having me around to torture.

But if she did make me into a vampire, would I revere her as Queen? Was loyalty to your maker part of the vampire transformation? That would explain Phil's weird behavior around her.

I stumbled again in an effort to keep up. Tepid hands gripped my hips to steady me. Phil's. His compassion spoke volumes, but his dread had me worried.

The dank air coated my lungs as the darkness closed in on me, making my skin crawl. If a vampiric makeover wasn't what Alora planned, locking me away for any length of time would push me over the edge. After a few more steps, my nerves snapped and fear took over.

"NO!" I yelled and clawed my way through whatever I could to get out of the tunnel—their limbs, skin, clothing. "I'm not going."

"Hush," Alora said and ran her fingers through my hair. "Just relax."

Something numbed my legs as the claustrophobia evaporated and things grew fuzzy. My eyelids flopped closed as happiness spread across my skin. I stopped fighting and collapsed downward.

"Catch her," Alora said through echoing tunnels.

And someone did.

# Chapter Twenty-Five

The chill of the salty air made me snuggle tighter into Nicholas' arms, but his body wasn't radiating the smoldering warmth like usual. I turned to focus on what he said as the waves crashed in the distance.

"Only the giver of the talisman can take it back. It'll burn anyone else who tries to touch it." He watched the angry surf just beyond us with glassy eyes. "But I'd never take it from you, no matter what my mother wants."

I reached up in thankfulness to caress his face, when my heart dropped. I no longer had the necklace. My hand groped my neck just to be sure. "Alora has it now." The words slipped from my lips, an accidental confession.

Nicholas shuddered behind me. "What? You have to take it back from her. She can't have it."

"But how?"

He groaned before he slumped over. "Hurry," he whispered and grew completely still.

"No!" I screamed and grabbed his hand. He melted through my fingers; his flesh nothing but sand. The infection continued to spread down his extremities, sucking with it all the color until his body solidified into a statue. Wind eroded the fine granules that made up his face and hair. I tried to shield him with my body, afraid to touch him for fear he'd fall apart and I'd never get him back.

"No!" My eyes jolted opened with a start.

Sledgehammers pounded into my temples as I pulled my face up off the cold floor, trying to get my bearings. I blinked, realizing I'd been dreaming and shifted to sit upright. My gaze trailed the bars that stood from floor to ceiling in front of me. I stretched and my foot bumped into something soft. Someone moaned in the corner and pulled whatever I kicked away from me. A leg?

A swath of yellow light from a torch illuminated a grey head of hair. Dad.

"Oh, dear God." I crawled to him and put my hands on his shoulders. Warmth greeted my fingertips. "Dad?"

Two hazel eyes opened under the grime and dirt covering his face. "Julia," he breathed with a scratchy voice. "How'd you get in here?"

"I've come to save you." I gave a weak smile.

"You did?" Hope entered his frightened eyes.

A tear splashed down onto his cheek, leaving a trail of white as it ran down his stubbly skin. I brushed the rest off my face with my sleeve and helped him up by the elbow into a sitting position. He winced and pulled his wrist from me. Multiple bloody crescents lined his skin.

I gasped in horror. "What are they doing to you?"

"Breaking me," he said in despair and quickly covered them up.

"Oh, Dad." I hugged his neck gingerly. His arms wove around me along with his anguish.

"They keep feeding off of me," he said. "I don't know how much more I can take."

"I have help. We're getting out." *I hope.*

He clung to me, disbelieving, and his body trembled. Helplessness reverberated out of his fragile aura. "I'm so sorry, Julia."

"No, Dad. Please don't talk."

"I've put us all in tremendous danger and asked you to do something I knew you couldn't. Now we're both trapped and they'll win. They always win."

Misery made a fast and furious whirlwind around us, sucking the hope out of me. "Don't talk like that. We are getting out."

I tried to channel all that was left of my optimism and push it his way, but his condition emptied my well. Would Phil be able to rescue us? What happened after they knocked me out? How long had I been unconscious?

"All I've ever wanted was to avenge your mother's death and prevent this from happening to anyone else and it backfired. They knew we were coming . . . somehow they knew."

Guilt tugged at my gut to confess and get the truth out in the open. Would he understand this wasn't my intention when I asked Nicholas to save the doctor? That the mission was ruined and more people were hurt or killed because I wanted to save Sam?

"Dad, I have something to tell you."

"It's not Luke, is it?"

"No. He's safe." *I hope.* Fear gripped me. How long had I been out? Was it morning already? Did he know to get Sam inside in time? I pushed my worry away and refocused on Dad. "It's my fault. I had Nicholas warn the doctor."

Horror crossed his weathered eyes. "Why, Julia?"

"Because," I said with a sniffle, the dam behind all my emotions bursting at the seams. "Sam would have died if I let you kill him."

Compassion slowly wafted from Dad as his shoulders slumped. "I see."

"It's like I told you. I have—that necklace. Sam tried to attack me like you said, but the necklace stopped her."

Dad's eyes opened wide then returned to normal, his heart flooded somewhat with relief. "And then what?"

"I took her to see Phil." I cringed, waiting for him to explode in an angry lecture, sleeper wave eyebrows and all.

He remained quiet for a long, torturous minute. Then curiosity leaked out. "How is that possible? He died. They found his teeth. There was a funeral. Was there a cover-up?"

"No. He did die, but he was resurrected."

Dad leaned his head against the wall and stared off into space. "This changes everything."

I touched his hand, pushing a little encouragement his way, reminding him this was good news. "But, because he'd experienced," I struggled to say the word and pointed downward instead, "he's reformed. Righteous even. And he'll be here shortly to get us out."

Dad blinked hard then laughed. "That'll be the day."

"I promise you," I whispered.

"You promise what?" Alora suddenly appeared at the bars, the doctor standing right next to her.

I stared back and clenched my jaw. Unlike Scarlett, Alora needed physical touch in order to read minds. A smile formed on my lips. *Wouldn't you like to know.*

She gave a curt smile.

"I saved her for you, Myhail. She has certain gifts that might be useful, if channeled correctly."

"Hmmm." He squinted, scrutinizing me. "Let's see if she passes the test. Or," he tapped his lip with his finger, "an offering is a good idea. She is so *appetizing.*"

Alora hummed in agreement, her face filled with giddiness. The talisman, though, continued to radiate out from within her cleavage like a strobe light. Could no one see it but me?

"My father is dying," I begged. "I'll do anything you want. Just please let him go."

Dad grunted next to me. "Take me and let her go."

"No, Dad." I took his hand.

Alora laughed and gave me a wink before they both vanished, leaving Dad and me alone.

"I don't want you to become a vamp," Dad said, touching my arm. "Swear to me you'll do everything in your power not to become a vamp."

"Okay." I looked away, ashamed at the lie I'd told.

Though most of my decisions stunk, this one I knew would rescue those I loved and be worth the sacrifice. I no longer believed Alora intended for me to die. And as a vampire, I'd become a powerful asset to her coven. But I could also eradicate the bad vamps in a snap. We could induce comas on those we couldn't kill, including Alora—once we trapped her somehow. Then, Phil, Sam, Nicholas, and I could live in peace and fight crime instead. We'd eliminate the need for the ET unit altogether. Dad could get a nice, safe desk job.

He lulled into my shoulder, overcome with exhaustion.

"Good," he mumbled, reassured.

# Chapter Twenty-Six

"You didn't tell me it was Julia," a female voice said, high pitched and whiney.

A thunderbolt of bloodlust blasted into my psyche. I yanked my eyes open. Beyond the bars stood Phil with Rochelle at his side. In one hand, she held a syringe and the other, the keys.

I moved over and shimmied up against the wall, tapping Dad so he'd wake up. I wasn't sure if the cavalry had arrived, or my worst nightmare—Todd's ex-girlfriend here for revenge.

Phil gave me a knowing smile. "We're here to collect your sample."

"Sample?" I asked.

"Yeah, so don't be difficult," Rochelle snipped as she unlocked the padlock.

I darted my gaze to Phil and tried to read him as I chewed the inside corner of my lip. Other than complete and utter boredom, he didn't exactly exude heroic chivalry. What was his plan? Just in case, I held the stake I'd found in my jacket earlier tight against my palm. If she got too close to me, she'd be dust—literally.

She watched me with her greedy black eyes like a tweaking drug addict.

"Just one taste. Please?" she moaned.

"No," Phil said, with a condescending glare. "They said just the sample. That's it."

She whimpered but latched her hand onto my arm in a flash anyway. I struggled as she plunged the needle into my vein. Silence followed as the ruby-red, hunger-enticing liquid poured into the tiny vial.

My blood. This life-giving liquid fueled the entire fight between man and vamp—such a small thing, yet so dangerous.

After what felt like forever, she extracted the needle. Her eyes glazed over as she rolled the vial between her fingers. I used my shirt sleeve to stop the blood flow and pressed down.

"A band aid would have been nice," I said.

"Shut it," she quipped.

"Thank you." Phil took the precious commodity from her hand.

Rochelle mashed her lips together as she continued to fix her stare at the blood that remained on her fingertips. Unable to control herself, she licked it off quickly.

She moaned again. "Holy . . ."

Her bliss knocked me off guard and before I could react, her snarling teeth snapped inches from my nose. Miraculously, Phil held her back. "Whoa there, partner."

She hissed and scratched at him to release her before her body went slack. Her face grew taut as she clutched her throat. The tiniest hint of pain shot out from her. I took the opportunity of distraction to plunge the stake into her chest.

Childlike fear crossed her eyes as she looked at me. "Why?"

I cringed and remembered Katie. A tear fell just before she sizzled into dust. I wanted to say sorry as the ash showered over my hand, the stake hovering in my hand in the air.

Phil cussed. "Why did you do that?"

I yanked my head up in surprise. "What do you mean? She was going to kill me."

"No she wasn't. I'm here. Geez, Julia. I haven't been able to get the antidote yet."

I dropped my hands to my side and let go of the stake, stung. Yet again, I'd messed up the plan. "I . . . I didn't know."

"I can't leave without it. For Sam."

"I'm sorry." I curled my arms around my knees and wished everything would go away, to return to a happier vampire-free life. "Then go get it now," I said.

"I can't. They'll know. And if we leave now, I'll never get the antidote."

I rocked back and forth, plagued with what to plead him to do, to save Sam or us.

"What's going on here?" Alora asked, her voice arriving before her body. "Oh, my . . . ."

Phil straightened up and handed her the vial. "I'm sorry. I must have missed it when I searched her."

Alora snatched Harry's venom laced stake from the ashes and inspected it.

"So clever." Her lips pulled into a line as her eyes raked over me. "Here," she said, handing Phil another syringe of golden liquid. "This is for Samantha. I'll take care of this mess. Transforming her here won't be a picnic, but she'll have sustenance at least." She motioned toward my father. "I hate sickly donors."

Phil grimaced slightly and studied the antidote in his hand. Victory with a price. My humanity. He formed a ball with his fingers and tucked her gift into his pocket. Sadness crossed over his face.

"Go," Alora said with more urgency. "They already know."

Phil shifted his weight and I wished for a joke—something to lighten the mood. He couldn't just leave us here alone with Alora, not when she'd promised to sire me. The corners of his lips turned up and hope poured out. Then his happiness dawned on me. He'd always wanted me to become a vampire and the day finally came.

But before I could beg for my humanity, Phil disappeared, leaving sadness in his wake.

"No," Dad growled and held out his arm to shield me. "I won't allow this."

"As if, old man. But there's no need to worry—well, not now that is. Julia and I have history and there's no way I'd ever sire her with *my* venom." She leaned forward and the talisman popped out of her shirt, sparking electric light. She touched my shoulder. *"And honestly, you're most useful to me dead."*

*Dead.* The word ricocheted in my head. She did hate me. She'd managed to take the only thing protecting me. And now, within her grasp, my minutes were numbered.

Phil left with high hopes I'd cross over and become like him. But instead, Alora tricked him and he'd discover he indirectly chose Sam over me. And in some respect, I deserved this outcome. I'd denied the responsibility of being a Seer, pushed Scarlett away, and rejected the sound advice Grandma had given. Where else could that logic have gotten me except inside a vampire lair and eventually a casket like the other Seers before me. Stubborn must be one of the prerequisites to be part of the club.

She inclined her head. *"Scarlett believed you're the Seer?"* She laughed caustically in my head. *"Unlikely, and to answer you question, yes, Julia. I really do hate you and you will end up in a casket after Cain is finished with you. And once you're gone for good, I can erase you from my son's mind forever."*

*"Where is Nicholas?"*

*"Wouldn't you like to know."*

She let go and left the cage, clicking the lock shut. I slunk into Dad's side as he put his arm over my shoulder. "Just let my father go."

She cackled and disappeared before I could beg.

❧

As Dad slipped in and out of consciousness, I tried to summon some hope his way through my hands from my empty well. Feverish heat radiated unnaturally from his body, riddling me with unease. Someone had to come and get us out of here soon, or he might not make it. He grabbed my hand and shot open his gray eyes.

"AnneMarie, don't let them take you!" he mumbled.

"Okay, I won't," I whispered back, pushing aside his damp hair.

He inhaled deeply before rolling back his eyes and sinking down. I moved his head onto my lap and stared at him helplessly. He continued to thrash about in his nightmare involving Mom.

"Please," I called out to anyone who might have pity. "We need help!"

My voiced echoed down the breezy cavern, welcomed with silence. Water would be a good start, but he needed a warm bed, food and possibly a blood transfusion. The bloodlust ebbed and flowed, but never came at me very strong. Everyone was far away from our location.

I mopped Dad's brow with my shirt sleeve and sobbed, unable to contain my grief anymore. Where was Nicholas? Was he still alive? I couldn't even be sure how long we'd been down here, other than thirst tore at my throat.

"Julia, are you okay?"

I swallowed hard and wiped my tears to look into Phil's sparkling eyes.

"Phil?" I had to be hallucinating. "I thought you left."

"How could I leave you alone with *her* after everything? Don't you know me better than that?"

I blinked back, disbelieving. "You took a big risk. She said she was going to sire me."

Phil clucked softly. "Yeah, right. I saw that lie a mile away. I overheard her tell Myhail you'd make a better offering than a vampire because you were a virgin." He jingled the keys and popped open the lock. "I had to wait until I knew for sure she'd left."

"What?" I gaped, accosted with the thought Cain would do much more to me than just drink my blood if I were offered to him. "How does she know?"

The shadows highlighted dimples tugging at his cheeks as he walked into the cell. "Not like that kind of virgin. A blood virgin. You've never been bitten before."

He reached out and helped me to my feet. His warm hand felt like a life preserver, pulling me from the stormy sea. "And you didn't have to doubt me. I did have a plan."

I let him hold me for a minute as my heart subsided. He pushed aside my bangs and kissed me gently on the forehead.

"Thank you," I whispered.

"Of course."

With my aid, Phil slung my father carefully over his shoulder and then wrapped his arm around my waist.

"You ready?"

I relaxed into his shoulder and nodded. Together, we glided super-fast through the dark caves toward the exit, just like the old days.

"One good thing," he whispered in my ear, "they've locked you away from the rest because you're too mouthwatering, so it's given us an easy exit."

I wanted to laugh. For once my scent worked in our favor. Instead, I closed my eyes and leaned against his shoulder.

After Phil maneuvered us through two more gates, the stairs came into view. Phil ascended them rapidly as if we were on a floating escalator. The cave entrance came into view and outside a huge moon hung in the sky, casting blue shards of light to greet us. Could only a few hours have passed? Would Luke and Sam be outside, still waiting for us in the car?

"Almost there," he said in victory.

Freedom. I could already feel the hot shower waiting for me at home. My eyes closed and I thanked God for answering my prayers when Phil stopped abruptly.

In a flash, someone separated me from his arms and restrained my hands. I threw open my eyes in the struggle to stare into a familiar face. One I'd seen on the wall in Dad's office: Rachel Delagrecca.

She inclined her head. "Do you know me?"

My voice locked in my aching throat. How did she know I recognized her? I swung my gaze around to find Phil and Dad when I saw him. Cain.

"Going somewhere?" He smiled, flashing striking blue eyes, black slicked hair, a strong jaw line, and flawless skin, all packaged in a six-foot-two frame.

A delicious, masculine scent wafted off of him, pulling out of me conflicting feelings. His picture didn't do him justice at all. My cheeks flushed in betrayal and I cursed internally at myself. How could I be this attracted to the enemy?

"I could say the same about you." Cain perused me up and down. "Of course, only after you've cleaned up a bit. Who's feeding you these lies about me?" he asked, his white teeth catching the moonlight.

I creased my brow before remembering Cain read minds like Scarlett did. Immediately, I went to hide in someone else's aura to stop him and hit a wall. None of them emitted any emotion—or at least what I could read. Not even Phil or my dad. No wonder they snuck up on us undetected.

Off to the side Phil grunted, struggling against the male behemoth that held him. Dad lay draped over the shoulder of another woman with a familiar face.

*"Please let him go,"* I thought, too frightened to speak.

*"And ruin all my fun?"* Cain replied. *"So sorry. He's a fugitive and must pay for his crimes against us. And—is that ash on your hand?"*

I hid my fist in my pocket and turned away. Rochelle and Katie's faces flipped through my mind anyway, revealing my past sins.

*"Hmmm. Runs in the family, I see."*

My fight evaporated with the adrenaline that had hyped me up moments ago. Judgment day for all those who had wronged Cain finally came. How the heck did Scarlett even dream I'd be his nemesis?

*"So you're Scarlett's little Seer."* he chuckled lightly. *"Interesting."*

I gritted my teeth and tried to wiggle out of Rachel's grasp. "I wouldn't do that. You're in quite a lot of trouble and Our Prince can make things much more difficult on you."

She glanced over to my dad and he twitched in pain. I froze instantly. "I'll behave."

Her grip lessened with her smile.

Cain's face grew hard as stone and everyone lunged forward as if he'd ordered them telepathically to move. "It's so disappointing my reputation no longer strikes fear in their hearts. That must be remedied."

The others laughed evilly and I shivered under the hidden implication. As we descended, the moon slipped out of sight, ripping freedom from my grasp.

"You never had a chance," Rachel said quietly to me.

# Chapter Twenty-Seven

*O*nce Cain and his vampires reached the main floor underground and entered a torch-lit hallway, Cain hummed. A crash of metal against the floor drew my attention away. One of the other vamps yanked a small cage containing a black furry shape inside up off the ground. A cat moaned, one that sounded awful close to Scarlett's meow.

*"Scarlett? Is that you?"*

*"Hush, I'm fine."*

A ringing shrill exploded in my head and drowned out her voice. I pressed my hands to my ears. "Stop!"

"What are you doing to her?" Phil asked, then grabbed his head too and groaned.

*"Please. I'll do anything,"* I begged.

"Of course, you will," Cain said. The ear shattering noise abruptly stopped. "No one talks to *her*, or you'll all suffer for it."

I nodded and bit my lip to keep from crying. Phil shot me a pained glance, all the spark I'd seen earlier had evaporated. He knew we weren't ever leaving here alive.

We entered a room half the size of a football field carved out of the stone, supported with steal girders. Shiny white marble covered the entire floor and golden chandeliers dangled from the ceiling, holding hundreds of lit candles.

I gasped at the vast sight and locked onto a fountain that bubbled out with water in the middle of the room—a horrible tease. Maybe an illusion? I licked my parched lips, wishing for just one cup for Dad and me.

Before I could ask, the behemoth whisked Phil away and someone forced my shoulders down so I'd sit. Dad appeared next to me in a rumpled heap on the floor, his shallow breathing barely audible. Further down the wall, they shackled Phil with cuffs. He shrugged and forced a smile.

Myhail appeared from nowhere. I braced for the confrontation, the throwing of fists and massive vamp carnage. Instead, he walked up and greeted Cain with a kiss on each cheek.

"You've come, My Prince. Excellent," he said in his thick Ukrainian accent.

*What?*

I tried to zero in on his feelings to see why, coming up blank. No fear, no worry, no apprehension—nothing. It was as if someone had put me in a bubble and shielded me from everyone.

"We ran into your fugitives on our way in." Cain inclined his hand toward us.

Surprise momentarily dotted the doctor's face, especially when he locked onto Phil's shameless smile. "I see. Thank you."

Alora entered in a black gown with a plunging neckline, setting off her fiery red hair. The bottom shushed along the floor as she sauntered towards Cain's people.

"My Prince," she said and took Cain's hand.

The talisman dangled down, accentuating her assets, and shone brightly for all to see. I expected Cain to snatch it from her chest or at least notice, but he did nothing.

Her gaze fell on me quickly as her lips pursed. She dropped his hand. "Yes, they've been quite difficult to keep."

Shock briefly crossed her face once she saw Phil.

Her head whipped back to Cain. "Are you hungry? I could have a meal prepared."

He smiled at her. "Actually, I am."

"Wonderful. Why don't you, Rachel, and Helena freshen up first? Then you can address the coven from your seats over there." She pointed to a set of thrones on a dais beyond the fountain. "Migdalia will take care of you."

A girl no older than me with platinum white hair materialized before Cain. She bowed and took his hand, kissing it. "Come."

Together, they disappeared into a room off to the side. Other escorts appeared to take the rest away. Alora watched them leave with a gleam in her eye before walking over to me. She leaned forward, hands fastened on her hips.

"You'll come in handy after all."

The talisman dangled in front of me within reaching distance. Something compelled me to snatch if off her neck when her claw-like hands fastened onto my shoulders, paralyzing me. Icy waves flowed from her fingers and probed into my mind. I closed my eyes and pulled away, unable to break the connection. Pictures of my life flashed on the backs of my eyelids as she rifled through me with what felt like a pointed rake.

*"Stop,"* I begged.

*"Shush and quit fighting me,"* she growled. *"There."*

She held up the memory where I'd first met Nicholas. He stood on the porch in all his rugged handsome glory and the green stone peeked out from under his shirt. I swooned, the vision so real I reached out to touch him.

Something pinched at my temple and when I opened my eyes, the vision dissipated like a fading dream. I recalled something having to do with Nicholas, something important, but what?

Revulsion crept across her features as she stayed connected and dug further, to when Nicholas had caught me when I fell off the cliff. My most treasured memory.

*"How sweet."* She began to twist again and I tried to resist. She couldn't take this from me, not Nicholas. Then something stopped her and she gasped. She released her hand like I'd electrically shocked her. Her eyes pulled into angry slits.

I looked up at her, knowing something important happened. Had she'd tampered with my memories? For some reason I couldn't remember.

The slide of her lips pulled into a sick smile and she sauntered over to the doctor's side, sweet and charming once again. She entwined her fingers with his. I wondered what Preston would think of her now, the cheating con artist. Was he going to rule by her side once she tired of Myhail?

Her snap echoed throughout the room, inciting blurs of vampires to buzz about. Tables appeared with linens, tapered candles, and fine china. A row of people assembled in a snaking line. I gasped, recognizing my classmates and, to my horror, Boba Fett and the others from Dad's ET unit. One shot me a helpless glance, then looked away, dejected.

*What's going on?*

*"They're preparing for the feast."*

*"Scarlett?"* I scanned the room and found her cage tucked under a small table.

*"Don't look at me or they'll know we're talking. I'm fine."*

I faced forward, tension wracking my body. *"Where have you been? What happened to you? What are they going to do with them?"*

*"Listen to me carefully. You will be offered as a live sacrifice to Cain. I've solicited your handmaiden to sneak you a stake when you're being prepared. I want you to try not to think about it. I'll*

*shield your thoughts the best I can. When he bites you, you'll have a clean shot. Stake him in the heart."*

My pulse jolted into hyper drive. *"You want me to what!?"*

*"And don't talk to me mentally. If Cain is within eyesight of either of us, he'll hear what your saying to me and kill us both. Do you understand?"*

*"You can't be serious!"* I formed my hands into fists.

*"Yes I am. If you don't, he'll drink you to your death and all of this will have been in vain."*

*"I can't. He'll stop me."*

*"You can do this. I know you don't want to kill us off, but we're all dead anyway. Even though Myhail has given the sleeping serum to Alora to inject into Cain, Cain knows. He's only playing along, participating in the dinner and allowing Myhail to be hospitable. Cain plans to kill every person in this room and leave with Myhail's genetic research and weapons. With the knowledge, he'll be able to make stronger, more impervious vampires that can't be destroyed. You're our only chance."*

I rested my hands on the floor to gain strength. This couldn't be happening. Not now. Not when I didn't know where Nicholas was.

*"Once you've staked him, you'll be free to rescue your family and the other humans here. Your father doesn't have much time."*

My breathing increased as I watched the wrists of the humans being sliced one by one to fill the glasses on the table.

*"But what about Nicholas?"*

*"I haven't caught word or seen him. Sorry."*

I clenched my jaw. He was probably outside, going crazy because he couldn't find me or get inside the lair. Maybe he ran into Luke and Sam. I needed him to come save the day.

"I invite you in, Nicholas," I whispered, unsure if I could even grant that permission.

"I'm here to take you," a soft female voice said.

I startled and blinked up into the pale face of a girl my age with sad, sallow eyes. Dark hair fell over her plain blue dress. She held out her hand to me, revealing rows of scars that lined her forearms. A blood slave.

I nodded and took her hand, allowing her to pull me upwards. She clunked slowly ahead in shoes too big for her feet toward a doorway at the end of the hall, completely ignoring the fact vampires drained humans to our right. I tried to keep the same demeanor, head down and arms to my sides, to minimize attention, but their faces—I couldn't keep from staring.

Each one looked so pale and weak. I assumed they all lived here underground, forced to serve Myhail's coven. At least Alora treated her slaves as gifts and let them enjoy the process, not bled them and treated them like dirt.

Their eyes all screamed for help. For a savior. For someone to free them from this nightmare. Did Scarlett promise the girl freedom if she helped me? How did Scarlett ever manage to convince her? I'm sure, living in this hellhole would make you pretty desperate for freedom. But to sneak me a weapon? I'd believe it when I saw it.

My eyes hit the floor as a tear trickled down my cheek. There was so much at stake beyond killing off the vampires. And once I returned, I'd need to make a decision. And more than likely between Nicholas and me, one of us would die and neither would get to say goodbye.

# Chapter Twenty-Eight

The girl took me into a breezeway and like a wrecking ball, not only did her fear hit me hard, but everyone else's bloodlust and anguish practically knocked me onto the floor. I grabbed the wall for support and pulled my force field in tight, astonished my power returned.

I followed her into a side room and closed the door. Electric light illuminated the oversized bathroom, complete with tub, vanity, and dressing curtain. She motioned for me to sit on the chaise as she began to draw the water and add various scented oils. At first sight of the water, I ran over and shoved my mouth under the tap, sucking down the hot goodness.

"No, don't do that. I've got water and food for you," she pulled at my arm, "over here." She gestured to a table in the corner.

I wiped off my mouth with my dirty sleeve and stumbled forward, engulfing two grapes, a cracker, a hunk of cheese and another gulp of water before sitting down. She removed my grimy shoes and socks, then inspected my chipped toenail polish with a tsk.

"What's your name?" I asked with a mouthful, suddenly

feeling self-conscious and wondering if she'd stay while I soaked in the tub.

She looked toward the door, her anxiety spiking. "Amanda."

"How long have you been here?"

Her eyes widened and she shook her head ever so slightly while removing my polish. I took the cue and stopped talking while I continued to eat, though my stomach felt it would burst.

Dad came to mind. I lifted my glass.

"Could you take this to my dad, please?"

Her shoulders tensed and she didn't respond. Guilt punched my gut for stuffing my face without a single thought for him and I stopped. Maybe I could smuggle some back with me.

She instructed me to take off all my clothes and get into the tub. I turned away from her and removed my pants, shirt and undergarments, uncomfortable about being naked. The heat of the water caressed my tired muscles as I sank down up to my neck, thankful the bubbles hid my body. She washed my hair and handed me a soapy washcloth. I wiped away the grime and thought it weird they'd want me so thoroughly clean when they planned on murdering me right away.

She pulled a white dress and an apron out of the closet and laid it on the chaise next to the vanity. Everything hit me— the delectable food, the hot running water, and electricity. A hotel under the ground. How did they manage all this? I bit my tongue, tempted to ask.

My eyelids shut in a futile attempt to wish everything away, to pretend I was back at the Beverly Hills Hilton and Nicholas was on the other side of the door. No vampires. No war. Amanda interrupted my daydream with a slight cough and held out a fluffy white towel.

She wrapped me up and led me to sit in front of the vanity while she combed out my hair. The silence began to wreak havoc on my sanity. I ached for conversation. For answers. Why couldn't she talk? Who was listening? How long had she been down here and who else was here?

Her eyes told me everything, her loneliness and despair. She needed me. She needed a Seer.

She eventually blew my hair dry and applied makeup before she left the room. I quickly shrugged on the dress and found within the folds of the apron, a stake—small and handmade. I tucked it into my pocket and studied my reflection, faking a smile. Amanda risked her life to give me the stake on the promise from Scarlett that I'd grant freedom to her and the rest of the blood slaves. But could I really do it?

A story Dad once told me as a child came to mind about a rail bridge operator. He'd taken his eight-year-old son to work with him to show him his job. The boy poked around the office and asked dozens of questions—just like all little boys do.

The bridge stood over the great Mississippi River and whenever a ship came, he'd open the bridge to allow the ships to pass. However, on this day after he'd opened up the drawbridge, he realized his son wasn't in the office. To his horror, he saw his son climbing around on the gears of the drawbridge. He hurried outside to rescue his son, when he heard a fast approaching passenger train, the Memphis Express, filled with 400 people. He'd yelled to his son, but the noise of the clearing ship and the oncoming train made it impossible for the boy to hear him. The man realized his horrible dilemma. If he took the time to rescue his son, the train would crash, killing all aboard, but if he closed the bridge, the boy would be crushed in the gears. After making the unfathomable decision, the father pulled the lever and closed the bridge.

Dad said, as the train went by, the man could see the faces of the passengers, some reading, some even waving, all of them oblivious to the sacrifice that had just been made for them.

I'd need to have as much courage as the operator in order to fulfill this horrific task. Sweat pooled under my fingertips as I grasped the stake. With a lift of my chin, I swiveled around and walked to the door. There was no turning back now.

# Chapter Twenty-Nine

Alora materialized next to me and took my arm. Amanda wasn't anywhere in sight.

"Don't you clean up nicely?" She pulled my leaded feet forward. Her happy grin revolted my stomach and I staved off a wave of nausea. Though puking might have stalled this deadly interaction, I eventually had to face Cain and my fate.

I wiped my mind clean of what I'd planned to do and kept my eyes forward. Katie's face came to mind. Originally, all I ever wanted from Alora was the resurrection ritual so I could bring her back.

"You killed Katie?"

I yanked my head up in shock she didn't know. "Accidentally . . ."

Alora shook her head and tsked. "Like Myhail would ever waste his blood to bring her sorry self back."

"You need the maker's blood?"

She sighed. "Yes . . . among other things."

What else? Their dust? Their teeth? "Why did you bring Phil back anyway?"

She chuckled for a moment as if at a private joke. I watched her expression darken. There was another reason. The answer lay on the tip of my tongue. She'd wanted something from me this whole time. Something that only Phil or Nicholas could get me to give. But what?

"Oh, sweetie, you think too much."

"Huh?"

She clamped her grip tighter on my shoulder. "I need to do something before you go inside. I can't have you thinking about the plans we have for him."

The icy tentacles returned, sucking with it our interaction about the sleeping serum at the storage shed. I yelped from the pinch as the thoughts dissolved from my mind.

I pulled away and studied her smug smile. "What were we talking about?"

"How you're going to be a good girl and cooperate. We must hurry. You can't keep Cain waiting." She shoved me forward, into the arched doorway.

A heavy sadness settled over my heart as I remembered her earlier promise. If I failed to stake Cain, she'd wipe Nicholas' mind clean of me. I could become a blood slave forever like Amanda, and Nicholas would never know what we meant to each other.

Upon entering the ballroom, I stepped into the impenetrable, emotionless bubble once again. All the humans had moved away from the table and were lined up against the wall, heads down. Vampires in various period dress stood in rows behind the chairs at the tables—girls in long, beautiful ball gowns and men in white shirts and coats. The royals, dressed in beautiful regalia as well, had all taken their seats on the dais.

Cain looked especially fetching in a black tailcoat and crisp white waistcoat with a matching neck cloth tied in a bow. In front of him stood a girl, grungy and bound in shackles.

"She killed Todd!" a guy yelled out from somewhere at the other end of the room.

The girl shuddered and turned toward me with a pitiful frown. Sam. I tripped forward, tempted to run and fall before Cain, begging for her life.

"Is this true?" he asked and watched her with fascination.

Sam kept her back stiff, her eyes down as more shouts came from the corner.

He tilted his head and waited. "Are you not going to beg for mercy?"

I probed to find out her feelings, blocked again. If she wasn't going to do or say something, I would. But fear glued my lips shut. Where was Phil? Why wasn't he begging for mercy? And surely Alora wouldn't allow Sam to be exterminated for Phil's sake.

Cain shrugged. "Then you'll die."

A small cheer erupted from Todd's friends, but abruptly stopped when Cain plunged a stake into her heart without hesitation. Sam coughed in surprise, and then jolted backward, collapsing into the floor while peering down at the gaping hole left from the weapon. It had pierced right through her venom soaked T-shirt. The glint of metal on the stake's hilt told me he'd procured the same stake I'd used on Rochelle, the one Alora took. She'd given it to him.

"NO!" I screamed, falling on my knees. "Dear God, no!"

Cain snapped his face in my direction, burning with anger.

*"Don't mention His name in my presence, ever!"* he snarled in my mind.

My body jerked involuntarily from a zap of pain, his voice slapping me across my psyche. A whimper slipped from my lips as Sam's body burned and crumbled to the floor. Her shackles slipped through her wrists and hit the ground next to a matching empty pair. My heart dropped as I scanned the room for Phil again, finally finding his spot through the wall of vampires— empty. Where'd he go?

"All right then, what's next?" Cain said brightly, as if he were picking out draperies.

I blinked and watched two vampires drag Nicholas to the front. The air pressed out of my lungs as my world swayed. They'd captured him. Alora's smug smile turned into brief terror. She vanished and reappeared at Cain's side.

"My Prince," she said, bowing before him. "Before you punish this one, aren't you thirsty? We've prepared your host just the way you like."

She swept her hand over toward me. Someone yanked me to my feet. Eyes from all over the room met my tear-streaked face. Many revealed their fangs. I could imagine the bloodlust emanating from the crowd at my delectable scent.

Alora reappeared next to me. "Let's go."

I couldn't move, let alone breathe. Somehow, I arrived at the dais, limp and numb, and I hated him with all my might. My arms fell limp to my sides.

"Here she is, My Prince." Alora curtsied before pushing me forward.

"No!" Nicholas' voice boomed through the hall.

I whipped my head around in time to see he'd shirked off both his handlers in one shake and charged the dais. My heart leapt as I imagined the impossible. Of Nicholas sweeping me off my feet and escaping out of here, of course with my Dad somehow.

Cain laughed and cast out his hand. Nicholas' body flew the opposite direction through the air and landed at the far end of the hall with a loud crash.

"Wait, My Prince," Alora exclaimed, staying his hand. "I'll handle this for you."

She emerged by Nicholas' side after he'd picked himself up and shook himself off, ready to charge again.

"Nicholas." She wiped his brow with her hand. "Stop this madness."

He attempted to push her off, but did a double take. He froze, staring deeply into her eyes. His shoulders relaxed.

"I apologize, My Prince," he stated robotically. "I don't know what came over me."

My mouth fell open as I watched Nicholas' fire melt into a blank expression. Then I saw Luke sitting behind him, bound and gagged, next to Dad's still body. Torment spread through his face, wrenching me with pain and helplessness. I cursed internally. Myhail's vamps must have found them together outside and brought them in. Why did he leave the car?

A woman stumbled past me into the hall and fell prostrate onto a table, knocking over a row of blood filled glasses. She shrieked something intelligible and clutched at her throat. Within seconds, her hair and skin turned to ash and she disintegrated into a puff, falling to the floor in a ball of dust.

"Myhail! What is this?" Cain got to his feet.

Myhail stood from his throne at the right of Cain's, face filled with panic, and rushed to the pile of smoldering ash on the floor. "I don't know. She was working in the lab."

The doctor motioned for some girls in blue dresses to come over. Together they cleaned up the remains of the vampire and procured clean linens.

"Do you not have control of your coven? It's been one thing after another. All I want is to have a peaceful dinner!" Cain yelled.

The occupants of the room cringed and Myhail bowed. "Of

course, My Prince. Let me handle this," he said, before giving Alora a look and leaving the hall in a frenzy.

Alora materialized in front of me and grabbed my hand. She turned it wrist up, placing it before Cain's mouth.

"Please, My Prince. Drink."

The crazed look in his eyes stopped as he inhaled, brushing his lips over my wrist. His breath tickled my skin as he pressed his canines against me, his eyes rich with a wanting gleam. Mesmerized at how he looked at me, I held my breath and waited.

*"What say you, Seer? Any last words?"* he spoke only to me.

My courage melted under the burning heat of his beautiful blue eyes. Though Luke and my father were inches from being enslaved and I would most likely die, the only thing stopping me from pulling out the stake and plunging it into his black heart was Nicholas. I had to trust Alora would save us someway, save her son so I didn't have to do it.

An easy grin pressed into Cain's lips. *"We all knew you'd be nothing more than a myth."*

A myth. His words crushed me. I'd die without a fight. Could I let the train fall into the river to everyone's doom and do nothing? Let Alora win after all she'd done? Only God knew the depths of the carnage they'd inflict if I didn't try to stop them.

I remained stiff, body trembling, hoping he'd bite me and get it over with when Alora appeared silently behind his chair with a hint of victory in her eye. I flicked my gaze to a syringe needle that briefly caught the light.

Cain let go of me, brushing against my stomach, and turned, grabbing her wrist with one hand and plunging something into her breastbone with the other. She dropped the needle as her torso bowed backward. The stake he'd attempted to kill her with shredded into sawdust onto the floor. Alora's eyes widened as Cain held her. Disbelief spread over his beautiful face.

I fumbled in my apron for the stake, my moment to fulfill my Seer duties finally here. But my pockets were empty.

"You! You have it," Cain said with controlled anger to Alora.

Alora threw him an evil smile and disappeared.

"Find her!" Cain bellowed. "And Myhail as well. I do believe this was a stunt for him to try to escape."

Rachel and the others vanished at his command. I stepped backward, preparing to run as the room burst into hysterical whispers.

"Silence!" he called out. "You still have a choice to whom you'll serve. Or I'll end your lives with Myhail's death if you continue to annoy me. We are here to have a party and I won't let a few ruin it for the rest of us. Sit and drink."

No one moved, the silence in the room thick with tension. Fear played visibly on all their faces. The corner of Cain's lip twisted upward.

*"See? I told you I'd strike fear in the hearts of vampires once again."*

He leaned forward. "I said to sit."

In unison, chairs scooted across the floor and the entire coven sat. They waited, glasses in hand, for Cain to take the first drink. Of course, that meant from me.

Cain snatched my wrist and sniffed again.

"You, my dear, are one of the most tantalizing creatures I've ever laid lips on. I must keep you for myself."

I pressed my brows together in confusion, still speechless.

*"You'll only be mine and come with me wherever I go, child. It will be fun."*

Heat spread from where he touched me, relaxing my muscles as I mulled over his invitation, flattered. All the vampires before him only wanted to use me, remake me, steal from me, or murder me, but not Cain. He was the first who saw me as something to be treasured and only wanted to enjoy me. I'd live to see another day.

A strange release flooded my bones. Seer duties could be postponed when I was stronger. And maybe someone could erase my memories, too. I didn't want to care anymore about what happened, or feel any more sadness. Anything to end this horrific day

"*Please. Just release my father and my brother,*" I begged.

"*Of course. Now can we get on with it? I'm starving.*"

# Chapter Thirty

As Cain's teeth sunk deep into my flesh, the room collectively sighed. I bit my lip at the initial sting, but relaxed once the mind-tingling euphoria took over, covering my skin with pinpricks of joy.

The fact I'd failed melted from my being and all I wanted was to stay here connected to him forever. We tumbled in bliss as my legs gave way and I collapsed into his waiting arms.

*"Far too delicious,"* I heard him whisper in my mind as he groaned in pleasure. *"Just a bit more."*

I didn't want him to stop either, but my lips were frozen, probably with an ecstatic grin. Entwined, we sunk onto his throne together in a heap. He kept drinking, gulp after gulp and I didn't care. The thought he'd drain me soon and my heart would stop didn't frighten me. No more pain. No more agony over the loss of Sam and Phil. No more nagging about the prophecy or overcoming Nicholas' amnesia. No worry about the future or if I'd marry. No more anything. Just a sweet white light with wings attached. I wanted to go, into the far beyond. Heaven. And effortlessly, my feet floated towards the starry rift in the sky, suspending in space. I was almost there. I just needed to take one more step.

But the air under my feet began to vibrate and the joy crumbled into pain. Somehow, I came to. Cain stopped, his blue eyes swirling with a nebulous smoke. Then the bubble previously withholding the room's emotions popped, flooding me with his formidable fear.

He coughed, then clutched his throat. Fire erupted under his skin, licking through his veins, singeing his luminous face.

"What did you do?" His voice crackled through parched lips. "What are you?"

I watched as he doubled over onto the floor, his skin shriveling into leather and his black hair streaking with white. Someone grabbed me from behind and a slap across my cheek doubled my vision. Rachel. She cursed and ran to Cain's side before she started wallowing in pain herself.

The goon quickly released my arms. Then the suffering whipped my psyche with a backlash of pain and confusion, doubling with each passing second. Every vampire rapidly aged before my eyes.

The blood slaves watched in astonishment then darted for the exit, gaining courage one by one. Amanda stood in shock, her hand holding a cage to her side. She released the spring and tilted the edge carefully to allow the ball of fur to fall free. Amanda stroked the cat and prodded it to run. Her face saddened as she stood. Then she turned to me. She mouthed a "thank you," and disappeared out of the hall.

The cat slowly lifted her head as her fur began to streak white and then thin.

I stepped forward, conflicted to go to her.

*"I did my best to help you stay focused,"* Scarlett said breathlessly. *"I blocked all the emotion. But once the girl came in from the lab and died, I knew the secret. She drank your blood. It's poisonous."*

*"My what?"* I clutched the spot Cain bit me and scanned the hall for Nicholas. They were all dying because of me.

*"You did it,"* she said before she took what looked like her last breath. *"It is finished now."*

I scanned the sea of writhing vampires to find Nicholas. He lay curled up on his side.

"No." I stumbled toward him and took his hand. "Please . . ."

He looked back with knowing eyes, no longer shrouded in ignorance. He gasped for air. "My memory, it's back. I'm so sorry," he said, reaching for my cheek.

"Shhh . . . don't talk. I'm the one who's sorry." I wished for water to quench his thirst, to stop the burning, and thought of the fountain.

I moved to leave him, but he gripped my arm hard.

"Please, I have to tell you how sorry I am. I treated you horribly on the beach . . . said cruel things. I wasn't in control. I couldn't stop the demon within."

"I know." Tears washed down my face.

"I love you and I've always loved you. And I've failed you. I'm so sorry." He gulped down air into his lungs. "But now you'll never be hunted again."

"No, don't say that. I love you, too. I—"

A rush of something warm pelted my brain and weird pictures suddenly popped into my mind—memories of wearing the talisman and Alora demanding it from me for Luke's life. And then Nicholas' words of how the necklace worked. The last owner of the talisman could take it back.

My gaze found Alora as she entered the hall unaffected, her face revealing her shock as vampires writhed and died all around us.

I stood up.

"Give me the talisman, Alora," I yelled. "I was the last owner and I demand it back."

Horror crossed her eyes and she clutched the necklace. "No."

"It was mine. I am entitled to it." I looked at the stone the same time she did.

Alora wheezed as the brilliant crystalline stone dimmed and faded into a deep onyx. Smoke rose up from her skin and she shrieked, yanking the necklace off. It fell to the floor between us with a heavy thud.

"No!" she cried out. "You can't do this to me."

She fastened her fingers over her throat and fell to the ground, gasping for air. I pursed my lips as I approached her, fighting my guilt in her suffering. She looked up at me with sunken eyes, her sallow skin retreating into her face, accentuating her skull.

"It's too late," I said, taking the talisman off the ground.

She grabbed my arm with spindly fingers, begging I give it back. I pulled away, ripping off a few of her phalanges. They skittered across the floor like dice.

I turned from her and closed my eyes. Remorse couldn't hit me now, especially after all she did—turned my friends, erased Nicholas' mind, and threatened to kill my brother. The stone warmed and radiated a luminous blue again. I ran to Nicholas' side.

He looked straight into my eyes, pained. "How did you do it? Kill everyone?"

"It's my blood. I'm poisonous." I mopped his brow with my sleeve. "Here . . .take this."

I clasped the chain around his neck. It glowed under my fingertips and changed to a luminous green again, just like when we met—the fateful night on my porch after he'd rescued me. It would save him, protect him from my deadly blood.

He sighed, deliverance flooding his face. The energy radiated out from the talisman like a cool glass of ice water. He laid his head in my lap and a peaceful smile tugged at his lips. I wove my fingers behind his neck and bent over to kiss his cheeks, my heart overflowing with thankfulness. His lips puckered momentarily and searched for me. I brushed mine over his, but his body went slack as he drifted off to sleep, exhausted. I tried to focus on his peaceful aura, not listen to the vampires dying around me. We'd survived, though I didn't know how I'd lug him out of this cave by myself.

Alora's screech drew my eyes away. She repeatedly morphed from cat to human, fur falling out of her body and bones protruding from graying skin. My heart pinched at the sight and I searched for Scarlett.

She didn't move, curled in a ball. I opened my feelings monitor to find she wasn't resisting. She'd accepted her fate and wanted to move onto her next life.

I marveled in how right she'd been all along, that I *was* the one to end everything, and do it innocently like she and the fortuneteller predicted. But my worst fear happened. People I loved did die in the process—Sam, Phil, Katie, and even Scarlett—and I didn't know how to bring them back. The only vampire to survive had been Nicholas. My heart tore in sadness, missing Phil and Sam. I hoped, somehow, they'd earned a place in Heaven for choosing to be good and helping me in my battle.

*God, please be merciful to them.*

Someone grunted in the corner. Luke and I locked eyes with one another. He hadn't been freed, tied and gagged still sitting next to Dad. Tears streamed down his cheeks.

My heart clenched as I studied Dad's still and lifeless body on the floor. I reached out internally and felt nothing.

"No!" I called out, my voice echoing over the sound of death.

I attempted to get up when a hiss came from the dais. Cain dragged his boney form against the floor, clawing towards me in slow, jerky movements. Paper wisps of skin clung to his bones in ragged sheets. His blue eyes, the only color, electrified out of hollow sockets.

*"You'll regret this,"* he snarled. *"The talisman was mine, only mine."*

My heart jerked as I looked down at Nicholas' neck, expecting the stone to change. I held my breath, but nothing happened.

Cain kept advancing towards us. I grabbed a broken chair leg and held it firmly in my hand as a warning.

*"Don't come any closer."*

He glanced up at the raised piece of wood and before I could plunge it into him, his bones splintered apart into a million, tiny pieces. I exhaled and tossed the wooden leg away, hugging Nicholas with all my might. With Cain's demise, the source of the vampire power turned off at its inception. And like a line of dominos, one by one the vampires puffed into pillars of dust.

Alora had been wrong. Cain couldn't take back the talisman by sheer will. He'd lost ownership a long time ago, and luckily, it had spared Nicholas' life. But to my horror, Nicholas started to moan. Then the talisman disintegrated before my eyes. I grabbed it as the sandy filaments slipped through my fingers.

Nicholas looked up at me, his green irises clouding over, dissolving to an eerie grey. "What's happening?"

"I . . ." I gulped down my fear and pushed off his hair from his forehead. "Nothing, you're fine."

"It hurts." He tore open his shirt and clutched at his heart. The pink skin on his chest began to fade from white to a shade of grey. My nightmare was playing out for real.

Panic surged inside me and I buried my head into his shoulder. "No," I moaned. "Fight . . . please . . . for us . . . for me. You're part human. You should live."

"Whatever happens—" he said in raspy breaths, "remember I love you." His hand found the nape of my neck and he held onto me, loosely.

I wouldn't accept it. I couldn't let him go. I'd fulfilled my part of the deal. God couldn't take the best part of my life from me.

"Please," I begged. "Don't leave me."

"I don't want to," Nicholas gulped back. He brushed away my tears. "But you'll be free now. They won't hunt you anymore. No one will."

The tears slipped down my cheeks and he pulled my lips to his. His tongue, warm and soft, teleported me to another place, far from the pain. To our cliff where we met. Where fate brought us together finally. "I will never forget you, Julia," he whispered. "I'll always be with you in your heart."

I wrapped my arms around his torso, and sobbed as his body chilled under my touch. Then he slid through, eroding into a pile of dust around me, like a sand castle hit by a wave.

"NO!"

I grabbed at the pieces that were once him and tried to collect them in my fingers.

*I can bring him back with Alora's blood! Of course!*

My eyes, wild and crazed, searched the room for her. And then pain gripped me once again as I remembered. There was nothing left of her either. I pounded my fists into the ground and wailed. This couldn't be happening. This couldn't be the end. But I was there, alone in the icy silence, surrounded by the stench of death. Bile rose up my throat. I puked. Dizziness took over. I crumpled onto the cold, marble floor, wishing for death to take me, too.

The ground beneath me began to tremble. I sat up as stones fell from the ceiling, crashing all around me. Luke let out another muffled cry from the corner. How had I forgotten him? Pushing away my grief before it killed us both, I picked myself up and fluttered to his side to untie his arms and remove his gag. A large boulder broke free from the ceiling and smashed down in front of the exit, blocking us in.

"What's happening?" he asked, terror in his eyes.

I couldn't speak. I still tasted Nicholas on my tongue. He couldn't be dead. This couldn't be real.

I gasped and looked at Luke. But the assault wasn't over. A hum of energy reverberated over our bodies, standing up the hairs on our arms. My limbs became weightless as a strange wind blew from the hole and swirled the dust in a whirlwind up and outside. My hair whipped around my face, sticking to my cheeks. I held tight onto Luke, expecting to be pulled out of the cave as well, maybe pulled to Heaven, maybe to Nicholas. Instead, a sonic pulse, as if from a bomb blast, ricocheted out from the dais and disintegrated everything in its path. Just as the wall billowed and threatened to slam into us, I screamed and everything went dark.

# Chapter Thirty-One

August 25

*Today is Julia's sixteenth birthday. She was having a great time at dinner with her friends until another close call, this time in the public restroom. Of course I couldn't stake the vamp without making a scene, so I yelled "Police" and pulled the bloodsucker outside. Luckily the restaurant is dark because everyone saw me, including Julia. But I worked fast and kept my head down. And actually, it made the evening exciting for her. She's still giggling over it with Sam on the phone right now.*

*But it's becoming a bigger problem than I imagined and I don't know how I can stay out of her life completely. 'Cause the older she gets, the more enticing her scent becomes and the attacks have been happening more frequently to where I can't leave her unguarded after dark for even a minute. Maybe I will put up those beacons like Harry suggested.*

*But it just hit me. That that's all I'm going to be for her—a nameless stalker. I hang out in this stupid redwood tree night after night and watch everything she does. I know her hurts,* fears, secret desires . . . and though I could make her happy, there's nothing I can do about it. Because I could never be him—the guy that wraps her up in his arms and makes her feel safe, the one who loves her unconditionally, the one she spends the rest of her life with. Not with my heritage.

And the idea of her eventually getting married and growing old sickens me. What am I going to do on her wedding day? Am I going to stalk her on her honeymoon of all places? Or what about when she does eventually die? I would have protected her her entire life and she'd never know it, or me. The pain will kill me, like it does daily for not saving her mother. Julia's beautiful smile will be gone forever. Her light she brings to so many, gone. And then what? I protect her children? I protect someone else just to repeat the process?

I'd rather find Cain and slaughter him for all the pain he's caused everyone for his sin. If only I knew where he was exactly. I'd just do it. I'd stake him without any regrets. Then I could die happy knowing Julia will live out her life in freedom. Then I'll be free too.

# Chapter Thirty-Two

"Julia," a familiar woman's voice said. "I'm serious. It's time to get up or you'll be late."

I pried my eyes open and sucked in a deep breath, amazed nothing ached. The peeling glow-in-the-dark star stickers on my bedroom ceiling looked down upon me. Was Heaven supposed to resemble earth?

The woman snatched my dirty laundry off the floor and turned to me with big hazel eyes and soft blonde hair. She looked like my mother, only older, wearing jeans and a pink tee-shirt. I sought to feel her out and came up empty. I blinked again. She couldn't be real. A figment of my imagination.

"Up," she said a little more firmly and tugged on my comforter, touching my skin.

I jerked my foot back. I'd been using my gift long enough to know figments don't touch people. I had to be dreaming.

"Mom?" My voice crackled out of my throat.

Her brow wrinkled as she met my gaze. She sat down on the side of my bed and brushed aside my hair with her hand. I felt tears well up automatically. I'd wanted to dream her into reality so many times I couldn't believe it was finally happening.

"What's wrong?" She put her hand on my cheek, warm and soft.

I sat up and hugged her as hard as I could.

"What's this all about? Are you okay?"

"Yes," I sniffled. "I just . . . miss you."

Mom petted my hair like I'd always imagined she'd do. "I was only gone for the weekend. Did something happen? Did you and Dad have a fight?"

"No," I said and drank her in, her smell, her smile, her beauty. "I had a really bad dream."

She patted my knee. "It was only just a dream. Now get up. I'm tired of getting those tardy warnings from your PE teacher."

As she disappeared from the room, my feet made contact with the carpet. The arrangement of my furniture appeared the same, but the bathroom door was missing. I poked my head into the hall to find I'd been moved into Dad's old room.

*That's weird.*

I turned back around and opened the closet. Three times the amount of clothes burgeoned out of the small enclosure and most of the items were a variety of colors other than black.

I shrugged on a pair of jeans and a cute blue top. If I was dreaming, I wanted to at least look good. I finished getting ready and trudged downstairs towards the noises in the kitchen, wondering why I couldn't sense anyone, and rounded the corner.

I froze midstride. A girl, roughly eight-years-old, hair color like mine in a pigtail, slurped milk from a spoon. The memories flooded me the instant I saw her. Rachel, my little sister.

"What are you looking at?" She stuck out her tongue.

I gaped, then recovered. *Too real to be a dream.*

"Nothing." I took a seat opposite her. She slid over the Shredded Wheat and Cheerios boxes to make a partition between us.

*I had a sister?*

The décor, the draperies, the paint, and even the furniture had changed, all screaming a woman's touch. Family pictures adorned the fridge—summers at the beach, camping at Lake Tahoe, Disneyland. As I soaked them in, each event came back to me. Mysteriously my brain contained memories of a life I hadn't lived.

Was that what Nicholas felt like when he read the journal? *Nicholas.*

My heart lurched, misfiring a beat. I'd watched him die. I'd watched everyone die. Everyone.

"'Morning, pumpkin," Dad said and breezed past me with a brush against my shoulder.

I jumped up as if he were a ghost, knocking my chair to the floor.

"I didn't mean to startle you." He pulled the chair upright.

I gaped at him.

"You okay?" he studied me quizzically.

I wrapped my arms around his torso so fast, and inhaled his fresh, soapy scent like it was my life force. His thicker middle surprised me.

He hummed and hugged back just as hard. "That's not a greeting you get everyday."

The vision of his lifeless body on the ground tensed my arms and I gripped him harder. I never wanted to wake up. I couldn't. He couldn't die. I had to stay here forever.

After he began to twitch in impatience, I let go and allowed him to pour himself a cup of coffee. Mom walked in and sidled up next to him, vying for the pot. Somewhere in the middle of the playful tussle, they kissed. Rachel made an "eww" noise and excused herself from the table.

Admiration flowed through me at the sight of the love they felt for one another, something I'd imagined so many times and never thought I'd experience. But my heart ached to see Luke. My last memory of us clinging to one another right before the blast ripped our bodies apart competed with the day he left for college at San Diego State.

Tears welled in my eyes and I darted toward the hall. This was too real to be a dream. And if I woke up, cold and alone on the marble floor of the vampire lair, I couldn't live after experiencing this. I touched the frame of a family photo of us in a field filled with wildflowers and gasped. It looked just like the one Mom had been buried in.

I shook my head back and forth super fast. Maybe I was in a coma. I couldn't possibly have dreamt the last sixteen years to wake up here. Or was this a glimpse of my life if Mom had never been murdered by a vampire? I continued down the row, each photo revealed a new memory in my head. We'd come to Scotts Valley because of Dad's new job at Alcon, a tech company. Mom, a writer, worked from home. Luke, of course, was at college. *Grandma.* Grandma moved here with her sister. They both were living together in a house by the beach.

I stopped at the next picture and froze in shock at of the sight of Aunt Jo and another man, not John. No. She married Rick, cool, fun Rick. And they had three kids, my cousins: Sophia, Piper, and Travis.

"Holy crap," I said within earshot of my parents.

"Well, excuse us," Dad said and moved past me, headed toward the garage.

Mom came around the corner, too, her hand fastened to her hip.

"You're going to be late." She handed me a homemade lunch. I almost fell over right then and there. "Don't forget your keys."

She placed the set in my hand and shooed me out the door. I squished across the lawn in a daze and turned the corner, expecting the Acura. I stopped in my tracks. The Quantum, alive and well, sat on the side of the road, waiting for me to start her up. I brushed my hand along her hood, as if welcoming an old friend.

Together, we bolted down the street and the gas gauge read full—not broken like before. I laughed, hard and long. And then it hit me; without the nuisance of empathy, today was going to be a cool day.

Before arriving at school, though illegal, I took out my phone and dialed Luke.

"Yeah," he answered, groggy and half-awake.

"Luke, I—" My breath came out too fast, drying out the inside of my mouth. I choked.

"Jules? What's wrong?" He instantly sounded more alert.

"No . . . I'm sorry to wake you. I just wanted to say hi."

Luke paused. Then something on the other end rustled around. "Hi? You woke me up to say hi?"

"Well . . ." My cheeks burned. "How's school going?"

A deep exhale, then another pause followed. "Good."

"And your classes?"

"They're all great."

Luke's voice, rich and clear, though totally annoyed, had no hint of unhappiness or pain. The reality that in this life we weren't as close, tugged at my heart. Mom's death had bonded us together like nothing else and without it, we'd carried on like typical siblings. But all I wanted to do was wrap my arms around him and squeeze tight. If only he could have known what had happened, what we used to share.

"Well, you sound busy, so . . . I'll let you go," I said.

"O-Okay," he said with a yawn. "Call later next time."

"Yeah, sorry. Bye."

I hung up quickly and squeezed into a parking space in the lot and darted inside. Unable to help it, I knocked into people while I moved through the hall. Sam stood by her locker, beautiful, happy, and alive. I ran and ambushed her with the biggest hug, definitely bruising some ribs.

"What's that about?" she asked as she pried me off her body. "Are you okay? You're crying."

I discreetly wiped away a tear. "I had a dream you died."

"You what? Really? " She shivered. "How did I die?"

"I can't even tell you it's so horrib—" I couldn't finish. Katie had turned the corner sporting her sassy black hair and attitude up the wazoo.

The hug fest repeated itself and Katie had to physically remove me from her body.

"What is with you?"

I shrugged. "Super bad dream."

"You need a psych ward."

I encircled my friends' arms and moved onto PE. The halls seemed the same, a few new faces here and there.

Justin turned the corner and I had to restrain myself. Our last interaction in vampire world involved a stake piercing through his heart. But there he stood, alive and well, a little less geeked out than before. He'd been the very first vamp I'd staked, defending myself in the warehouse.

"Hey," I said with a smile.

His eyes grew and he mumbled a "hey" back before he rushed off to his class.

⁙

At lunch we all sat around our regular spot and everything felt right with the world.

"Where's Phil?" I slyly asked Sam, my leg twitching to an unheard beat.

"Who?"

I nudged her in the side. "You know. Sandy blonde hair, blue eyes, amazing basketball player: Phil."

"Is he a transfer?"

"Um, well . . ." *He was supposed to be.*

My heart sank. Were we never going to meet? Did something happen in this alter-universe and the D'Elia's didn't move here after all?

"He sounds pretty cute—" Sam lifted the corner of her lip. "But only if you guys aren't hooking up or something . . ."

"Oh, no. Aren't you and Todd—?"

Sam let out a huff. "Didn't I tell you? I dumped him. He's such a selfish jerk."

"Oh."

I took another bite of the yummy tuna sandwich Mom made to keep from saying anything else totally stupid. The "I love you" Mom had written on my napkin peeked out of my bag. Though any other student at SVH would have been embarrassed, I refolded it neatly and put it in my binder. Who knew how long this alter-existence would last and I planned to treasure every moment of it.

"So, what kind of secret super power would you like, Jules?" Katie asked, interrupting my thoughts.

I sat up straight as the déjà vu punched across my brain. Hadn't we had this conversation before? I blinked at her, when everything clicked. I'd gone back in time, to September, when I didn't know vampires existed—the day I'd met Nicholas.

"Oh my gosh," I whispered, catching my breath.

Maybe he was here, in this time continuum. He had to be. We'd see each other again. I wanted to jump out of my seat and race in my car over to the cliff so I could wait for him right now.

"What's wrong with you today?" Katie watched me

suspiciously while arching her pierced brow. "It's just a question."

"Right. Time travel," I said without flinching.

"Oh," she took a second, then shrugged. "That's cool."

As Cameron, Dina, Morgan, and Sam answered the same answers as before, I couldn't concentrate. I had to get to the cliff right away. Now, in fact.

❦

Unable to ditch school early, I raced home to change before I headed over to the cliff. I figured he wouldn't show up until the evening anyway, since that's when the stalking mishap took place. Did I need to recreate the event? Fall and call out for help?

Once I got home, I felt compelled to double-check Dad's secret room in the garage. When I couldn't find the button inside the drawer, I yanked them all out of the wall and accidentally cut my hand.

"Hey," Dad barked. "What did the drawers ever do to you?"

"Oh." My cheeks flushed as I swiveled around to meet his scowl. I held up my bloodied hand.

He sucked in the air between his teeth. "Let me get you a towel."

"Wait. Where's the—you know." I pointed to the drawer-less cabinet where the floor was supposed to open up to his secret room. "Where you study the—" I made the universal fang sign with my non-injured fingers.

"What are you talking about? Is there a black widow in there?"

I let out a huff. "I know, Dad. Don't hide it from me," I whispered.

"Know about what?" he whispered back.

He wrinkled up his brow pretty convincingly and waited. Without my powers, I couldn't tell if he was lying or not.

"Never mind," I said and stormed out of the garage.

"You forgot to put back the drawers," he called behind me.

My head reeled as I quickly changed and tried not to get blood on my outfit. The more I went through my day, the more I began to believe this wasn't a dream, especially after being injured. And my cut hurt pretty badly. I wanted more than anything for this alter universe to be real, but Nicholas had to be a part of it. Had to.

If somehow we time traveled or jumped time continuums, could I be the only one who remembered? My "thank you" for saving the world and sacrificing everything so people could live free of vampires. If Nicholas wasn't at the cliff right now, waiting for me, I'd spend each day remembering how the love of my life disintegrated through my hands, never to see him again. How would that be fair?

Yes, I was extremely thankful to have my mother back, and my family and friends. But to not be with Nicholas, too? He had to be there. I wouldn't rest until I found him.

I ran out of the house without telling my parents. The Quantum, unused to me driving her like a maniac, took her time to get to the trail entrance, though I floored it. I parked and bolted down the railroad tie stairs. Breathless, I ran with all my might intending to leap into his arms once we saw one another. My feet skidded around the corner, a huge smile on my face, as I neared the cliff. The fallen log sat empty on the trail.

I caught my breath and shook off my disappointment. I took a seat, nervous and twitching for time to pass. Once the chill of evening settled down amongst the redwoods, I chastised myself for not bringing a coat. When the sun completely set, taking with it the light and my security, I tucked my arms around my legs and shivered.

The past played through my mind, yet again. I'd left work and run out of gas, then trudged through the forest around dinnertime. I checked my watch again . . .only eight o'clock. How long would I have to wait? And why didn't I bring my cell phone? After twenty more minutes, I yelped out a little. "Help."

Nothing.

"Help me," I cried out a little louder.

Something moved in the brush, jolting my heart rate. I took off running, unable to stop myself. Once out of the trail and in my car, I panted for air. Thinking he'd show up like before was ludicrous unless . . .

I flipped the key and sped towards Nicholas' house. I knew where he lived. What was I thinking waiting outside in the dark?

Out front stood a for-sale sign.

I bounced my fist against the steering wheel. "No fair!"

My head fell back and the tears dropped down my cheeks. Who was I kidding?

Both parents greeted me at the door when I returned.

"Julia," Mom said in exasperation. "Where have you been? I've been calling you. You missed dinner."

"Sorry." My eyes hit the wood floor. How could I even begin to tell them what I suffered from?

"What's wrong? This morning you cried and Dad said you'd behaved weird in the garage and then you left without telling us where you were going and didn't answer your phone. I was worried. This isn't like you."

"And disassembled my workbench, too," Dad added.

I circled my foot around on the floor, noting the dirt from the trail had stuck to the sides. "I know. I had a crazy dream and it's just haunting me. I'm sorry."

"Where did you go?" Dad asked.

"For a drive."

Mom tilted her head and looked at me softly. "Sweetie, if you are struggling with something, you can tell us. We can help."

"I know. Really, it's nothing to worry about." I forced a smile. "It was just a really horrible dream."

Mom pulled her lips into a line, the worry still evident. "Well, I've saved you a plate."

My stomach lurched, rejecting the idea of food. All I could think about was going back to the cliff and waiting tomorrow. Maybe Nicholas would miraculously show up. I'd wait everyday if I had to.

After dinner, I found my phone on my bed—tons of missed calls from my parents and a few texts from Sam and Katie. Out of curiosity, I flipped through my contacts. Nicholas didn't happen to be one.

On a whim, I texted a < to his number. Maybe he had a phone. Maybe he had the same number. Maybe he didn't know where to find me. Maybe, if he didn't know me, we could accidentally meet in this life somewhere else. Maybe I could go to L.A. to Preston's house and find him.

The phone vibrated with a return text. My pulse zipped through my veins.

**- Who is this?**

My fingers shook as I texted back.

**- It's Julia. Nicholas?**

The seconds ticked by, dragging the wait out way too long. *Please be him . . . please, please, please.*

**- You've got the wrong number.**

My chest caved and I burst into tears again. Nicholas couldn't possibly have existed in this universe. His father, a thousand-year-old, full-blooded vampire, would have needed to hook up with Alora present day in order for Nicholas to be born during my lifetime. Completely impossible.

I quickly looked between the mattress and box spring for the journal. Nothing.

With a soft moan, I curled up and clutched my blankets, hoping tomorrow I'd wake up and forget it all happened. The old me would fade away and I'd forget the love of my life before it tore my heart in two.

# Chapter Thirty-Three

T he next day came. I pried open my puffy eyes to look at the same stars on the ceiling, the same pajamas on my body, the same memories stuck in my head, grieving over the same guy. I curled up and moaned. Though I'd longed my entire life to be with my mother, the knowledge Nicholas might not be in this existence bludgeoned my insides to smithereens.

Rachel hogged the bathroom most of the morning and breakfast didn't sit right in my stomach. All I wanted was to hurry through my day so I could wait again at the cliff. But when I drove away from the house, the wheel didn't head to school. There wasn't anywhere else in the world I'd rather be.

With my hot coffee heating my hands, I padded down the trail, noting the same familiar landmarks. I mindlessly turned the corner, ready to sit on my fallen log when I plowed straight into someone.

"Excuse me," I said, unable to tear my eyes away.

A boy with piercing blue eyes, light brown hair, and a chiseled chin stared back at me, assaulting me with his beauty.

"Julia?" he whispered as if speaking my name would change that fact.

My tongue lulled around in my mouth, impeding my voice. I crinkled up my brow. "Do I know you?"

He stared for a moment before disappointment crossed his face. Then he hung his head and looked away.

"Never mind" he said softly and moved past me, down the trail I'd just walked on.

"Wait," I called out. Something about his gait and the way he held himself was familiar. "I'm serious. Do I know you?"

He turned, pain pressing into his face. "No. I don't think so."

"But you know my name. How?"

With a tuck of his hands in his pockets, he pushed his foot against the dirt. "Lucky guess."

I bit my lip. A lucky guess? No. Something inside insisted I not let him go until he told me. "What's your name?"

His jaw clenched. "Nicholas."

I clutched my heart and studied him harder. Could it be him somehow?

"Nicholas Kendrick?" I swallowed hard.

Light entered his eyes as he walked closer. "Yes."

"Nicholas Kendrick who promised to protect me forever. Who lied and said he killed a mountain lion on this spot. The one I can't live without?"

He closed the gap between us and brought his hands to my face. "That and so much more."

Our lips crashed into one another's, hungry and untamed. I didn't know how it was possible, but with my eyes closed and his hands touching me, I knew beyond a shadow of a doubt I kissed Nicholas, my Nicholas.

"How?" I said between rough gasps, tears streaming down my face.

"I don't know," he said, running his lips along my jaw line. "I woke up at my home in Texas with my mom and dad, and the first chance I had, I bought a plane ticket and flew out here to find you. I figured you had to be here. I just hoped you'd remember me."

I ran my hands through his hair and admired his eyes. He slightly resembled the Nicholas from before. "How? Preston was a vampire. He couldn't have been your father in this life."

"I thought the same thing and looked up my family tree. Preston Alaster Kendrick happens to be one of my great-grandfathers from way back. Alora, my mom, who's actually a very nice person by the way, married William Preston Kendrick III. With everything I know from the past and this consecutive life, I don't know how I could possibly be both Nicholases, or what it all means. I just woke up with his memories and I had to find you."

"So you aren't really Nicholas, but you are?" I reeled back. "This is insane. Why do you live in Texas?"

"But, I am Nicholas and we've always lived in Texas. In my other life, Preston relocated us to L.A. to hide from Alora. That's the only reason we'd left."

"I don't get it."

"I don't get it, either, but I assure you I'm him, though I don't look like him."

I touched his face, tracing his cheeks and lips. He kissed my fingers. "So why do we remember? No one else does. Not Sam, my dad, Katie. What happened?"

"I think since you stopped them, the curse broke and returned us to the timeline without vampires. But in order for us to find each other, we needed our memories, because I look different and I live in Texas."

I gawked. "So, I get everyone I loved back?"

"I guess." He shrugged.

I wrapped my arms around his waist and squeezed. "This

has been so horrible. I waited here for you all evening last night and wracked my brain over it."

"I got here as soon as I could." Nicholas took my hand. "All I know is that I love you and I can't live without you. And if God is going to go through such lengths to bring us together, what we have is Heaven-sent. I don't ever want to be apart again."

I exhaled and snuggled deeper into his chest. "I couldn't agree more."

The rest of the day I didn't worry I'd skipped school as we recalled and compared memories from our two different timelines. I kept catching myself, wanting so badly to read his emotions and had to rely on my powers of intuition and observation instead. But nothing felt more complete than sharing this experience together. I wasn't going crazy after all.

We eventually ended up on the cliff overlooking our beach and stood together, eyeing the sand with jealousy as the seashells below mocked us. He no longer had the power to fly down so we had to watch the waves from afar.

"We'll have to find another way down."

I bit my lip and looked up into his blue eyes. "Want to go to the cave?"

"The sea cave?"

"No." I pierced him with a look of sincerity. "The lair."

Nicholas raised an eyebrow. "Are you sure?"

Something inside me needed to know that chapter was truly over. If we got there and the cave wasn't there or was empty, I could live my life in confidence, knowing without a shadow of a doubt vampires didn't exist.

"I just need to see it, to be sure."

Darkness shrouded Nicholas' face. "If that's what you need, then okay."

The past mingled with the present as we drove down Bonny Doons Road. The memories struck me hard, of Sam slowly dying in the backseat and Luke's fear mingling all around us. I had to remember they were alive and well in this world. But were the vamps really gone? Could they never take my loved ones away from me again? As we pulled off onto the gravel road and parked, I clutched Nicholas' hand tight.

"This is it," I whispered and we looked at one another.

My heart began to rattle my body once I touched the car door handle.

Together we exited the Quantum and moved silently toward the spot where it all ended. The memory of the bloodlust vibrating up from the ground sent a chill over my bones. Deep underneath all the rock and sand, we'd all been buried. Everything felt recent and distant all at the same time, fighting my reasoning.

"How did you get caught anyway?" I asked.

"I found Sam and Luke in the car. When he said you went inside, I freaked. You were in the den of vipers and I couldn't get in to get you out. Before I knew it, we were surrounded. Cain's men were fast and furious."

I glanced over at the ridge Phil and I hid behind, and pointed. "Alora found Phil and me over there and made us go inside. Since the vamps had killed the cell phone network, I couldn't call you."

Phil.

Nicholas' grip tightened on mine. "I know he was your friend and I'm glad he didn't let me bite you, but . . ."

"It's over," I said, smiling up at him. "My guess is he's in L.A. and he won't remember. He'll never come between us again."

Nicholas smiled reassuringly and tucked me under his arm.

As we approached the cave and looked inside, the earth began to shake. I clutched onto Nicholas' arm and screamed, expecting the ground to open up and suck us down inside, starting the nightmare over.

"Whoa, dude," a guy said, blasting out of the cave like a bat out of Hell. "Not a cool time for an earthquake."

He flipped the dirt out of his sandy blonde hair and turned toward us with a grin. I almost fell over.

"Phil!" I wanted to say as my mouth hung open unnaturally.

He cocked an eyebrow and then smiled smugly. "Do we know each other?"

My mouth slammed shut, unsure what to say. I looked to Nicholas for some help.

"I don't think so," I finally said.

"I thought maybe we'd met. You look really familiar." He squinted and glanced casually over at Nicholas. I wished for my empathic powers to read him. "I'm Phil. I'm new in town and starting SVH tomorrow. Do you go there?"

"I—yeah. I do. I'm Julia." I held out my hand. "And this is Nicholas."

I nudged Nicholas in the side, hoping he'd be cordial and let bygones of the parallel universe be bygones, since Phil obviously didn't remember.

"Hey," Nicholas said flatly, but didn't offer his hand.

Phil gave Nicholas a once over with a scrupulous grin and tilted his head. "Hey, man."

I tightened my grip on Nicholas' fingers. "We were out exploring, and I wanted to check out this cave."

Phil shrugged. "Yeah, it's kinda cool. But be careful, it might be a den. I saw paw prints inside—possibly wolf."

"Really? Wolves? Don't you mean mountain lions?" I

chewed on the inside of my cheek, remembering back to Nicholas' initial lie to explain what stalked me in the forest.

"Maybe . . . you can never be too sure," Phil said and moved off the rocks and onto the trail. "Anyway, be careful."

"Sure thing," I called out. "See you at school."

He disappeared out of sight. "Yeah, Parker. See ya."

I froze and swiveled around to Nicholas. "Did you hear that?"

Nicholas' lips pulled into a straight line. "Apparently, we aren't the only ones who retained our memories."

I dropped Nicholas' hand and moved to catch up with Phil. I couldn't let this go. We had so much to talk about.

"Whoa, where are you going?" Nicholas asked, wrapping me up in his arms.

"I have to talk to him."

"No, you don't." A sexy smile tugged at his lips, revealing two adorable dimples. I melted. "We've got other things we need to take care of."

"Like?" I furrowed my brow.

"Like the rest of our lives and the details of the latest incoming transfer at SVH."

"What do you mean?"

He grinned. "Me."

My mouth fell open. "You're transferring to my high school? How?"

"I'll move here, of course." He laughed, his electric blue eyes lighting up his face. "How else am I going to keep you out of trouble?"

I chuckled, squeezing his torso tighter. "That might be a lot easier considering the obvious." I grazed my teeth over his neck and pretended to bite.

He shivered like he enjoyed it and dropped a kiss on my

temple. "We've been given a second chance, and I plan to be worthy of that gift."

I took a deep breath and drank him in, his smell, his warmth.

"I love you, Julia," he breathed in my ear.

I looked up into his baby blues and smiled. "I love you, too, Nicholas." And I will for forever.

Then he kissed me.

# Acknowledgements

I can't believe this day is finally here and the Talisman Trilogy has come to a close. I'm going to miss Julia, Nicholas and especially Phil, who will always have a soft spot in my heart.

First, I thank God for being patient with me and still showing His mighty blessings. Second, to my husband Mike: we've survived yet another book release. Thank you for keeping our house together while I buried myself in this fantasy world. I love you. Third, to Kristie Cook: your encouragement, your assistance, your insight, and pushing me to do my very best. I can keep going on. I'm blessed we are friends and am still dreaming the KM dream for us!

To Lisa Sanchez and Lisa Langdale: both of you are bomb-betas and your magic pulls life from those infamous, confusing dead paragraphs. To Jaime from Two Chicks on Books and Nicole from Books Complete Me: Thank you for hopping up to the plate and begging to give me feedback. To Donna Wright and Lori Moreland: for making me look smarter than I am. To my family: thanks for putting up with me, helping me in my times of need, and cheering me over the finish line. To my friends: for telling me I could do it and being excited with me when I do. To all the aspiring writers out there: if this is your dream, don't ever let anyone tell you you can't. Dream big! Live the life you've imagined!

To you, my fans: this book is really for you. From all the letters, tweets, messages on Facebook, and emails, you didn't give up on my characters and I hope this ending is all that you craved. Maybe . . . if I hear enough rumblings, someone may need a story of their own.

To the book bloggers: thank you for all your promotion and endless excitement of books. You put my work in front of eyes I'd never reach and continue because you love good stories. I'm forever grateful.

To Rachel Clarke: for donating to such a worthy cause and earning your name in the book, twice.

A special shout out to my street team: Lenore Merritt, Leticia Garcia, Karen Stephens, Aeicha Matteson, Jennifer Gonzalez, Jaime from Two Chicks on Books, Jayne Lombardo, Cassay C, Aurora Momcilovich, Laurie, Meghan and Caitlin T from Reader Girls, Martha Schlegel, Joseph McGarry, Jodi Morgan, Audris Jimenez, Jennifer Howell, Heather A. McBride, Zanda Orgil, Bailey, Christine Ko, and Rhonda Helton—my #1 fan.

This year has been one of the hardest and most thrilling years of my life. My son, who's so typical now you wouldn't know he didn't speak at age three, is thriving at school and preparing to graduate from his four-year journey of in-home therapy. This is the entire reason I started writing and will continue. To all the tutors: thank you for investing in my son's life. Thank you for helping our dreams for his success come true.

Because of confusion/greed in the medical industry, the environment, and our poisoned food supply, autism isn't going to go away. My family is a success story, but there are so many who deal with incredible sadness and difficulties everyday because they love someone with autism. To up and coming parents: don't believe the media. Don't believe your doctor. Do your research before you vaccinate and don't let anyone bully you once you've made your decision. Stand firm. Be a warrior. It could save you or your child's life. For more info, go to www.ageofautism.org.

# Follow the Author

Sign up for the author's newsletter to enter contests and find out about future installments at: www.brendapandos.com
Twitter: @BrendaPandos
Facebook: Brenda Pandos – Author
Email: brendapandos@gmail.com
Connect on Goodreads

# Also by Brenda

*Everblue* – Book #1 Mer Tales (Available Now)
*Evergreen* – Book #2 Mer Tales (Coming 2012)

# About the Author

Brenda Pandos lives in California with her husband and two boys. She attempts to balance her busy life filled with writing, being a mother and wife, helping at her church and spending time with friends and family.

Working formerly as an I.T. Administrator, she never believed her imagination would be put to good use. After her son was diagnosed with an autism spectrum disorder, her life completely changed. Writing fantasy became something she could do at home while tending to the new needs of her children, household, and herself.

You can find out more about her daily challenges and discoveries on her blog at brendapandos.blogspot.com.

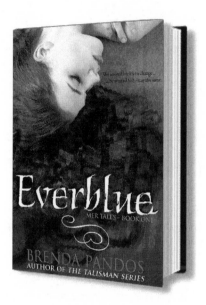

1

## ASH

"So, tell me everything, Ash." Tatiana stretched out on her blanket in rapt attention. Her toes—complete with ruby-red polish—were out of her flip-flops and curled into the sand as if it was summer, though the chill of March lingered in the air and patches of snow dotted the coastline.

"Nothing exciting happened today." I shivered in my jacket, sitting on a nearby boulder with my arms looped around my folded legs to keep warm. "I swear."

"I'll be the judge of that."

Out of the corner of my eye, I watched her bask in a little bit of sunlight and wait in anticipation while the icy water lapped the beach just beyond us. Daily we did this—the drama report from South Tahoe High. Her home-schooled existence left little to no excitement, which meant I couldn't start talking about anything else until I'd dished out every dirty detail from my craptastic day.

"Fine." I rolled my eyes.

After I filled her in on the drama, I studied and secretly envied our differences. Tatchi, with her long, tan legs could have any guy at South Tahoe High School she wanted. Her iridescent blonde hair flowed like cascading water down her shoulders; a perfect match to her azure eyes. I, on the other hand, the Irish redhead that freckled in the sun, walked around school unnoticed by guys. Constantly smelling like sunscreen and chlorine didn't help either.

She lapped up my account like a lonely dog whose master had just come home. She never cared how similar the stories were. To Tatchi, my words were her lifeline to society, to a real life she craved—her live reality show with me as the narrator.

"Oh, wow. What did he do?" Tatchi rolled over onto her stomach and kneaded her hands together, hungry for more.

"Nothing. He acted like nothing happened. The whole thing kinda backfired."

Tatchi laughed and laid her chin on her folded hands. "Serves her right. Then what happened?"

The longing on her face tugged at my heart. I turned away to watch the endless span of sparkling water across the lake—only the snow-covered mountains gave away its end—and shook my head. "Nothing. I came home. Just another totally boring day."

"Not in the slightest," Tatchi giggled. "I can't wait 'til this is our life."

I smiled, knowing we'd be breaking out of this tourist trap

soon enough and she'd be free. Then she'd finally see that living the drama was vastly different than hearing about it—especially when the heartache happened personally.

We sat in silence for a moment as the past drifted in like the tide in my mind. Tatchi would love nothing more than to finish her senior year in public school, but her parents were super strict—similar to mine. Only, their concern didn't lay with what kind of education she'd get at STHS or the influence from her peers. No, they hid a big secret. One I'd discovered a long time ago and was the reason I avoided her house.

"Do you have swim practice tonight?" Tatchi asked, interrupting my thoughts.

"No." I jumped back into reality. "There's some banquet for the teachers so it was cancelled."

"Nice to have a break, huh?"

"Meh. I like practice and it's not like you can do anything anyway. You've got a curfew—"

"Not for much longer. How many days again?" Tatchi sat up and copied my pose by curling her arms around her legs too.

"Like I have to tell you." I scrambled over and pulled the tattered brochure from my book bag. Every word on that thing had been read at least a hundred times.

Last summer, I'd gotten the hair-brained idea to get a post-office box so Tatchi could apply to colleges in secret. She wasn't thrilled about the idea, afraid how her family would react, but after we sent out applications and were accepted to Florida Atlantic University, we both became excited about the possibilities.

"Only five months and six days 'til we're free," she said with a coy smile, though nervously fidgeting with her charm bracelet, the vial of blue liquid sparkling in the sun just right.

I grabbed her hand. "Your family will be thrilled, I know

they'll be. You're the first to go to college *and* on a scholarship. They'll be happy for your accomplishment."

Tatchi and her twin brother Fin helped run the family sailing business, Captain Jack's Charters. My Gran's curio shop, Tahoe Tessie's Treasures happened to be on the same pier. Without college, both of us would be slated to stay and eventually take over the family business, putting down roots like our parents.

"Well . . .," she said with a sigh, a glint of worry reflected in her eyes, "you just don't know them."

The childhood flashback of her dad's angry face shimmered across my vision. I gulped down my hesitation. She needed me to be strong for her when she finally told them.

With a deep breath and as much compassion as I could muster, I looked her in the eye. "How could they not be proud of you? Sure, they'll have to find someone to take your place in the office, but that's nothing. And you can't pass up a scholarship—"

"It's not that. It's other things."

My stomach clenched. Now seemed like an opportune time to finally discuss what I saw so many years ago. Her dad had a serious problem. In fact, keeping the family secret to herself wasn't healthy, constantly living vicariously through my warped interpretations of other teens.

I'd just about broached the subject when Tatchi suddenly gasped.

"What's wrong?" I asked and glanced over to where she looked, afraid her father might be storming down the beach towards us. Instead, a red Jeep rolled over the ridge and down the rocky path that separated our neighborhoods.

She tsked. "What does he want?"

My mouth parched as I caught a glimpse of Tatchi's twin brother through his windshield. He wore his usual black baseball hat, and looked nothing short of adorable.

"He's coming here?" My voice cracked.

"Apparently." She pressed her brows together and looked toward her house. "Let me find out what he wants."

Fin parked and got out before she could intercept him.

"Hey, Ash," he called out with a wave.

My stomach flipped into a knot as I smiled and waved back.

They argued for a minute, but I didn't catch what about. I stood, trying not to gawk, as I shamelessly adored his broad shoulders and beautiful blonde hair. Under the bill would be his piercing blue eyes fringed with paintbrush lashes—the ones that always melted my knees.

My crush started years ago, right after we'd met when we were ten—right on this beach. With a deep breath, I tried to relax and not dream of a relationship that probably wouldn't be. As far as I knew, he didn't think much of me beyond meaningless flirting.

Tatchi threw her hands in the air and stormed back in my direction.

"Drama on the home front. I have to go," she mumbled as she snagged her blanket off the sand. "Sorry."

"Is everything okay?"

Fin watched us, which made me even more nervous.

"Yeah, it should be fine. I'll try to call later." She smiled and gave me a hug. But more of a "I'm leaving for a trip and saying goodbye" tighter kind of hug. I grimaced, unsure what to say.

She left with a sigh and headed toward their house, brushing past Fin without even a look. Once she was out of view, Fin turned and instead of going back to his Jeep, he walked towards me. My pulse quickened.

# 2

## FIN

Ashlyn stood awkwardly as I approached. Her curvy hips and wavy red hair took my breath away. For a moment, I caught her scent and hummed—honeysuckle with just a hint of chlorine from her morning swim. Briefly, I imagined us playing in the water. She'd give me a run for my money in a race.

"What's going on?" I asked.

Her green eyes darted away. "Not much."

"Sorry I interrupted—" I pointed towards the imprint of my sister's towel in the sand.

"Oh," she said with a gulp and a smile. "It's okay."

She pressed her lips together and suddenly all I wanted to do was kiss her right then and there. I took a deep breath and glanced at my feet.

"Is school going good?" I asked, kicking a rock.

"Yeah." She shrugged and then shot me that look—one with a hint of yearning behind it. I couldn't help myself. I stepped forward and cupped her cheek. Her skin was soft as a rose petal, but within her startled eyes I caught my reflection—my very selfish expression.

Her whole life flashed before me. This kiss I desired to give her would change everything—her dreams, her life with her family, her future. Innocent and trusting, she closed her eyes and tilted her chin upward in anticipation anyway. My soul protested, but I did the only thing I could—the responsible thing.

"You've got something on your cheek," I said, wiping my thumb over her skin.

She opened her eyes and pulled away, her cheeks reddening. "I do?"

I stepped back and grimaced at myself. I was being one of

*those* guys, the jerk who led girls on and toyed with their emotions.

"I'm going to go," she said, rubbing her hand where I'd touched, and faked a smile. "See ya later."

She quickly stumbled up the path towards her Grandmother's house before I could comment, but I heard what she said under her breath. *"I'm so stupid."*

I sulked back to the Jeep and slammed the door, hating myself for being such an ass. The only reason I'd come in the first place was to tell Tatch about the meeting we had to attend, not get distracted by Ashlyn's captivating beauty. And I'd made a complete mess of things.

I spun out of the spot, and drove the small distance back to our house.

When I went inside, I spotted Mom in the kitchen, eyes wild with frustration, her waterproof bag and random stuff spread out over the countertop.

"Where have you been?" she barked, hands on her hips.

"Sorry." I lowered my head.

Mom's right eye twitched, as if she couldn't decide whether to yell at me or just move on with things. I noticed she had changed into her most ornate, beaded bikini top and skirt—obviously for the meeting.

I casually took a seat on the bar stool.

"We've still got time." I gestured toward the bay windows. The sun still peaked above the horizon.

"Close enough. Your father has already left to meet with everyone. I guess you look okay. Just put on whatever you're going to wear to the hatch." She grabbed Great-Grandmother Sadie's sacred shell-encrusted bikini top. "Tatiana!"

Tatch came around the corner, taking a second to sneer at me. "What?"

"I want you to wear this."

Tatch cringed. "What's wrong with this bikini top?"

"It's a special meeting. I want you to look your best."

"But that's for like . . . a *promising* or something." Her face wrinkled up in horror.

Could this be a trick and not a standard meeting? Promisings in our world were the equivalent of weddings but prearranged between parents. Our parents, who fell in love before getting promised, didn't think the arranged unions were fair. They said, when the time came, we could make up our own minds. At least that's what I thought they'd said.

Tatiana blanched. "Oh, dear Poseidon. Please don't tell me you have arranged someone for me to—? Is it Azor?"

Mom chuckled. "Of course not. It's just an important meeting and I want us to look our best. Please, for me?"

Tatch groaned and grabbed the overly ornate thing from Mom's clutches and marched toward the bathroom, mumbling threats. I let go of the breath I didn't realize I'd held and darted into my room as well. Off came the jeans in a rumpled heap along with my shirt. I put on my tear-away board shorts and my waterproof sling pack over my shoulder—anything to stay on Mom's good side.

We reconvened in the living room at the same time and gave each other a fast once-over.

"Happy?" Tatch twirled in a circle, but I avoided looking at her chest.

"Beautiful." Mom's shoulders relaxed until she looked down at the lower half of her body. Tatch still wore her skinny jeans. "Are you planning to *wear* those?"

"No." Tatch rolled her eyes. "Sea serpents! Of course I'm going to change."

She stormed off and Mom resumed pulling cans of food from the pantry. Why would we need food when we were coming right back? Would we be staying the night?

"What's the meeting about, Mom?" Tatiana asked, walking back wearing her swim skirt.

Mom kept a straight face as she took dry goods out of the cupboards: flour, sugar, coffee, noodles, and beans. "We'll find out in a few minutes, but just in case, why don't you pack a few of your things."

"Are you serious?" Tatiana gasped. "Can I at least make a phone call before we go?"

Mom turned and tilted her head. "Who do you want to call?"

Tatch's eyes made their way to the linoleum. "Ash."

A jolt hit my stomach at the mention of her name.

Mom used her low lecture voice. "I'm not sure how long we'll be gone. What will you tell her this time? There's a family emergency? We've had a death?" She shook her head and tsked. Close human friendships were discouraged due to the risk of exposure and Tatch hid how much time they'd spent together, as well as her secret plans for college. "We have to leave in five minutes."

Tatch huffed and stamped her foot. But I already knew we were running out of time. Under my skin, scales began to form and ached for the refreshing cool water to relieve the growing itch.

But if we weren't returning for a while, then someone else would be assigned to guard the gate. Last time, the privilege became my Uncle Alaster's and his son Colin while we were in Fiji on vacation. Colin, who was our age, broke the lock on my closet and used all of my stuff. I couldn't let that happen again.

I ran to my room and put my belongings into the new secret hiding spot under the wooden floorboards: my laptop, iPod, all my shoes, and keys to the Jeep. I pushed my bed over so a leg secured the loose board in place. The rest of my clothes and underwear, I packed in a duffle bag and slid it into the attic. I shivered at the thought of him wearing my boxers again.

"Hey, Tatch. Will you lock this in your room?" I called

across the hall, showing her my guitar.

"Yeah, whatever."

She was scrambling around, hiding stuff too. Luckily, my cousin never touched her room, but we could never be too careful.

"Fin," Tatch whispered. "Sweet talk Mom for me, will ya? Get her to let me stay."

"We have to go. Azor said."

"What?!" Tatch stood, wide-eyed and frantic. "He's going to be there, too? Why didn't you tell me?"

I shifted my weight from side to side, angry with myself for telling her accidentally. Azor, the King's son, made no secret of his desires for Tatch, but she couldn't stand him.

She shoved me aside and clutched her pink sparkly bag under her arm as she headed down the hall, her top jangling with each step. I half listened as she complained to Mom, begging to use the phone again.

I returned to my room, did one last sweep to make sure I'd hidden everything important, and grabbed a few extra board shorts for the road.

"Let's go, Fin!" Mom called from down the hall.

"Okay." I closed my door and paused, hoping this wasn't the last time I'd cross the threshold.

Mom saw me and sighed, frustrated with Tatchi's reaction— no doubt. I picked up the bag at her feet with little effort and offered my arm as we walked down the steps. She squeezed my hand to console me, but I remained positive things would work the way I'd envisioned.

Together, we walked across the bridge that stretched over the pool in our basement. On the other side was the metal hatch attached to the floor, leading out to the lake. Tatiana had already left, her pink bag resting on the cement ledge. With a shake of her head, Mom shoved it in with the rest of our things, sealed the bag, and dropped it down the hole. We watched it sink out of sight—the collection of our lives in one small bag.

"Don't be long," Mom said, and slipped into the water.

I frowned as I looked around at our huge recreational center, with the large TV suspended in the corner, swim-up bar with anything you wanted to drink hooked up to taps and swim mats to lounge on. Most likely, Colin and Uncle Alaster would soon be here, enjoying our stuff and having the time of their lives without having earned it. I wanted to punch something.

With two claps the lights shut off, leaving me in complete darkness. I ripped off my board shorts and plunged my body into the icy water. With an ache the muscles in my legs fused together and scales burst across my skin from my toes up to my waist. A wicked, black fin spread out where my feet used to be. I was sleek, fast, and dangerous—like a shark ready to hunt. I shot down the passageway and came out into the lake on the other side.

Riddled with guilt, I went back up to the lake's surface a hundred feet off shore. I looked towards Ash's house, already missing her. What was wrong with me? How could I let things go that far? I felt wretched for hurting her and vowed to never do it again. Feelings aside, I had to remind myself of the consequences and stay away from her. For her sake.

In the window, a silhouette of someone appeared. Was it Ash? I wanted to apologize in person and confess the truth about who we really were. *If only* . . .

"Sorry," I said right before diving down into the frigid lake.

I tucked my shorts in my sling pack and swam towards my family who waited a few feet underwater in the distance. When the sun returned, along with my legs, I'd need something to cover myself with so I wasn't walking around in the nude.

*EVERBLUE* – Available Now!

Made in the USA
Columbia, SC
15 November 2017